Forever and a Knight

Bridget Essex

Books by Bridget Essex

A Knight to Remember
Don't Say Goodbye
A Wolf for Valentine's Day
A Wolf for the Holidays
Wolf Town
Dark Angel
Big, Bad Wolf
The Protector (Lone Wolf, Book 1)
Meeting Eternity: The Sullivan Vampires, Vol. 1
Trusting Eternity: The Sullivan Vampires, Vol 2

About the Author

My name is Bridget Essex, and I've been writing about vampires for almost two decades. I'm influenced most by classic vampires– the vision of CARMILLA (it's one of the oldest lesbian novels!) and DRACULA. My vampires have always been kind of traditional (powerful), but with the added self-torture of regret and the human touch of guilt.

I have a vast collection of knitting needles and teacups, and like to listen to classical music when I write. My first date with my wife was strolling in a garden, so it's safe to say I'm a bit old fashioned. I have a black cat I love very much, and a brown dog who actually convinces me to go outside. When I'm actually outside, I begin to realize that writing isn't all there is to life. Just most of it! I'm married to the love of my life, author Natalie Vivien.

The love story of the beautiful but tragic vampire Kane Sullivan and her sweetheart Rose Clyde is my magnum opus, and I'm thrilled to share it with you in The Sullivan Vampires series, published by Rose and Star Press! Find out more at www.LesbianRomance.org and http://BridgetEssex.Wordpress.com

ISBN: 1502453452
ISBN-13: 978-1502453457

FOREVER AND A KNIGHT

DEDICATION

For Natalie, the love of my life, my beautiful knight in shining armor who wields a pen (which is, as the old saying goes, much mightier than a sword). A present et toujours. Now and always.

And this book is especially dedicated to our beloved cat, Kit. Every day, I miss you. Always, I will love you.

Chapter 1: The Shutdown

"Good *morning*, Boston! This is Josie Beckett with LEM 100.5, Public Access Radio, here to tell you that it's going to be a *really* good morning," I purr into the microphone, pushing down the level for the start music as I chuckle. No one can see me in the sound booth, but that doesn't stop me from rolling my eyes.

Yeah, it's not *really* going to be a good morning. But then, I'm pretty sure my listeners can hear the dripping sarcasm in my voice.

"I've got some great stuff for you on this gloomy Monday, folks," I say with a smirk. "Today," I growl, dropping my voice and almost whispering in suspense, "I have supposed eyewitness accounts"—skepticism that I can't quite hide makes the next few words sharp—"who *swear* they saw the 'Boston Beast.'"

I punch one of my buttons that gives me a sustained "sad trombone" sound effect, pressing the laugh track button right after that as I chuckle myself. "Of course," I sigh, "I don't need to remind you—but I will, anyway!—what the Boston Beast *supposedly* was, or how it *supposedly* terrorized the docks down at the harbor. Yeah, folks, you remember how people were saying they saw a, and I quote, 'creature' out in the water about a month ago. It 'looked like the Loch

Ness Monster but with more teeth,' said a guy in one of the most popular news clips that the news stations have been playing. You will *also* remember that our sister station, LEM, Public Access Television, was the first station to pick up this ridiculous story, thus kind of destroying our credibility, but there you go." I shrug, cue up my fade-to-commercial music. "Don't go away!" I tell my listeners. "I'll be right back with eyewitness accounts that'll make you roll your eyes, but at least," I purr, "it'll start your day off right, like I always do here on Josie in the Morning."

I set the commercials to play and stand up, stretching overhead and massaging the back of my neck. My mind is racing a mile a minute. I have the supposed eyewitness accounts blinking on my phone panel. My assistant already set up the interviews and has them waiting on standby, but the eyewitnesses are also probably listening to the radio station, waiting to be put on the air. So they've likely heard how I'm framing these interviewees: as the nutballs they are. As a shock jock, I'm used to diffusing anger and using it to make the on-air interview even better, but I also don't want to lose those interviews and deal with dead air.

"Hey, Stella?" I yell out into the corridor. My assistant, Stella—a poor college kid who got roped into doing this as an internship (i.e., she's not even being *paid* to put up with me)—trots down the aisle in her ridiculously high heels (I'm thinking today's pair are six inches, which—to me—translates as stilts, but then what do I know? I'm a sneaker lady). Stella has her clipboard clutched tightly against her and is looking a bit perplexed. "Sorry to bug you, but can you make sure," I tell her, stretching overhead again, "that the interview folks are still on the line?"

"I just did," she says, one brow raised as she looks at me a little funny, her head to the side. "Great lead-in, by the way," she mutters with a frown. She bites her lip, and she looks like she's going to say something before she shakes her head. "You know Deb wants to speak with you still..."

I grimace and massage the back of my neck a little deeper, trying not to sigh. Deb Oliver, my station manager, put a memo in my inbox that it was urgent I speak with her this morning, but there was so much to do for today's show (and so much to tackle from over the weekend) that I hadn't had the chance to answer her yet.

"Tell her I'll see her soon," I say to Stella, who widens her eyes.

"You can't blow off the station manager, Josie," she tells me briskly. "My business relationships professor says—"

I raise my eyebrows and lean on the door frame with a sigh. Stella's a great kid, and I'm lucky to have her as my intern, but nobody's perfect. "Did he talk to you about prioritizing?" I ask, raising a brow. "Because I have a show to run, and I'm sure Deb, of all people, wants to make certain I run it."

Stella bites her lip and rocks forward a little as she sighs, too. "Point taken. Just...talk to her as soon as you can, okay?" She glances at me worriedly. "She *really* didn't look happy this morning."

For some reason, a foreboding feeling twists my gut for half a second. But then I shove it down and straighten. I have a show to do.

"Knock 'em dead," Stella tells me sincerely, and shuts the door behind me as I return to my seat, the last commercial fading out.

"Always do," I mutter, silencing the butterflies in my stomach as I pull my headphones back on and turn up the start music again.

"You're listening to Josie in the Morning on Boston's LEM Public Access Radio," I say into the microphone with an exaggerated smile. Listeners can *definitely* hear if I'm smiling or not. "Up next for your listening pleasure," I purr smoothly, glancing at the still-blinking phone panel, "we have some local folks who *swear* they saw the Boston Beast...in the supposed flesh. If," I snort, "it even *had* flesh, since the Boston ghost hunting group PARECs tells us that it might have actually been the *ghost* of an old sea monster... Yeah, you heard me right. Honestly, I *can't make this up*, guys. Our first caller, Garth Bradbury, thinks the Boston Beast was, at the very least, a *living* monster. Garth owns a commercial fishing vessel that was out in the bay the first morning that eyewitness accounts saw the Beast. Welcome to Josie in the Morning, Garth. You're on the air." I cross my fingers and flick the lit-up caller button.

"Hi, Josie," drawls a strong southern accent into my ears. "Glad to be here."

"Garth, can we hear in your words exactly what you saw that morning?" I ask him, picking up my coffee cup, relaxing just a little.

"Sure can!" he says, too excitedly. "Well, ya know, we had the boat out like we always do, and we were looking back toward Boston when we saw a dark hump in the water. I thought it might be a whale, 'cause we have a lot of whales in these parts, ya know, but then the Beast stuck its head *out* of the water, and I can tell you—it weren't no whale. Was the scariest thing I ever saw in my life, after my wife when she gets up in the morning." He laughs at his own ridiculous joke, and I congratulate myself for not sighing audibly into the microphone.

"Can you describe the supposed Beast?" I ask, letting a little sarcasm leak into my voice.

"It looked sort of like one of them plesiosaurus things," the guy says promptly. He probably pulled that line from one of the newspaper articles or news spots about the Beast. For some reason, I doubt most people could conjure a comparison to 'plesiosaurus' out of their asses. "The Beast had a big, long neck, and a hell of a lot of teeth," he continues, still talking a little too quickly, like he's nervous to be on-air. "But it didn't pay no mind to my boat," he says then. "It just kept going in the direction it was headed—toward Boston."

"And you're sure you weren't, uh, under the influence of anything stronger than salt water that morning?" I chuckle a little into the microphone. "Was anyone else with you? Can anyone else corroborate your story? Garth, did anyone else *see* what you *saw*?"

"A *lot* of folk saw what I saw, missy," mutters the guy, going from nervous to irate in about half a second flat. "Ask anyone! Hell, everyone near the harbor or shore saw what I saw that day, and—"

"Actually, there are only about ten people coming forward *willingly* with a similar story right now, Garth," I tell him briskly, flicking on the next caller button and ending Garth's call. "Like Susan Redding from Gloucester, who—like you—was out in her boat that morning, harvesting her lobster pots. Welcome to the show, Susan," I tell her.

"Hi, Josie—I love your show, listen to it every morning," she gushes. She sounds like a nice lady; I'd hate to rip her apart on air. But *all* these people swear up and down that they saw something that is utterly and obviously not possible.

I take a deep breath.

"Glad to have you, Susan," I tell her, glancing up at the window connecting my recording booth to the hallway.

Stella is out there, grimacing and flicking her red-nailed index finger over her neck again and again.

It's a cue to cut to commercial break.

And, *usually* this cue is only used when something is desperately wrong.

My stomach turns again, but I'm all business. "And we'll hear more from Susan," I say quickly, cutting Susan's first syllable off before she can say any more, "after the break." I flick on the commercials, frowning as I take off my headphones and stand up.

Stella's already in the booth, shutting the soundproof door behind her and leaning against it with a deep frown. "Josie, we've got trouble," she tells me, her brown eyes wide.

I sigh and roll back on my heels, running a hand through my hair. "The other callers dropped off because I think they're all crazy?"

"No," she tells me, licking her lips. Her eyes are wide, she's as pale as bad milk, and she actually looks like she might throw up at any moment.

That's when I realize that it's much, much worse than a few irate callers.

"I don't really know how to say this," she tells me, her voice weak and shaky. She glances at the big clock on the other side of the room. "Um..."

With absolutely no warning at all, the lights overhead go out. We're plunged into darkness.

"Um," repeats Stella miserably in the dark. "We lost the Moran grant."

The lights on my equipment go out, followed almost instantly by the lights in the hallway. Far, far down at the end of the hall is a window to the outside world which sheds a moderate amount of light down the hall and a little into my studio—just enough to see how upset Stella appears, and how bulky and unhelpful my equipment looks when it's not—you know—actually *running*.

I stare at her, my mind running on overdrive. I have no idea how to even process this. It's as if Stella told me a mythical unicorn walked into the radio station and wanted to volunteer as a paper puncher.

"Where the hell is Deb?" I mutter, tossing my silent headphones into my chair and prowling past Stella, half seething and half completely numb.

It can't *possibly* be true, is the thing. Stella is the best assistant I've ever not paid (and better than the ones I *have* paid), but she must have gotten her wires crossed in communication or something. It *can't be true*.

Once upon a time, Old Uncle Sam gave public access radio and television a break in the form of cash. But that was a long time ago. These days, the only way that public radio and TV stays on the air is because (really) "viewers like you" donate money to the cause. Grants, especially, are one of the best ways to keep us afloat.

The Moran grant was our biggest grant. And if we *did* actually lose the grant, this means that LEM Public Access Radio is toast. And LEM Public Access Television will be able to run for only about an hour a day, but would—essentially—be toast, too.

It would mean that LEM Public Access Radio was off the air.

It's not really possible that we lost the grant. Maybe Stella misheard or there was a massive miscommunication. Maybe some *really* unfortunate squirrel got zapped by the power lines outside, and that's why our power was cut and the generators aren't working. Yeah. Totally. I mean, there was *talk* that the grant might not exactly be secure, that the grant's trust committee had been considering pulling funding from LEM Public Access and giving the money to some other organization (and I quote) "more respectable than public radio."

But it was *all just talk*.

They hadn't *meant* it.

They *couldn't* mean it. Because if they did...well, Boston would be losing one hell of a fine radio station, for one. It would mean that I, and everyone else here, would be losing our jobs.

And it would mean that Boston's public radio and television would, technically, go the way of the dinosaur.

I stalk down the labyrinthine hallways until I

get to Deb's office. But I don't actually *reach* my station manager's office... I sort of just join the line of unhappy people outside said office, standing around, leaning against the walls and uneasily muttering under their breath as they wait to be heard.

"This is shit," says Carly Aisley, as she huffs out her breath and pages through her smartphone. She turns to look back at me and raises an eyebrow.

Carly is a producer for the television side of things—we're about equal as far as rank goes, and we really have nothing to do with each other, but it's kind of a small station.

And it's pretty much public knowledge that we can't stand the sight of each other.

This hasn't always been the case. It is true that from the get-go we've been at odds. You know how sometimes you meet someone and you don't like them from the very first moment, but you would never be able to explain exactly *why*? That was Carly and me. And the feeling was utterly mutual. I mean, it's no secret that I'm an eternal skeptic and Sarcasm is my primary language. Carly's the exact opposite: she believes anything and everything and runs one of Boston's biggest ghost hunting groups.

You can see that we'd have a lot to clash over.

But that was all okay. All of it. We were friendly to one another and agreed to disagree.

Until Carly brought the Boston Beast to air on the television network. And our acquaintanceship went downhill from there.

"I heard you were going to interview the Beast's eyewitnesses this morning," Carly growls at me, glancing me up and down. Her eyes narrow as she tosses curly hair over her shoulder "Did we have fun ripping apart innocent bystanders who saw something they can't explain and are getting tremendous flack for being brave enough to talk about it publicly?"

I cross my arms and frown, raising a single eyebrow. I don't need this right now. "I interviewed people who are trying to get their five minutes of fame," I mutter back, rolling my eyes. "This Boston Beast stuff is all tabloid crap, and you know it—"

"You *saw* my footage, and you *know* that it wasn't fabricated," she starts in on me, immediately heated.

But just at that moment, Deb Oliver—our station manager, and the most frazzled woman I've ever met in my life—pushes her office door open and prowls out of her office to stand in the center of the hallway. Her tight gray curls are waving around her face, and the plaid suit she's wearing—a classic from the eighties that she still swears up and down is fashionable since "these damn fashions cycle around even ten years or so"—is all shoulder pads. But even her shoulder pads are drooping with dejection today. Not a good sign.

Deb glances up and down at the line of people gathered and waiting for her outside her office. She sighs for a long moment before upending a small palmful of white pills she was holding into her mouth and washing them down with a couple of generous gulps of coffee. She brandishes her large coffee mug toward us.

"Ladies and gentlemen, you probably already know that something's very wrong," she drones and frowns. "I'm sorry, but we appear to have lost the Moran Grant. It's not a rumor. It's the truth. I don't have much more information than that right now. I'm waiting on a call with the chief trust holder for the Moran association, but since he hung up on me in the last hour..." She waves her coffee mug to the side and shrugs. "I doubt that he's going to be receptive to another begging session." Her mouth goes into a thin, hard line. "Without the grant's monthly check, we don't have the money to pay last month's debts, so the power had to be cut immediately before we go into a black hole we can't return from. This means that, as of immediately, LEM Public Access Radio is no longer, and LEM Public Access Television is close to dead."

"How did this *happen*?" asks Carly, stepping forward and spreading her hands. "Deb, seriously—"

"You kids know that funding for public television and radio has been on the downward slope for years, thanks to that damn Internet," says Deb, patting her pockets in her search for the bulge of her cigarette pack. She finds it and takes it out of her breast pocket, tapping the cardboard container irritably against her right palm. "And we've already lost grants left and right, and we haven't been getting funding from the public, and we really, *really* counted on the Moran grant. They were stringing us along this last month, or I would have known sooner. I'm sorry, kids—it's been a blast," she mutters, fitting an unlit cigarette to her frowning lips. "I'm going to do my best to get to the bottom of this and get some answers. But until that time...there's really no reason for you to stay here. I'll keep in touch. On your way out, please don't riot or spray paint our walls or steal our equipment; it's all second-rate, anyway. Questions?"

I thought that everyone would start yelling at once, but in all seriousness, we *are* a bunch of liberals who have been criminally underpaid for years in service to public radio and television. We just aren't the rioting type.

"I hope we get severance pay," mutters a guy near the front. "Will we get severance pay?"

"Yeah, right," laughs Deb ruefully, then starts to fiddle with her lighter, turning it over and over in her nervous fingers. "Look, I wish I had better news. You're a damn good team, all of you..." She sort of deflates at that moment, shrinking smaller than I've ever seen her.

Deb has such a glowering personality and air of command that she could get paint to peel on her orders, and I've seen big, burly guys easily cowed by a few choice words from her. She's one of the most terrifying and intimidating women I've ever met, and she's always daunted the hell out of me. And, truth be told, inspired me. Seeing someone I've always thought was so strong grow so sad and small...well, it's heartbreaking. And I can't stand it.

"Look," I say then, stepping forward and taking a deep breath. Carly raises her eyebrow at me, and every single person in the station turns to look at me, waiting to see what I'm going to say. *I'm* not even sure what I'm going to say, not until I'm talking. Call it the gift of the radio host: my mouth is always thinking before my brain.

This can sometimes be a good thing. Or a

very, very bad thing.

"The Moran Trust needs to understand that public radio is very important," I say quickly. "They need to understand that public access programming can't go the way of the dinosaur, and that it's important enough to support." I realize I'm preaching to the choir, so I cut to the chase: "Could we get a meeting with the trust committee, do you think? Have the Moran trust guys meet with a couple of people from the station? Like...like me and..." I turn to glance back at Carly, brows raised.

We see eye to eye on almost nothing in this whole big world. But we do both believe completely in these stations. It's the one thing we have in common.

"I can go, too. Together, I think we can convince them," Carly says smoothly, stepping forward and running a hand through her tightly coiled curls. She casts another glance at me as she bites at her lip. "We got the highest viewership *ever* with that Boston Beast stuff," she says, shoving her hands deep into her jeans pockets. "I don't understand why they'd pull the grant *now,* and I think they're making a big mistake. If they heard succinct and passionate reasoning to the contrary, they would listen and reinstate the grant."

Overhead, the last lights in the building—the ones in the managers' hallway—go out with an undignified sizzle.

"It's a sweet thought, ladies," intones Deb in her gravelly voice. Though there are many "no smoking" signs posted up and down the corridor, she has obviously stopped caring and lights up the cigarette, the lighter flashing brightly in the now-dim hallway. She takes a deep inhale and closes her eyes, holding her breath for a long moment. "Look, if *you* think you can actually convince them," she mutters, blowing the smoke out with her words, "I think I can probably get you a meeting with the trust committee tomorrow morning. Possibly. But I hope you both know that it's a fool's errand."

"Those are my favorite type," says Carly, with a quick nod and wide, encouraging smile. "And I think we can do it, Deb." She starts to tick a list of things to do off her fingers. "I'll get all the viewership reports pulled, run the statistics on everything we've done here at the station. We're such a part of Boston's culture that—"

"It was our viewership that most concerned them, Aisley," says Deb, taking another drag on her cigarette with a frown.

"Viewership isn't everything," Carly huffs, "and our viewership was *growing*. Seriously, we doubled day over day with the Boston Beast stuff. We were starting to head toward the right direction and really fast. I mean, why pull the funding *now*? It makes no sense."

"I don't know," says Deb, blowing out a puff of smoke. "But if you want to talk to them, you can."

Carly and I glance at one another, then at all of the waiting faces, a little hard to see now that there isn't much light in the corridor. All of our fellow coworkers look at us hopefully, expectantly. A few of them are staring at us like we're nuts.

But every single person in this room will be out of a job if we don't try, don't give this a shot.

Hell, we'll all probably still be out of a job, but at least we're going to attempt to *do* something about it.

"We'll do it," Carly and I say at the same time.

"I'll go try calling 'em. Again," says Deb with a shrug, shoving her way back into her office and shutting the door sharply behind her.

In the dim silence that follows, Carly glances over her shoulder at me with a frown and raised eyebrows. "We're in deep shit," she mutters to me then, turning on her heel to walk back down the hallway.

I run a hand through my hair, take a deep breath.

God, what did I just get myself into?

⊗

Carly and I meet for our "war council" at the coffeeshop around the corner from the station, if only for the electrical outlet to plug our laptops into.

And the light. Having light is good, I've just realized, since my sound room and office currently lack light of any kind.

"So, we don't have much time," says Carly, setting her steaming latte down next to her closed laptop and placing her elbows on the table. Carly's very pretty, a fact that has never been lost on me. I lean back in my seat and let my eyes have a moment of appreciation as I glance her up and down. She's wearing long, black slacks and a poufy white blouse, all very elegant. But it's *also* never been lost on me that Carly's as straight as an arrow and in a relationship.

And there's the small problem that we dislike each other extremely...

I sigh and glance at her, hooking my elbows over the back of the chair, and stretch. "And...?"

Carly straightens, her mouth in a thin, hard line. "I would like to get some things out of the way before we begin."

I raise one eyebrow.

"The only reason I'm working with you is to try and save the station," she says succinctly, her head to the side. Her lips are pursed together, and her eyes are flashing aggressively.

I smile at her as I shrug slowly. It's a fake smile I'm sporting, but, hey—it's still a smile. "Don't worry. I wouldn't dream that we were working together for any other reason," I tell her blandly.

"You're not on my list of favorite people, Josie. I don't enjoy being called an idiot," says Carly, placing her chin in one hand and staring at me while her nostrils flare.

I bite my lip. "I never called you an idiot," I tell her, wracking my brains as I try to think of the incident in question.

"You called me an idiot to my *face*, Josie," she says, snatching up her latte cup and blowing on it. "Remember? Last month?"

"I think the word I used was *stupid*," I tell her with a small grimace. Oh, yeah—she's talking about the conversation in the break room when I was toasting a bagel. God, that was weeks ago. I spread my hands. "I still think that the footage you *think* you got of the Boston Beast was actually of a tarp in tree branches, and you were probably on some pretty strong drugs when you took said footage and thought it was an actual, honest-to-goodness, real-life monster, *but*"—I hold up my hand before she can protest, and I fake-smile at her again—"I don't think that means we can't work together on making certain Boston still has public access programming to...not watch."

She stares at me and snorts over her cup. "You're a piece of work, Josie."

"I try," I tell her, booting up my laptop. "And, for the record," I say, with a long-suffering sigh, "I don't think you're stupid. Misguided, perhaps. But it takes a lot of balls to stake your reputation on what was probably a tarp in some tree branches and some pretty terrible, grainy footage. So, for that, I commend you."

She stares at me for a long moment before she shakes her head slowly. "Thanks. I won't let it get to my head."

"So, you have all of the statistics for the stations?" I ask her, bringing up a blank Notepad document. I just want to take down a few notes to go off of for our meeting and appeal. Honestly, I think and speak best when I'm not going off a script.

"Yeah, I have the stats," she tells me, patting her laptop but not opening it. "I had this idea that I'd take one of the cameras out into the city this afternoon, maybe near Quincy, and get some footage of people saying they love the stations, get some real feel-good stuff about growing up with the station and its programming and then use that footage in our presentation to the trust members." She stiffens, tapping her foot against the tiles under the table. "Honestly, I can't just...just *sit* here and talk about why the station's great. We both know why," she tells me, and I glance up at her.

Her eyes are full of tears.

I'm rattled by that. First off, sarcasm is my default setting. I'm not that big into emotions. Second off, Carly's just not the crying type. Or, at least, I assumed she wasn't.

But here she is, taking a deep breath as tears begin to fall down her face, gently at first, then a bit quicker as she grabs a handful of napkins from the dispenser on the table, presses them to her nose and breathes out.

"I need to *do* something, Josie. We can't just let the stations go like this. Not like this. Not now. Not on our watch. Not without a fight." She glances up and holds my gaze. "Tomorrow morning at nine o'clock, we're going to go in there to that meeting with the trust guys, and we're going to do what we do best, okay?"

"What's that?" I ask, surprised.

"We're going to talk the station out of this," Carly says firmly. "And that's all there is to it. Meet you out front of the building, okay? Nine o'clock tomorrow?" She stands up and picks up the news camera that she'd placed under the table.

"Yeah, sure," I tell her, still surprised, and without another word, Carly picks up her latte and storms out of the coffeeshop, into the bright August warmth of Boston in summer. Usually, Boston in summer is the best place to be. But as I look after her, with her shoulders slumped, diving into the laughter and happy faces of the sidewalk and bright sunshine...I wish I wasn't here.

Carly's coping with the trauma of not only losing our jobs but losing the stations that we passionately love by going out and asking people why they love our stations and why they should remain on air.

I can't think of any other way to cope with all of this than...

I take a deep breath.

I can't believe that's the first thing I thought of.

But I go with my gut, pick up my to-go coffee cup, and step out onto the warm streets of Boston.

My feet point toward the West Side Methodist Church graveyard.

I need to go visit my sister.

Chapter 2: The Laundry

The cicadas are out in full force, droning on and on as I walk the couple of blocks to West Side Methodist Church. My hands are deep in my jeans pockets, and as I make the walk, putting one foot in front of the other, I realize that I'm perfectly calm. My brain, which races at a speed that cheetahs would probably envy, is—for the moment—stilled.

I always get like this when I visit my sister's grave.

The graveyard is right off the sidewalk. You cut in through the little wrought-iron gate (that's about three feet high, and wouldn't even keep out a toddler) and walk down three rows of gravestones and to the right.

And there's her stone.

My heart rises into my throat when I see it. I stare at that stone, crouch down in front of it, pressing my palm to the words carved into the granite, and then I sit down on top of my sister's grave.

Ellie Beckett, the granite reads. June 18, 1976 - December 31, 1999.

I reach forward and again press my fingers into the different indentations in the granite of her name, tracing the big "e." I take a deep breath.

"Hey, El," I say, and my voice is already thick, but I keep going. "Hope you're doing okay. I miss you..." I trail off, wipe a single tear from my right eye that I won't let shed. I lean back on my hands on the grass and sprawl my legs out in front of me with a sigh. "So, I've got some problems," I tell her gravestone, clearing my throat. "The station's in trouble."

I've been coming out here to the West Side Methodist Church cemetery and talking to Ellie's gravestone once a week for fifteen years. When I was younger (I was born in '79, so when Ellie died, I was only twenty), a family counselor told me it might be a good idea to not actually *talk* to the gravestone since people might think I'm nuts. The problem is, I've never much cared what people think.

So I kept doing it.

Yeah, I know Ellie's not really there, not sitting six feet underneath me, placing her ear to the underside of her coffin and listening for her kid sister to tell her all her woes. And I don't claim to know what I think happens after you die.

But I still believe that there's some small part of Ellie still here in this world. Still looking out for me.

At least, I like to think that.

I've come out here to the graveyard and poured out my heart to Ellie about girlfriends and love troubles, about the time that I received the death threat because of a controversial show I did on commercial fishing. I've told Ellie everything good that's happened in my life and everything bad. And, in a lot of ways, being that vulnerable (if only to a slab of granite) has helped me move through some pretty rough patches.

It helped me cope with her death. It helped me move on.

Though not entirely...because how can you ever move on, really? You cope and you keep living. And that's good enough.

Because someone you've loved so deeply is never truly gone—they're always with you. They've marked your heart forever, and that mark remains, long after they've left. And, in that way, they live on.

"I'm not nervous about going in front of the trust committee, El," I tell her, rolling my shoulders back and staring up at the bright blue sky and the unrelenting sun. It's a pretty hot day here, the sun beating down at me with relentless warmth that sinks deeply into my bones. "I'm just..." I trail off, shake my head. "I'm just worried about what's going to happen if I *fail*. All of those people at the station are depending on me to make a difference... I mean, in all honesty, all those people, *including* me. All of our jobs are on the line, but it's not just that. The station's done so much in the community. We can't lose that..."

I trail off again, running my fingers through the warm blades of grass beside me as I close my eyes and listen to the cicadas. Their steady thrum, and the steady lull of the traffic, soothes me.

I know it's kind of weird, but there's no place on earth more peaceful than a graveyard. I mean, yeah, it's a place filled with dead people—there's no getting around that fact—and I guess it's kind of spooky if you think of it like that. But said dead people aren't exactly bothering you very much, and they're certainly not worried about anything at the moment. They're, in fact, pretty chill about *everything*, and that kind of rubs off on you. You start to realize that a lot of the problems in your life? They're really not so terrible.

A graveyard is such a restful place, a quiet place that reminds you of the stuff that *really* matters. You can't come to a graveyard and be worried about the argument you got into on your ex-girlfriend's Facebook wall, for example. Because you realize, in a graveyard, that trivial things are exactly that: trivial.

"Thanks for the chat, El," I mutter, rising and patting off the seat of my pants before reaching out and pressing my fingers to the warm granite of the gravestone.

But I snatch my hand back as if singed.

I gasp, my heart thundering through me.

Well, that was...weird.

Granite can't conduct electricity, right? I mean, it's a rock, right?

But when I reached out and touched her gravestone, it was as if a surge of electricity had moved through the rock and into me, as if I got a sudden charge of electricity. Like a really strong static shock.

That shock rushed through me for only an instant. Only an instant, and then it was completely gone. And I don't feel it anymore...but I can't explain it away. I don't know how it could have possibly happened. All that I know is that it happened.

I frown and hover my fingers over the top of her gravestone again. I take a deep breath, and I press my hand to the sun-warmed granite.

But absolutely nothing happens. The granite

is hot because of the heat and sunshine. But that's it.

No static electricity.

God, I need more coffee; I must be missing something very simple, a very easy explanation for what just happened. Hell, maybe there's electricity pouring through the ground from some faulty wiring or something. That must be it. And maybe I missed the science class where we learned that granite conducts electricity just a little.

I shrug and, slinging my book bag over my shoulder, I turn to head out of the graveyard.

Weirdly, the hair on the back of my neck stands up at that moment. Like someone's watching me.

I turn and glance casually behind me. There are some birds singing in a nearby tree, cicadas screaming their little insect heads off all around me, and a delivery truck that whooshes by down the side street, going way faster than the speed limit.

But there's no one watching me, because there's no one there.

Weird. But, then, I've not had the most normal day. I scrub irritably at the back of my neck, raise an eyebrow and make my way back to my apartment building.

Still, that odd, surreal feeling of being watched doesn't go away until I'm actually in my apartment building, the door swinging heavily shut behind me. It's only then that the hairs on the back of my neck go down, only then that my hackles go down, too, my shoulders drooping. That was really weird. But, again, I've got to remember: it's been a weird day.

I put it out of my head.

I trot up the three flights of stairs because it's good for me to get some exercise, and because Mrs. Thorton was headed into the elevator on the ground floor, and if I have to be stuck with her in an elevator even for just three floors, I might be convicted of homicide.

For the record, Mrs. Thorton is the peach who tries to convert me to her brand of born-again Christianity every single time she sees me. No exceptions. For Christmas last year, she gave me a dozen Christmas cookies, which is nice, right? But they came with a Biblical tract slipped into the wrapper. The tract had a picture of Santa Claus on the front sporting horns and went on to talk about how the devil is actually Santa Claus. Or something. I used the tract to line my cat's litter box, so I'm kind of hazy on the details.

Once I get to my floor and reach my door, I slide my keys into my front door's lock and sigh, leaning my forehead on the cold metal door and feeling the chill of the metal bring me back to reality.

Home sweet home.

I don't even get the door open a crack before my loudmouth cat, Wonder (short for "Wonder Woman," but if I called her that all the time, she'd get a bigger head than she already has), is meowing very (*very*) loudly as she sticks her paw through the opening in said door and tries to push out onto the landing.

The thing about Wonder is that she really and truly believes that she is some enormous wildcat who belongs out in the untamed wilderness of the jungles or desert, certainly not cooped up in a pretty nice apartment in Boston where her every need is taken care of, night and day. She protests her cruel and unusual captivity by flinging herself out the door every time it's open even a quarter inch.

"Wonder, *no*," I sigh as she somehow (because she's made of liquid, I'm certain of it) slips past my leg that I've wedged into the opening of the door and out into the hallway. She bolts down the stretch of dirty gray carpeting toward the elevator.

Exactly as the elevator doors *ding* open, and Mrs. Thorton steps out.

Wonder is a gorgeous dark gray tabby, which is just fine on any normal day and is utter crap when she's out in the dark hallway of my apartment building and blending seamlessly in with the dark gray carpeting of the floor. Thankfully, even with her superior camouflage skills, we've both been through this too many times for me to *not* spot her, her fluffy little ass prowling down the side of the hallway like she owns the place.

"Gotcha," I mutter, sprinting after her and scooping up my bad cat as Mrs. Thorton begins to make a bee-line toward me down the hallway, closing in like *she's* the big cat on the prowl now.

Well, damn. It's too late. She's spotted me, and the inevitable is at hand...

"Hello, Miss Beckett," Mrs. Thorton purrs, sugar dripping off her words as she smiles at me a little too widely. Mrs. Thorton always dresses to impress, with suits bearing shoulder pads that make walking straight through doorways slightly difficult. Today she's wearing a beige pants suit with shoulder pads so wide, she had to step sideways to get off the elevator. Her enormous, permed brown curls are struggling out of their loose ponytail toward me, and her makeup is overly done but utterly perfect for a preacher's wife...which she is.

"Hi, Mrs. Thorton," I manage, before Wonder starts to insert her claws into my shoulder like she's intent on ripping out my heart. "Sorry," I mutter, trying to detangle my cat's razor-sharp claws from my skin (good God, I've got to trim her nails). "I've just have to get her inside... She's such a little *stinker*!" I say, with hopefully toned-down sarcasm. I turn to get Wonder back into the apartment.

"I heard your radio station went off the air today, dear," Mrs. Thorton says now, her smile never wavering an inch.

That smile is starting to look a little deadly.

I shake my head, wincing a little as Wonder digs in deeper. "Yeah, but we'll get it back. Don't you worry about that," I tell her, pulling one of Wonder's sharper claws from my shoulder with a grimace.

Mrs. Thorton's eyes glitter in the dark hallway as she gazes at me, and with dripping condescension, she says, "I don't know about that."

And that's when I realize there's something slightly fishy going on.

It's no secret that the Thortons are the king and queen of one of the larger born-again gospel-type churches in Boston, Great Hope Church (they have actual *commercials,* they're so big and well known). I don't have anything against religion and am really a live-and-let-live kind of lady, but they're the type of mega-church I can't stand: the one with parishioners who hold up angry, hate-filled signs and protest everything fun and wonderful in this big world. The entire church heads up to Salem every year to protest at their Halloween celebration; they protest (pulling out the big guns like bullhorns and the really *big* hate-filled signs) at Boston's gay pride parade. Hell, they even protest at the annual *vegetarian* convention. What vegetarians ever did to piss off Great Hope Church, I'll never know.

And, as Mrs. Thorton stares me down now, I'm beginning to get a sinking suspicion...

"Mrs. Thorton," I say, taking a deep breath and speaking with as much civility as I can muster, "is there something you'd like to tell me?"

"Liberal media is dying, dear," she says, her smile actually deepening. She's starting to look a little like a shark, actually, all big, sharp teeth and deadly grin. Mrs. Thorton does a little sniff, then, her nose in the air, as she straightens. "And I think we both know that the Moran grant is better allocated to entertainment that doesn't corrupt the family values America was founded on."

I stare at her. I'm pretty sure my mouth is open and my jaw is on the floor, but I don't give a damn, because then my quick mouth takes over.

I could say anything in this moment. I could tell her how outdated her views are, how most of America no longer agrees with her last-century way of thinking. I could tell her that the Moran grant was well utilized by the station and that we've done a hell of a lot of good for Boston.

But I don't say any of that.

"You've got to be fucking kidding me," is what I so eloquently tell her.

The color drains from her face, and her expression changes from acute smugness to disgust in a single heartbeat. It *might* be my imagination, but I think I see her shoulder pads deflate a little at the expletive. But then she straightens up again, like a marionette whose strings have been pulled tightly, and I think I begin to see steam pouring out of her ears.

"I...I...I'm going to lodge a complaint with our landlord," she snarls then, turning on her heel and beginning to stalk toward her apartment door, at the other end of the hallway.

It's not a complete lie when I tell you that my grip on Wonder somehow just...*slips* in that moment. It *slips* pretty deliberately, actually, as I set my tabby on the floor and stand up, crossing my arms.

Wonder had been terribly fascinated with the shoelaces on the sneakers Mrs. Thorton had changed into after a day of work. Wonder, in fact, had been *so* fascinated with those shoelaces while Mrs. Thorton and I had been having our little "discussion" that, free, she now makes a beeline for Mrs. Thorton's feet.

Mrs. Thorton, not expecting my tiny tigress to be anywhere in relation to her feet, doesn't look when Wonder darts in front of her. Nothing actually happens—Mrs. Thorton doesn't step on my cat or any part of my cat. But she *does* brush her pant leg lightly against the fur of Wonder's tail as cat and woman cross each other's paths.

Wonder is a lot of things, but—first and foremost—she is utterly in love with her tail, spending about nineteen hours a day grooming it until it shines like the sun. If you *touch* Wonder's tail, she will tell you, in no uncertain (and often violent) terms, that such a gesture is completely off limits.

This is something that Mrs. Thorton could never have known, of course.

Wonder rounds, instantly a ball of hissing, spitting rage—the personification of everything I'm feeling inside, quite honestly. My cat lunges, paws wide, claws extended...but Mrs. Thorton is quick, and reacts almost instantly, leaping out of the way as Wonder dives for her.

"You'll be hearing about this!" is screeched at me, and then Mrs. Thorton's door is opened and slammed shut, and she is safely in her apartment, my cat clawing at her door, for once her claws utterly useless against the metal barrier.

While I could *swear* that Wonder can occasionally walk through walls, this is probably not the day for such things.

"Come on, Wonder... There's my pretty kitty," I purr at her, scooping up her fluffy, yowling mass and holding it close to my stomach. Wonder goes a little limp at that (despite her aggression and temperamental personality, and though she'd never admit it under oath, Wonder's always had a soft spot for me) and allows me to carry her, unprotesting, into my own apartment, shutting the big metal door behind us.

I sigh and lean against that door as Wonder begins a deep, rumbling purr, pressing herself against me and rubbing the top of her head snugly against my chin.

"Thanks for trying to help, babe," I tell her, knuckling her gently behind the ears.

My cat's smug, blissful expression conveys that she would have killed Mrs. Thorton for me had she been given half the chance.

And I appreciate that.

I set Wonder gently on the floor and go through the motions of opening up a can of wet food for her while she aggressively rubs herself against my legs, purring like a motorboat. I'm lost deep in thought, and I almost cut myself on the can's lid as I wash it in the sink, ready to toss into the recycling bin. I set the plate of gooey food down in front of Wonder and am instantly my cat's hero. I grab myself a beer from the fridge and pop open the top, hooking one of my kitchen's stools out with my foot and sinking down onto it.

Truth be told, my head's reeling quite a bit at this moment.

Honestly? I can't believe this. Either Mrs. Thorton was on the trust committee at the Moran group, or she had her claws into someone who was, someone who could influence where the committee allocated their funds. I feel sick to my stomach now when I think about tomorrow and going in front of said committee, trying to plead a case that may already be—to them, at least—a completely lost cause.

Liberal media, *really*? What a stupid-ass reason to remove funding. I take a sip of my beer and bury my other hand in my hair, tugging at the ends of it. I'm so frustrated in this moment, I could scream. Or take out my aggression on my punching bag that sits gathering dust in the corner.

But, instead, I decide that I'm going to do what I always do when I'm angry and frustrated. It also helps that pretty much the only clean clothes I have left at this point are a gigantic shirt with Scooby Doo's face on it and some leopard-print pajama bottoms. Hardly the stuff to strike respect into the hearts of the Morgan trust committee tomorrow morning.

So it's time to do laundry.

Laundry in Casa de Beckett is a time-honored tradition that involves a lot of expletives. Honestly, I *hate* doing laundry. Granted, it's not one of the most beloved chores on the planet, but that's not the main reason for the hatred.

Mostly, it's because the washers and dryers in our apartment building are located in the Basement of Evil.

Okay, so you may think "Basement of Evil" is a little strong, but then you've probably never visited the Basement of Evil. Let me paint you a picture: long-standing water on the floor, *one* guttering light overhead in the entire expanse of the basement, the scent of the dead mouse that's been stuck under Mrs. Dalton's washer for the last month providing a rather atmospheric perfume to the whole scene. There are *holes* in the concrete walls that lead back into *crawlspaces in the ground*, not totally unlike holes that would store bodies, and I've had more than one nightmare where I'm stuck down in the basement, that one lone light guttering overhead, and zombies start crawling out of those holes.

No one in my entire apartment building ever

comes down to the basement. Only a few tenants have washers and dryers down there, not because we can't afford them, but because *everyone* thinks this place is haunted, even the guy on the third floor who's an ex-Marine, and thinks—in his words— "everything is bullshit."

Even *that* guy thinks this basement is haunted.

Don't ask me how the rumor of the basement being haunted got started in the building; it began long before I got here. There are stories that a murder actually *did* take place down there, and the murderer stashed the body in one of the holes in the concrete wall. But then there's *also* a rumor that a killer clown lives in the farthest hole from the door, so I don't know how much stock I put in these stories.

Either way, doing laundry down in the basement is enough to give you nightmares. So when I'm pissed, it's the perfect time to do it.

Because if there *was* a murderer (or, you know, killer clown) hiding out in the basement, waiting for a victim, he'd have to contend with *me*.

I'm not a betting woman, but my wager would be on me winning that one right now.

I still haven't unpacked my dirty clothes from the short vacation to Provincetown I took last weekend (don't ask—it was a royal bust, and the most action I got was the bed-and-breakfast owner patting my arm when she told me that "you'll find the right girl someday. Don't lose hope!"), so the suitcase full of dirty clothes is as good a place to start as any. I grab some more clothes from my hamper and stuff them into the laundry basket, and then I just grab my suitcase's handle. With my basket balanced on my hip and lugging my suitcase behind me, I exit my apartment (narrowly closing the door just in time to keep Wonder in captivity) and begin the long haul down to the basement.

"Hello, highly esteemed board members," I mutter under my breath, my mind racing as I try to figure out an eloquent way to address the Moran board of trustees. Nah, "highly esteemed board members" sounds too formal (and a little too much like I'm trying to kiss their asses, which—admittedly—I am, but still). I get into the elevator and press the grimy "B" button while watching myself in the floor-length mirror of the elevator's walls.

God, I look like hell. My long highlighted blonde hair, normally straightened to within an inch of its life, is sticking out in all directions (because I keep running my hands through it in agitation), and my makeup is beginning to smear at the corners of my eyes.

Honestly, I look like I'm in need of a stiff drink. But there's no time for that now.

"Hello, board members," I mutter again, as I punch the elevator door's "open" button, as the elevator drifts gently (and with a great deal of creaking and groaning) down to settle onto the basement floor. Even though the elevator has come to a complete stop, its door opens only partially (another lovely basement "perk"), and my suitcase gets stuck in the door opening as I try to wrestle myself, my laundry basket *and* the suitcase through the narrow gap.

I get through it somehow, and the elevator

dings pleasantly closed behind me.

So. I'm in the Basement of Evil.

The dead mouse smells especially pungent this evening, as I lug my laundry through the puddles of standing water and set my suitcase on top of my dryer. I'm purposefully trying not to figure out what else I think I might be smelling as I open my washer, toss in the clothes from my laundry basket, and grimace as I gingerly set the basket on the ground, managing to avoid setting it in a puddle.

I unzip my suitcase, trying to figure out what I'm going to wear tomorrow, thinking about a million things, actually, as I begin to pull my underwear out and toss them one by one into the washer. I have to call Deb and get Carly's number, because I want to go over some last minute things with her...

But I stop cold in the middle of my very long train of thought.

The light overhead is guttering a little more erratically than usual. That's the first thing I notice. Also...when the hell did it get so cold?

As I breathe out one long breath, I stare in shock as I watch that exhale hanging suspended in the air in front of me like smoke.

Like it's winter. When it most definitely is not. It's a gorgeous, sweltering August night out there.

So how is it this cold in here?

And that's when I hear the whistling.

I have to tell you: there are few things more terrifying than being in an *already* creepy basement *alone* and hearing distant but clear *whistling*. For the second time today, the hair on the back of my neck stands up, and I straighten, glancing toward the rear of the basement. The back part of the basement that *no one goes near* because, of course, the one guttering light doesn't reach back there, and some of the deepest holes in the wall are back in the dark. It's also rumored that there's a hole in the cement floor, like a well, but I've never gotten near enough to verify whether that particular story is true or not.

And it's in that darkest, uninhabitable, nobody-ever-goes-there section of the basement...where the whistling is coming from.

The tune is unrecognizable but very crisp and clear. That whistle sounds almost...jaunty.

Okay, so on a normal day, I'll not lie: I'd already be in the elevator and on my way up to my apartment, my heart pounding hard enough to bruise the insides of my ribs, and vowing never, *ever* to return to the basement, not even to grab my clean underwear from the washer.

But it's not exactly a normal day. This has, actually, been a completely shitty day.

So I don't even think—my whole body begins to move on instinct. I zip up my suitcase, and I lift it up, holding it in front of me like a shield. It's the only thing I have on hand to use as a weapon, besides my dirty clothes and the laundry basket, and I don't think anyone ever got injured by a plastic laundry basket (though there is, admittedly, a first time for everything). I think my suitcase is the best bet: I *could* hurl it at my would-be murderer (because, of course, that's where my mind is going right now: that the whistler is a murderer). It's a very *heavy* suitcase, and it would probably do at least a little damage.

At least, that's what I'm hoping.

I creep toward the back part of the basement. The pitch-black part of the basement. The part of the basement that the light doesn't even try to penetrate, and—if I wasn't completely hyped up on adrenaline—I would realize it is a completely *crazy place* to follow a whistle.

But this is *my* basement. Or at least partially my basement. And it was supposed to be a safe place to be. And the fact that it doesn't feel particularly safe right now has made me *pissed.*

Even through the haze of anger, however, I still have my wits about me, the wits that are telling me that this is a completely crazy thing I'm doing.

But I do it, anyway.

"Is anyone down here?" I yell out, congratulating myself that my voice didn't shake.

But there's no answer. And the whistling keeps going without even a waver, like whoever is doing the whistling didn't hear me, even though I shouted. The whistling seems to be getting farther away now, actually...which is totally impossible. The basement's not *that* big. The whistler doesn't have anywhere else to go...

What's really odd is that I think I see something light and large in the darkness. Something big and white in the far shadows. That makes no sense...

I take one more step.

I fall forward.

Where I'd placed my foot, where I'd expected there to be concrete floor...there had been nothing. Because my suitcase is in front of me, and very heavy, in that split heartbeat, there's no way that I can catch myself. I fall forward, and I gasp, waiting for impact, eyes tightly shut, body completely tense and bracing for that *slam* against concrete that's supposed to happen any second now...

I hit with so much force, my middle banging against the hard top of my suitcase, that the wind's completely knocked out of me. I roll over instinctively, onto my side, curling up into a ball, gasping and wheezing as my breath finally comes back after an extraordinarily painful moment. I roll onto my hands and knees, and I look up.

My hands are in cold, wet mud. I try not to think about what *else* could be in that mud (did whatever I fall into connect to the sewers? At least it doesn't *smell* like it connects to sewers) as I take a ragged breath in. It's so damn *dark* that I can hardly make out anything at all, not even shadows against the black.

I struggle to get up, my knees aching fiercely from the fall as I draw in a deep breath, putting my hands out in front of myself to steady my wobbling form. I assume that there's a wall in front of me, but my fingers brush against nothing. I take a step forward, my hands out before me as I glance up, wondering how deep whatever I fell into *is*. I should see a little bit of the guttering light bulb overhead, no matter how far I fell.

But I stop dead. Because my eyes are finally adjusting to the lack of light...

And overhead, there's no crappy, horror-movie light bulb flickering away.

There are *stars*.

My breath catches in my throat. It's utterly *impossible*, what I'm seeing. There's no way that I fell down a shaft or a corridor or into anything that would make me land *outside* of the basement.

But that's where I am, I realize. Somehow. Impossibly.

I'm outside.

My fingers brush against something nubbly and ridged, something that feels exactly like the bark of a tree, and then I'm taking another step before I can think about what, exactly, is going on, my head reeling so fast I feel sick, and—again—in that very confusing instant, I'm falling forward. I stepped into mid-air because my eyes haven't fully adjusted, but I'm not falling into a hole this time: I'm falling down the side of a hill, branches and scree rushing out away from under me as I roll against the earth.

There's a great *oof* as air is, again, knocked out of my lungs and I fall against something.

But I didn't fall against my suitcase this time.

I fell against some*one.*

There's the resounding smack of two bodies colliding, and then a startled animal noise that I can't quite pinpoint as I roll, and everything seems to roll together in that moment.

And then *finally*, it all stops, and the entire world stops moving.

Because I've stopped falling.

And I'm definitely on top of someone.

I am so far out of my element, as I push up and off of whoever it was, blood rushing to my cheeks in an instant. Because there are a lot of things I realize all at once:

It doesn't really matter that I have no idea where the hell I am or how the hell I got here. Because, no matter what, I'm always pretty damn adept at recognizing a woman's body. Even in *crazy* circumstances, like these ones. And even in the dark.

And I do recognize it right now.

Because I landed on top of a woman. And this woman isn't your average woman....not that any woman is really average, but *this* woman? The woman I fell on top of?

She's wearing *metal*.

Yeah. That's just not average in my book.

Her clothes are *made of metal*.

Before I can really register how utterly bizarre all of this is, there's this strange sound, suddenly, like metal sliding quickly on metal, and then I'm moving again, but this time not of my own accord, as I'm shoved off of her so quickly that I can't even catch a breath before I realize that I'm on my knees on cold ground (which, thankfully, is no longer muddy), and as my eyes adjust to the dark, I realize that this woman is standing over me...

Pointing a sword at my heart.

A sword.

A freakin' *sword.*

My eyes have adjusted enough for me to stare down the blade of the sword at the woman holding it. She's tall, impressively so, but then I'm on my knees in the dirt, so my judgment of size is a little skewed. In the dark, I can see that the metal bits she's wearing are glinting in the starlight. It looks like pretty much every part of her is covered in wrought, filigreed metal, actually.

It's like she's wearing...armor?

Her shoulder-length hair (it's impossible to tell what color it is in the dark) swishes over one shoulder as she stares at me with wide, glinting eyes that begin to harden and narrow. Her mouth already in a thin, hard line, and...well. What I can see of her is kind of scary. She's muscular, tall, standing over me with a sword... Not exactly a favorable first impression.

But also, in the deep, dark, instinctual back part of my brain, neurons begin to fire, or whatever the hell happens when your attraction meter shakes off some dust and starts operating again...

Because, come on: a woman in armor is standing in front of me holding a sword.

I...think that's kind of hot.

But then, of course, the rest of my brain catches up with the misfiring attraction part and slaps it silly.

What the *hell* am I doing on my knees, on the ground, in front of a woman holding a sword in a threatening manner?

And better yet: *where the hell am I?*

"Who sent you?" she asks me then.

The woman with the sword? She has the kind of voice that I could listen to all day. It's warm and multilayered and low and velvety. If she was narrating a book, I'd have to be listening to it in bed.

Admittedly, that voice isn't so warm when it's being directed at me full of agitation and anger, exactly as it is now.

But I can *imagine* it being warm.

Seriously, what's wrong with me? Did I hit

my head? Even though I have my arms open instinctively in the "don't shoot" or "I surrender" pose in front of me, I still reach up and brush my fingers over my forehead, just to make sure. Okay, that's good—I don't *feel* any blood, but that doesn't mean that I didn't clock my head terribly.

Because this *has* to be a hallucination, right?

Which would, of course, explain my attraction to the woman pointing a sword at my heart.

"What are you talking about?" I say sharply then, staring up at her while I try (desperately) to piece together what could possibly be going on. "Nobody *sent* me. What's going on? Where am I? What the hell are you doing in our basement?"

She thankfully drops the point of the sword now, lowering the blade until the sharp part is about an inch off the ground. She holds that very heavy-looking sword, by the way, without a single glimmer of the weight showing in her stance. She stands there unwavering, her expression unchanging as she stares down at me with a hard frown.

And then, she offers me her other hand.

For a long moment, I don't take it. I mean, she *is* still holding a sword. But then I place my hand in her gloved one, and with a single, fluid motion, she pulls me to my feet as if I have the weight of a feather, which I most certainly do not. The grip of her hand is tight and warm, warm even through the leather of her glove.

"Where do you *think* you are?" she asks me then, gruffly, glancing me up and down with eyes that narrow as she gives me a thorough look-over. There's absolutely nothing suggestive about her gaze, but like some fifteen-year-old girl, I find myself *blushing*.

Me.

Blushing.

God, maybe this *is* a dream.

"Look, this is all funny, ha, ha, look, I'm laughing," I tell her, pointing to my not-smiling-at-all mouth. "But we've had our little joke, right? Are you some weird maintenance lady I've never seen before, doing some Live Action Role Playing in our basement? Because if you are, I mean, I don't judge," I tell her, putting my hands in the "surrender" position again, as I try to balance my weight on both feet, my knees aching terribly from the fall. "I just want to go back to my washer, put the rest of the load in, and go back up to my apartment," I tell her, my voice raising as I take a step backward, while very consciously keeping the front of my body turned toward her. I dart my glance over my shoulder.

I take a big gulp.

Towering over me is a tree that's about twenty feet around. It just goes up and up and up like a skyscraper, and all I can really make out is the bark and the size, but when I peer up and squint, I think I see pine branches. It's a pine tree?

Last time I checked, there are no ten-story tall pine trees in downtown Boston.

Much less a forest of them.

I'm finally beginning to realize where I am. And it's not in the basement of my apartment building. Somehow, impossibly, I'm in a forest, in the middle of the night. A forest of gargantuan old trees...

And I'm standing next to a woman in armor.

"Ah, I think I...ah...hit my head," I tell her, scrabbling sideways to the hillside that I fell down. It's more of an angled cliff than a hillside, but I still try to climb up it, and because adrenaline is pounding through me, and even through the earth is crumbling under my hands and feet, and there's a ton of scree, I manage to get to the top of it.

I look back down at the woman in armor, who's glancing up at me with her sword sheathed now on her back.

"Wait!" she calls after me, and she sounds concerned, and that's nice and all, but this can't *possibly* be happening. It *must* be a dream.

I stumble into my suitcase at that moment (because my eyes aren't *that* well adjusted to the dark), and I fall over it, face first into the dirt. I'm apparently doing a lot of falling tonight. Okay, I can handle falling a lot. I scrabble up onto my hands and knees, and then I yelp, snatching back my hand as if it was stung.

It actually *felt* like it was being stung, but it was a bit worse than that. As I cradle my hand to my chest, pain roars through me from the prick in my palm I got from something very, very sharp on the forest floor.

In half a heartbeat, the woman in armor is beside me (how she bounded up that cliffside in an instant I'll never know), kneeling down in one smooth motion as she grimaces and—none too gently—takes my hand in hers and brings it closer to her face for inspection.

"You can't possibly be from around here," she

says then, a bit exasperated, as she helps me stand again, her other hand at my waist.

"Why do you say that?" I ask her, suddenly not feeling so great. The ground beneath us is beginning to buck in synchronized waves, and it feels like my heartbeat is centered in my palm.

The woman sighs patiently as she grips my hand with a tightness that almost hurts. Then, with her leather-gloved hand, she reaches down into the palm of my hand and, with as much nonchalance as if she was picking a bit of pet fur off a piece of clothing, she removes a two-inch thorn from my skin. A two-inch thorn, I realize, that had gone *completely through the palm of my hand and out the other side.*

I feel like I'm going to pass out for a full moment, as blood begins to seep out of my palm, brimming over and *plinking* quietly onto the forest floor at our feet. As I sway a little (I've always been woozy at the sight of blood), the stranger wraps her other arm around my waist a little tighter.

"Because if you *were* from around here," she replies with that same maddening patience, "you would have known that patches of poisoned thorns smell overpoweringly and sickeningly sweet, and you should avoid them at all costs. *Milady.*" The last is a fairly scorching bit of sarcasm.

Now that she mentions it, I *do* detect a clinging sweetness to the air. It just wasn't the first thing that had my attention in this woman-holding-sword, forest-where-there-shouldn't-be-one scenario that I happen to be living currently.

I really feel like I'm going to black out. I lean heavily on this complete stranger.

"You're going to feel a little dizzy," she says, in a very conversational tone, as I fall backwards and she catches me with no effort at all. The last thing I remember is being lifted into her arms. "You might lose consciousness, but it's a straightforward poisoning," she continues and then...

I black out.

❦

Chapter 3: The Bear

I wake up with my head pounding just as badly as it does when I drink too much tequila. The crappy part is that I'm *fairly* certain I didn't even get the enjoyment of said tequila. My blood roars through my brain, and I take a deep, quavering breath, feeling the world spin beneath me.

I painfully squint, opening my eyes, and then—like being beneath an avalanche of cold, sopping wet snow that covers (and soaks) you instantly—I remember.

"Oh, God," I mutter, sitting bolt upright, and immediately pressing my hand to my forehead, because everything's spinning so badly I feel like I'm going to black out again. And I remember that. I remember blacking out before.

And I remember a woman, covered in armor, her eyes intense and piercing as she held a sword to my heart...

I stare up at the impossibly tall pine trees that tower around me. I'm lying on the ground, but even if I wasn't, it's almost impossible to see the tops of those trees: they seem as far away as a ten-story building, and some seem even taller, reaching toward the sky. I've never *seen* trees that tall, didn't know trees could actually reach that height.

As I stare up at the trees, I realize that my breath is coming out like smoke into the air. It's freezing out, as cold as if winter were coming, which I know it isn't. It's *August*. I shiver a little, drawing the coarse blanket up and around my shoulders, before blinking in surprise and peering down at that blanket.

It's the color of earth, and roughly woven, like the kind of stuff you could get at a fair trade store. This wasn't made by a machine; it was made by a *person*. I finger the fabric in my hand, then shiver a little again and pull it closer to my shoulders.

I'm lying on the ground, on another blanket of the same stuff. To my left is a patch of dirt that's been cleared of fallen leaves and pine needles, and a tiny fire is eating up a small tepee of sticks that's been erected in the center of that ring of dirt. On the other side of the fire is a bedroll and some coarse-looking woven bags, and beyond that...

Is a massive horse.

The horse and I stare at one another, each of us utterly surprised.

Now, when I tell you that this horse is *massive,* I mean *utterly enormous*. Even though I'm still sitting on the ground, it towers above me. I know the perspective is a little off—I *am* sitting on the ground—but even if I was standing upright, I'm pretty sure its shoulders would still be a full head above *my* head.

The horse is jet black and has feathery hair cascading all around its huge hooves. It has a very muscular build, and it reminds me a little of the Budweiser Clydesdales, if the Clydesdales were pure black and looked angry. The horse has a long mane and forelock, and it's not wearing a saddle, bridle or anything tying it to a specific spot.

It could, for example, saunter on over here and crush me in a heartbeat—if it wanted to.

But it doesn't *seem* to want to, which—in that moment—provides a small measure of comfort. It stares at me for a long moment from beneath long, black lashes; then realizing that I'm really no threat to it, it goes back to tearing up the grass around the campfire in gigantic mouthfuls, chewing them aggressively before tearing up *more* grass and repeating the process.

"Nice horsey," I mutter, standing up. I start shivering almost immediately. I'm only wearing my Scooby Doo bed shirt and those leopard-print bottoms (a fact that horrifies me, but what can I do?), and August has apparently given us a raincheck on that whole summer thing.

But, if I'm being honest with myself, I know that it's not really August.

I don't exactly think we're in Kansas anymore.

I pick up the top blanket and wrap it around my shoulders, glancing around at the drab, gray surroundings and the utter lack of gorgeous-woman-wearing-metal-pants.

"Hello?" I call out into the clearing.

The horse snorts and takes a step away from me, like I offended it, shaking its head and blowing air out of its nose.

But other than that, there's no reply.

Well, the knight lady couldn't have gotten far. I'm assuming this is her horse and this is her stuff. If I can find that woman, maybe I can get some answers out of her, figure out where the hell I am.

And where the hell Boston disappeared to.

I take a deep breath and hold the blanket tighter against myself, but a twinge of pain makes me glance down at my right palm—the palm that somehow, impossibly, I'd gotten a massive thorn stuck into last night, a thorn that went through my entire hand.

It's been bandaged carefully with thin strips of white cloth. And though it occasionally twinges, the pain is pretty minor, considering my hand was pierced through. It makes no sense that I'm not in a ton of pain.

I stare down at the bandages with a brow raised for a long moment. Part of me wants to unwrap them, see what's going on beneath them, see what happened to that wound, but I'm still a little woozy-feeling from blacking out, and I don't want to encourage unconsciousness by staring at a gaping wound. I sigh and wrap the blanket tighter around my shoulders, ears pricked for any sound. Then I hold my breath and listen very carefully.

The forest is purely silent. Except...

I think I hear something off in the far distance, the *really* far distance. It sounds like murmuring. I don't exactly want to get lost in these woods, but my stomach is beginning to turn in panic when I wonder what time it is, if I've missed the board meeting...

Where the hell I am—stuff like that.

So I set out toward that murmuring sound, making certain that I do my best to walk in a very straight line into the woods. I was in the Girl Scouts for all of one week when I was a kid, but I think I remember a few tips on how not to get lost in the wilderness. I think. Shivering and stepping very carefully around branches, vines and dead plants (I'm only wearing slippers), I walk forward slowly.

I pause, turning to look back at the camp, making certain I can still see it. And I can: there's that enormous black horse, not giving me the time of day and eating like grass is going out of style. There's the small fire, busily licking at the remaining bits of wood in the circle of earth. There's the brown blanket that I spent the night on.

I hear the *snap* of a small branch close to me, and I jump out of my skin, turning to look back the way I was going. It was probably just a squirrel, I think, licking my lips, my mouth suddenly dry.

But there's nothing there.

I'm not an outdoorsy kind of lady—not that you didn't already realize that, since I live in the heart of Boston and rarely leave my beloved city. It's not that these woods, as impossible and improbable as they are, aren't gorgeous. Because they are.

There's just a lot that's very strange about this situation.

Obviously, numero uno: *there shouldn't be a forest in the middle of Boston.* But let's take that factor out of it.

In Boston? It's *August.* It's sweltering out on the coolest of days. It's a gorgeous, hot, end-of-summer time full of bikini-topped women, cold beers and hot dog vendors on the corners yelling about their famous mustard.

Here, wherever the hell "here" is?

It's *freezing.* There are leaves on the ground, like it's the end of *fall,* not the end of *summer.* There are bare bones trees in between the towering pine trees, and these bare bones trees are already bare because they've shed their leaves. The colorful carpet at my feet is made entirely of fallen leaves. There's hardly any grass on the ground (though that horse back there is still finding a pretty great breakfast), and what's left is dying or browning.

It doesn't make any sense. But when I hear another twig snapping, this time behind me, I'm expecting *something* to make sense. I'm expecting to see a squirrel, or absolutely nothing, like just a moment ago. And I do turn to look at what's behind me, because I'm a little freaked out right now, and I'd really like to see something familiar. Like a squirrel.

But that's not what I see when I turn around and look back the way I've come.

If I thought an enormous forest in the middle of Boston was weird, I had no idea how weird things could get.

Because, right now, I'm staring at an enormous silver bear.

To call it white wouldn't be right. Its coat is absolutely the color of silver, and its fur shimmers in the half-light of the clouded sky overhead as if it's lit from within. It looks like its fur is actually *glowing,* throwing light like an enormous, living disco ball, but that metaphor isn't elegant enough for how the bear actually looks.

Sometimes, really late at night (which is early morning for me, since I have to get up so early for my morning radio show), I watch nature documentaries, and while I've always thought there was a lot that's noble about the polar bear, at the same time, I've always thought they're kind of hilarious, too, the way they slip and slide on the ice, the way they play with each other like enormous puppies.

There's absolutely nothing funny or puppy-like about this bear.

It isn't a polar bear, for one. It can't be—not with that color of fur. Also, it stands much taller than a polar bear. I know that the shoulders of a polar bear are about level with the head of a man...

But this bear? This bear is *twice as tall* as I am.

This seems to be the morning of enormous animals.

But whereas I know that horse back at the camp—the horse I can see just beyond the bear's shoulder, who keeps cropping grass like this isn't a big deal, like it sees enormous predators all the time and finds them kind of boring—is completely domesticated...

Somehow I know, deep down, that this bear is all wild.

It moves slowly, lumbering along with a great deal of grace between the enormous trees, putting each paw down deliberately, and when I catch its eyes, it stands still on its four massive paws, paws that are the size of garbage can lids.

It's only about ten feet away from me as it lifts its massive head, blinking large, deep, bright eyes at me, sniffing the wind, its great nose wrinkling. If it wants to kill me right now, I know I'm dead. I'm already dead. There's absolutely no way that I can outrun this thing in my *slippers*, and there's no way I can evade her.

I don't know why I think this bear is a female; something just tells me that she's a she.

But the bear doesn't look hungry, and for some reason, I don't think that she looks like she wants to kill me. In fact, her eyes are actually quite peaceful, the kind of eyes I associate with cows or other herbivores—really quiet and gentle. But her eyes aren't brown, like most animal eyes.

In fact, they're blue.

They're a kind of glacial blue, the soft blue that snow can become at twilight. They're so light-colored, actually, that they seem to glow, just like her coat.

The bear rambles forward slowly, taking one step at a time, and I'm too afraid—and, really, mesmerized—to move. So by the time she's standing right in front of me, my heart rate is accelerated, yeah.

But I'm also filled with the kind of wonder I haven't felt since I was a kid.

Her massive head bends toward me, and then, very slowly and thoughtfully, the bear sniffs my face, her nose wrinkling about an inch from my own.

I stay perfectly still, not breathing. I should be shaking in my slippers, should be bracing myself for her to open her large jaws and bite my head off, or rear up and swipe me with a single paw to oblivion. There's something deep inside of me that's telling me those should be my logical, instinctual reactions, instincts that have been finely honed over millions of years thanks to my cavewoman ancestors, running from predators to live another day.

But as I stare up at this silver bear, as the breath finally comes out of my nose because I can't hold it in any longer, as that single gust of mine fills up the air in front of both of us like smoke...I realize something extremely odd.

I'm not afraid of her at all.

She gazes down at me with those wide, blue eyes, and I stare back at her with my chin tilted up, holding that eye contact.

There's something so gentle in that deep, blue gaze that it takes my breath away.

It reminds me of when I was a little kid, and I went to see Santa Claus for the first time (that I can remember, anyway). I went with my sister, Ellie, to see him, holding her hand tightly while we stood in line, being scared senseless, because our parents had told us how important this was, going to see Santa and tell him what presents we wanted. We weren't a religious family, so I'd never had any experience with the idea of someone who was so much vaster than me. And, to my kid mind, being able to give presents to children all in one night was pretty damn vast.

Now, don't laugh—but when I went up to sit on his lap that first time, when I looked into his kind, blue eyes...I felt a lot of awe. I was six years old. I believed, utterly, that this was the guy who could travel the entire world in a single evening and give presents to every single good girl and boy.

He was a miracle to me. And it was, of

course, just some guy in a suit, hired to be a mall Santa...but he certainly played the part very well. He was kind and really did laugh like a bowl full of jelly when I told him that I didn't want a Barbie—I wanted a G.I. Joe. He put his finger alongside his nose and winked at me warmly. He talked with me a long while, I remember. It was probably only a minute or so, but to a kid in awe of something so much bigger than her, it meant a lot to me. I can say that that's the first time that I felt awe or wonder that big, as I talked to Santa.

And that's what this bear reminds me of, as I stand nose to nose with her and am not afraid: awe, wonder and magic. Stuff I've not thought about in a very long time.

I sigh, then, and that's what makes the moment pass. She blinks her eyes slowly, and then, tortoise-like, she turns her bulk gently to the left, like a Mack truck backing up, and she begins to lumber back the way she came, putting one paw in front of the other and not looking back.

But, as she turns from me, her shoulder brushes against the front of my blanket just a little. I didn't think to move out of the way (I'm pretty sure I'm in some sort of shock). I glance down to look at the few silver hairs she left behind on my blanket, and I glance up just as quickly.

But when I glance up?

She's completely gone. Disappeared. Like she was never here at all.

I stand stock still for a moment, my heartbeat beginning to thrum loudly against my ribs.

What just happened?

I look back down at the blanket covering me and reach up my hand, brushing my fingers against the few silver hairs that are still there. They glimmer in the soft light beneath the trees. These prove she was here, that this just happened.

I glance around again wildly, but there's absolutely no place she could have disappeared to. She's simply vanished, and though the silver hairs remaining prove that she actually existed, that I did actually see her with my own two eyes...it's still the weirdest thing out of many weird things that have happened to me recently.

I blink, turning, dazed, and keep making my way further into the forest, stumbling forward.

I have no idea what to think about what just happened, so I simply don't.

But it's not long—only a few more steps, really—until I find out the source of the murmuring that led me deep into the woods and, for a heartbeat, I can take my mind off of the disappearing bear. I've reached the top of a little embankment, and down below me a small creek winds its way through the woods, bubbling happily over stones. That's what was making the murmuring sound—the water. It's bubbling cheerfully enough, in fact, that it looks like this is one of those settings used for filming a magical fairy tale movie.

But magical fairy tale movies, that *I* can recall, don't usually feature a naked woman swimming in a creek.

I stare, because I can't *help* but stare.

She hasn't seen me yet, where I'm standing up on the bank. Even though it was pitch black last night, I still recognize her as the woman I fell into, the woman who pointed a sword at my heart, the woman who'd worn armor...but she's certainly not wearing armor right now. Or anything else for that matter. Okay, maybe it's been awhile since I saw a naked woman, but it's not just that (or the fact that I, occasionally, have the mind of a twelve-year-old boy) that keeps me staring.

I mean...she's *beautiful*.

Maybe not everyone would think she's beautiful. You'd have to like her type, but I do. God, I do. In the daylight, I can see that she's completely muscular, with very few soft inches of skin. She's pale, which somehow surprises me (I don't know—I guess I thought a woman riding around on a horse would be a bit more tan), but then I note her shoulder-length straight hair is dark red as she rises out of the water a little, running her hands over her wet hair after she's surfaced, eyes closed, head thrown back as the water drips into the creek from her body.

It's one of the most erotic things I've ever seen, her standing up in that creek, arching her back and letting her face curve toward the sun as she lets her head fall back, her hair dripping. My heart is thudding against my chest about a mile a minute, and there's such a fierce ache and want that moves through me, I catch my breath.

She straightens, running a hand over her face to wipe away the water, and that's when she sees me. Even across the space between us, I can see that her eyes are dark brown amber, the kind of brown that glints and shimmers, like it has flecks of gold hidden deep within. She has a full mouth, and it's soft now, with water pouring down her face, but it hardens into a thin line when she spots me. Her cheekbones are high, the curve of her neck leads down to her chest, and I can't help but stare for a few seconds at her small, round breasts that float above the water.

"Hello," she says gruffly, thrusting her chin up as she narrows her eyes and stands up in the creek. Water pours down her body, and she strides out of that creek like she does this sort of thing—walks around naked—all the time. She has the confidant prowl of a predatory big cat. "Did you sleep well?" she asks me, and then she's standing on the creek bank, sluicing water off her arms with her hands.

"Uh..." I say with maximum articulateness. She glances over her sculpted shoulder at me with a single brow raised. When she raises that single brow, I go a little weak in the knees.

Okay. I *must* have hit my head. What the hell is *wrong* with me? Yeah, as much as I'm devoted to my job and don't go on as many dates as I used to, I'm not actually dead inside: I find random women attractive all the time.

But when I look at her, it's like a sucker punch to the gut. Well, a little more pleasant than a sucker punch—but it's just as strong of a sensation. My attraction to her is off the charts, and all I've done is fall into her.

I normally don't *literally* fall for women. It usually takes a bit more than that to get the old heart knocking against the ribs so much.

"Let me look at your wound," she tells me, her voice rumbling and deep, and with dripping hands, she turns and takes my bandaged hand. She undoes the bandage, wrapping the white cloth backwards around her palm, and her fingers are gentle, but I still wince and shiver as she unwraps that cloth and exposes the wound beneath. For half a moment, my focus shifts away from her gorgeous nakedness.

I steel myself, take a big inhale of air, and then I chance looking down at my hand.

The wound itself is about an inch long, which—on my palm—appears massive, but the gash in my palm is covered in a thick coating of cream-colored salve, and appears to no longer be bleeding, which I'm pretty sure is a good sign.

"You heal well," she tells me gruffly, spreading my fingers wide and peering down at the wound this way and that. Her fingers on the back of my hand are gentle as she raises my hand to her eye level and stares down into my palm.

She inhales deeply, and then, rounding her mouth into a soft "o," she blows warm air onto the center of my palm.

My heart rate right now is off the charts, and little black points are starting to hover at the corners of my vision, not from seeing the wound, but because of *her.* There's this unbelievably gorgeous woman, standing naked *right in front of me,* holding gently onto my hand and *blowing* onto it.

"Uh," I say again, ever so articulately, "what are you doing?"

She glances at me, and once more she raises that single brow, her head to the side a little. "Close your eyes, milady," she tells me in a soft growl.

My cheeks are so red that I probably look just

like that long-ago Santa Claus did, but for some reason, her tone brooks no argument. So I do it. I find myself closing my eyes.

I'm hyper aware of everything in that moment. Of the fact that she's holding gently to my hand, that her skin is warm, even though she just got out of a freezing creek, and even when everything else in the world (including me) seems so cold. That the heels of my slippers are sinking into the mud along the bank of the creek, and that my nose is so chilled that it feels like it's falling off.

But everything else is taking a backseat to the fact that this woman is still holding my hand, her fingers still gentle, her breath still warm against the skin of my palm.

And then, behind my eyelids, something begins to...well, *glow*. The day itself has been gray and drab, with the sun showing no possibility of peeking out from behind clouds. But now, just the same, there's a warm glow happening right in front of me, the light as soft and subdued as a candle's flame, or a match being struck. And, at the same time, my palm feels warmer than it did, even when she was blowing on it.

"All right," she says smoothly, the words rolling out like velvet, and—sadly (much to my dismay)—her fingers leave my hand. "You can open your eyes now," she tells me.

I do. And I stare down at the palm of my hand, spellbound.

There's...no wound.

That's the best way I can describe it: it's as if the wound on my palm never existed. Which I know it most certainly did. I'd seen it with my own two eyes just a moment ago, and I'd felt the pain of it with my whole body. It had hurt like a mother. It was *real*.

But it isn't there anymore.

"Okay," I say, taking a deep breath and clenching my hand into a fist. When there's no pain in my fist, I open up my palm again, staring down into it. "Um..." I glance up at her, biting my lip as my brain cycles through the millions of things I could possibly say in this moment.

Unfortunately, my quick mouth works before my brain can catch up with it.

"What the hell?" I manage, as that mysterious, gorgeous, naked woman folds her arms in front of her chest and smiles ruefully, shaking her head.

"That's not how we say 'thank you,'" she murmurs, her one brow artfully up, and then I'm blushing again, because she moves past me easily, toward the edge of the forest and a low leaf-less shrub that has a white blouse and what looks like deerskin pants hanging from its branches. Her silver armor is stacked neatly on the ground on top of her cloak.

I stare at that pile of metal armor, at her sword and scabbard, leaning against a large pine tree. I try not to stare at her nude form, and I fail, so then I drink in the curves of her rear for a long moment before I open my mouth again.

"What the hell is going on?" I persist then, steeling myself and following her. If she doesn't care that she's naked, I'm going to do my absolute best not to care, either (I'm currently failing at that, but hell, at least I'm trying).

She glances at me over her shoulder and shakes her head, little droplets of water dripping off her hair and flying in different directions. "You tell me," she growls, picking up a piece of cloth from the bushes.

I watch, mesmerized, as she pulls on what I can really only describe as panties. They don't look like the normal, Fruit of the Loom stuff you can get at Target, but they're still similar enough that I know exactly what they are. I guess the best way to describe them would be tight-fitting boxers. They appear to be made out of silk, or something like that—they shimmer in the clouded light as she pulls them on, as they hug the muscular contours of her body as if they're a second skin.

She places her hands on her hips again, and stands strongly, one brow raised, her mouth turning up at the corners as she catches me staring at her.

I blush a shade of red so deep, I wonder if I'll ever not look like a beet again.

The woman shakes her head, and I can tell she's doing her best not to chuckle. She sighs for a long moment, pulling the pants (which are made of something like deerskin, now that I can see them up close; they look like leather) on each leg and pulling them over her hips in a single fluid motion. She knots the leather thong at the waist.

"Look," the woman tells me, then, shaking her head. She's pulling the blouse, which resembles something medieval men might have worn while penning poetry (I just get that impression when staring at it; it also looks like something Fabio might have worn on a romance novel cover), over her head, letting it settle over her breasts. She pulls her hair out of the shirt and shakes it again in her hand, droplets flying from her red mane. "I don't know where you came from," she says succinctly then, pulling socks that look hand-knit onto her feet after she sprawls down onto the cloak next to her armor. "I don't know why you're here. But as lovely as it's been," she says wryly, "I must be leaving you."

"*What*?" I squeak, moving past my outrage that she has no idea what's going on right into the fear that she's not going to stay to help me get back home. It's a quick change in my rotating inner list of things-to-worry-about. "How...how can I get back home? Where *is* home? Where's Boston?" I ask her, realizing that I sound like I'm pleading, but I'm actually kind of nervous, in that moment.

She wouldn't really leave me here, all alone in this enormous forest, to fend for myself.

Would she?

"Hey," I persist as she stands, shaking her head, her long, knee-length boots pulled on. She picks up the chest piece and back piece of armor and lifts them overhead, draping them over her shoulders, so that they fall over her front and back. The two pieces of metal are attached by leather straps on her shoulders and sides, and she's tugging them tighter.

The chest piece of the armor is sculpted for her breasts, which I actually don't stare at, at that moment. Instead, I hold her deep, amber gaze.

"Look at me," I tell her, gesturing down to my Scooby Doo pajama top, leopard-print bottoms and the blanket wrapped around my shoulders. I hope that she can sufficiently see how *not cut out for this* I am. I step forward. "I have no idea where I am, and I have no idea how to get home, and you're the *only* person I've met so far in a forest that shouldn't even exist. You can't just *leave* me here," I tell her as she raises that eyebrow again, pulling shining metal gauntlets over her arms and wrists and drawing their leather straps tighter, too.

"What kingdom do you hail from?" she asks me, her head to the side as her eyes rake over my body. There's absolutely nothing sexual in the way that she looks at me, which is in turns disappointing (I mean, what are the chances she's gay?) and also horrifying, because, again—*I'm wearing a Scooby Doo shirt.* I doubt that anyone has ever found someone wearing a Scooby Doo shirt utterly attractive.

I blink, then, processing what she just said. *Kingdom?*

"Look," I tell her, taking a deep breath and hoping that my voice doesn't shake. It shakes only a little, at the end of the word. "I was just doing laundry in my basement, minding my own damn business, and then I fell into a hole in the floor. My basement is in Boston, which is in the *kingdom* of the United States." I take another deep breath and hold it for a moment while she considers my words, and not a single bit of understanding or recognition passes over her face. She's never heard of the United States. "What kingdom am I in right now?" I ask her, squeaking a little as I do my best to play along and not to feel overwhelmed.

"The kingdom of Arktos," she says promptly, her face growing a little stony as she slips a leather skirt over her feet and shimmies it up to her hips, over the leather pants. It's not a long leather skirt—it only reaches about mid-thigh, but each feather of leather also has a metal plate on top of it, so it's part of the armor. Normally, a skirt looks feminine on someone—but pulled over the leather pants and with the metal plates, it doesn't look feminine in the slightest on her.

She looks like a warrior.

"Arktos," I repeat in a whisper.

She sighs, then, turning as she hooks her scabbard over her shoulder and plucks up her cloak. She walks toward me, the metal clinking where her arm gauntlet brushes against the stomach of her armored chest piece. I think she's going to walk past me, but then she pauses.

She stares, her amber eyes dark and deep, as she glances down at my front.

"Where did this come from?" she breathes, and she reaches out and brushes her fingers against the blanket that's over my chest.

I'm red again and finding it difficult to breathe, but then I realize that she's talking about the silver hairs on the blanket. The silver hairs from the bear.

"Um," I mutter, clearing my throat again. "They came from the bear I just saw."

I mean, what else am I going to say? It's the truth. But when she stares at me, her eyes are so wide, and her lips are parted, like she's finally the one who's surprised about something.

"A bear?" she asks me then, narrowing her eyes and stepping forward, even closer to me. We're almost touching, and then we are, because she's gripping my shoulders in her gloved hands, holding me tightly, staring down into my eyes with her own dark ones as she frowns deeply, her lips in a thin, tight line. "You saw a bear? A *silver* bear?" she growls. "What did it look like? When did you see it?"

She's holding me so tightly that I wince, and only then does she blink, stepping back and releasing my arms. She takes a deep breath, folding her arms in front of her.

"Just now. It was back there—in the woods. But it disappeared," I tell her, straightening my blanket in front of me.

She stares at me, as if mesmerized for a long moment, as if I'm something magical.

I don't mind at all that she's looking at me like that. For the first time since I came to this crazy place, I feel something good unfurling deep inside of me. I *love* how she's looking at me...

But just as quickly, she glances away, darting past me in a graceful trot, up the bank of the creek and back into the forest proper.

"Over here?" she calls over her shoulder. "Where exactly did you see her?"

"Over there, I guess?" I call after her, following, but a bit more slowly. "I'm not exactly familiar with this area," I tell her sarcastically, as I stand, wrapped tightly in my blanket, following her back the way I came. "Look, she *disappeared*," I reiterate, as she crouches on the ground, pressing her gloved fingers to the earth with a frown.

She's pressing her fingers, I realize just then,

into an enormous paw print.

She appears deep in thought for a long moment, and though I can't see her face, the sweep of hair in front of her features, the curve of her shoulders...there's something bothering her.

The woman stands fluidly, turning on her heel and prowling toward me, then. She stops in front of me, reaching out with her hand and fingering the blanket as she stares down at the silver hairs with a deep frown.

My heart is threatening to launch itself right out of my rib cage.

Her fingers are directly *over* my heart, and as she turns the blanket this way and that, her gloved hand brushes against my left breast.

A shiver races through me, even as I try to stomp it down. She flicks her gaze into my eyes then, and for a moment, I think she's amused, but then her intensity comes back.

"What did she do?" she asks, her voice low.

"She...uh...came up to me," I tell her, clearing my throat. "And she sort of stood there for a while. We were nose to nose. And then she just turned, and she walked away. She brushed her shoulder against the blanket, and that's where the hairs came from. But when I looked back up, she was completely gone, like she'd disappeared. Which," I add, chuckling a little, though it's high-pitched and desperate-sounding, "there's no way that she could just have *disappeared*. I mean, right?" I ask her, swallowing.

She gazes deeply into my eyes for a long moment.

I notice that she hasn't let go of the blanket.

That the backs of her fingers are still against my heart.

"What is your name?" she asks me, mystified.

"I'm Josie Beckett," I tell her easily, the words rolling out of my mouth, sounding exactly as they do when I announce that fact a thousand times every morning on the radio. That's because I'm smiling like I do when I announce it into my microphone, I realize with no small amount of chagrin, as I stare up into this stranger's eyes.

"Josie Beckett," she says, one eyebrow artfully raised, "I am Attis. And you are in great danger. You are not safe in these woods."

I blink up at her, smile fading. I'm not exactly certain what I thought she'd say, but this...isn't it.

"What do you mean, I'm not safe? I don't even want to *be* in these woods," I tell her miserably. "I just want to go home. I have a meeting today, and I've probably already missed it, and that means that my radio station..." I trail off, taking in the blankness of Attis' expression. She has no idea what I'm talking about. "I have to go home," I tell her then, simply, shaking my head. "I *need* to go home."

"What kingdom did you say you were from?" she asks, stepping back, her hand falling to her side as she stands surely, feet hip-width apart, her head to the side as she considers me like a difficult problem that needs to be solved.

"I'm from *Boston*," I tell her. "It's not a kingdom. It's a city."

"Well," she says, folding her arms in front of her, "there is no Boston that I know of." She considers me with shrewd eyes. "And what world are you from, Josie Beckett?"

"Just call me Josie," I tell her, before I fully understand that she's asking me *what planet I'm from.* "For real?" I ask her, blinking, but she looks dead serious, her mouth in that thin, hard line and her amber eyes glinting. I wait for a long moment for the punchline, but there isn't one.

"Earth," I finally tell her in the tiniest voice I've ever used. "I'm from Earth."

The woman stares at me for a long moment before shaking her head. "You are on Earth no longer, Josie," she growls, not unkindly. "This is Agrotera."

Chapter 4: The Cat

"You're joking," I tell Attis, stepping forward and wrapping my fingers around the edges of the metal chest piece of her armor and holding her tightly. I shake her a little, panicked. "You're *joking*, right? You're telling me I'm on a *different world*?"

Attis allows me to cling to her, but one of her eyebrows arches high to the sky. "I'm *telling* you," she says, surprisingly gentle, reaching up with her gloved hands to curl her fingers over mine, "that you're on *Agrotera*."

"How is this... How is this possible?" I ask her, letting her go and stepping backward as I wrap the blanket so tightly around myself that I cough a little. "I'm on another world? How am I going to get home?" I take a deep breath, my heart rate skyrocketing. I take a few more deep breaths, calming myself down. I close my eyes, swallow. "What am I going to *do*?" I say then, softly.

The woman clears her throat and shifts her weight back into her heels. "Well," she says, drawing out the word a little, her head to the side again. She watches me for a long moment, her piercing gaze unwavering until she says in a soft growl, "You could come with me."

I stare at her. Go with her? "Where are you going?" I ask, uncertainly.

She's the only human (God, I *hope* she's human. She *looks* human—that's got to count for something) I've met since I came to this place. I don't want to let her out of my sight, but at the same time, a complete stranger is telling me to come with her to God knows where. I was raised in Boston. I wasn't born yesterday. For all I know, she wants to eat me (though, I admit, she doesn't exactly look like a cannibal. Whatever a cannibal looks like. I've...never thought about what a cannibal looks like before, but Attis isn't what I might have imagined).

"I'm journeying to Arktos City," she says smoothly, chin up as she regards me with her warm amber eyes. "I'm on my way there for the Festival of Stars."

"I'd prefer the Festival of Getting Me Back to My Own Damn Planet," I tell her, voice sharp, but she actually laughs, lifting her head up, tilting her chin back, and letting out peals of laughter.

It's the first time I've seen her smile, like, *actually* smile, and the first time I've seen her laugh. God, she's gorgeous when she laughs. Her hard exterior sort of melts, and all of her strength remains, but there's a sort of gentleness there, too, in the way that she lets her head tilt back, exposing the sweet, cream-colored skin of her neck, the way she sounds. It's bright and warm, her laughter. I love it.

She's also laughing at my joke, which warms me from the inside out.

But I've currently got problems, and I shouldn't be paying so much attention to what she sounds like (or, you know, looks like) when she's laughing. I shouldn't be paying so much attention to how she stands, her gloved hands on her hips, or how the armor clings to her body because of the leather straps, or how gorgeous her hips and thighs look, encased in that leather.

I'm on another planet, and I'm standing next to a gorgeous woman wearing armor.

I've got to try to look on the bright side, if only for a moment. And I have to admit: things could be worse.

"Okay, Arktos City," I say, softening a bit. "What's there?"

She's stopped laughing, but she's still smiling, her full lips turning up at the corners as she gazes at me with bemusement. But when I speak, she puts her head to the side again, and again considers me.

"Well," she says, straightening, "there just might be someone in Arktos City who could help you, possibly show you a way to get back to your world. But," she says sharply, when I gasp, "it's just a guess. I'm not certain she can help at all. Still, it's worth a try."

I might *(might)* just have a ticket *home*.

"Oh, my God!" I squeal, and then I'm so damn excited—like, little-kid-at-Christmas excited— that I bounce in place for a moment. All I can think about is the fact that, yeah, maybe I couldn't make the board meeting, but maybe I can reschedule if they'll give me another chance... "So, we're heading to that city now? Like, *right* now? Let's go!" I tell her, jerking my thumb back toward the encampment. "Is it, like, a couple of miles from here?" She stares at me blankly, and I try to curb my enthusiasm. "Um...how far is it?"

"Oh...it's a quarter moon's worth of travel," says Attis easily, turning on her heel and marching back toward the encampment.

"A quarter moon? How long is a quarter moon?" I ask, trailing after her.

"Seven days," Attis replies over her shoulder.

I stop cold.

"Seven *days?*"

When she doesn't answer me, I trot to catch up with her. She's already reached the camp and is stomping nonchalantly on the little fire in the circle of earth. I stare at her leather boot pummeling the fire, and then I swallow.

"Seven days is a *really* long time... Is there any way we can speed things up just a bit?" I ask her, nervously fingering the edge of the blanket wrapped around my shoulders. Attis glances at me, surprised, grinding out the last of the flame with the heel of her boot.

"No," she tells me crisply. "Seven days is the length of time that Zilla can get us there, and that's already pushing her more than I'm comfortable with."

"Who's Zilla?" I ask, utterly confused.

Attis jerks her thumb over her shoulder. But when I glance over her shoulder, all I see is the horse.

Oh. Zilla is the horse.

"Zilla...like Godzilla?" I quip immediately, because it's the first thing that comes to mind. Attis glances back at me with continued bemusement.

"I'm sure she thinks she's a god," says Attis thoughtfully.

I roll my eyes and follow after her again. "Can't we ask...uh, *Zilla* to speed things just up a *little*?" I mutter, as Attis bends down and picks up the blanket I'd been sleeping on. She shakes it out with a smart *snap* and then folds it as quickly as Martha Stewart can fold a pillowcase.

Attis casts me a single, pointed look. "No," she growls.

I shiver a little under my completely inadequate blanket. A soft, insistent, utterly chill breeze has begun to pick up beneath the trees, and it's starting to blow a little harder. The leaves at my feet shift and begin to dance across the forest floor.

Attis glances up at me from her crouched position, stuffing the blanket into one of her packs. "Look, if you're going to travel with me, I think it'd be highly insulting if I let my charge die of frostbite," she tells me mildly, untying the knot on one of the larger woven bags at her feet. She casts a glance back at me, as if sizing me up, and then she pulls what looks to be a fur jacket out of that pack. The coat is big and warm and so utterly inviting.

"How many bunnies were harmed in the making of this?" I ask her, as she offers the coat to me.

"There were no *bunnies* harmed in the making of this," she says, her jaw hard as she helps me into the coat. "It is made from the skin of a cannibal werewolf. He devoured three children before I cut his throat."

I shrug the coat onto my shoulders and then

stare at her for a long moment, waiting for the punchline.

But there, of course, isn't one. She's serious.

"Cannibal werewolf," I repeat, my voice wooden as I finger the soft fur, suddenly wondering if I really want to be wearing this, after all.

"Well," she says, stopping to consider as her mouth curls up at the corners. "He isn't a cannibal werewolf *anymore*," she tells me, smiling a little at her own joke.

"Tell me about it," I mutter, and because the choice is either to put on this fur coat that once belonged to a *cannibal werewolf* (where the hell am I?) or freeze to death...I keep the damn cannibal werewolf coat on.

I wrap my arms around myself. The coat's pretty warm, which is awesome, but I'm still just wearing slippers and leopard print PJs on the bottom, so I feel the cold. But I'm a lot warmer than I was a moment ago, just wearing the blanket.

I glance up at the little knoll, along the side of the encampment. "Is this where I came from last night?" I ask her, shoving my hands into—blessedly—pockets. The coat has pockets. Thank heaven for small favors.

"Yes, but do not go up that hill," Attis warns me, her voice sharp as she rolls up her own blanket and lashes it to one of the packs, tying the leather tightly. "Remember what those thorns did to you last night. I don't have enough energy to heal you again this day," she says, all business as she chirps toward Zilla. The big, black horse snorts out of her nose and swallows one last enormous mouthful of grass before sauntering on over to Attis.

I glance down at my palm, the palm that's completely devoid of any wound. "You healed me? With what?"

Attis glances up at me in surprise as she rises, placing one gloved hand along her horse's neck and patting her twice. "With magic, of course," she tells me, in the same tone of voice that people say "duh."

Magic. Sure. Why not. I mean, after cannibal werewolves and finding myself in another world, it's par for the course for magic to come into the picture.

I swallow and glance up at the knoll, wondering what's just out of sight beyond the edge of the hill and those trees. I wonder if there's a hole in the ground just past that one big pine tree, a hole that—if I fell into it, just like I fell into one last night—I'd appear back in my world, in my own, stupid Basement of Evil, a place that I would never, ever complain about again, having just fallen against something and knocked my head pretty badly. A knock that made me hallucinate all of this while I was unconscious.

But I'm pretty damn sure, at this point, that this is no hallucination. This is too damn real, all of this. It's impossibly real.

I still wonder if there's a hole up there—a portal back to my own world.

Attis catches me glancing wistfully up toward the trees, and she shakes her head as she lifts a thick blanket up from the ground and places it on her horse's back. "I scouted the area, Josie. There is no trace of the portal that you fell through. I'm sorry.

You're stuck with me for the time being."

I look at her in surprise. She genuinely *does* sound sorry. I wrap my arms tightly around myself, glance at her a little sheepishly.

"I'm grateful for the coat. Thank you," I tell her, my voice quiet.

A softness comes over her face, and her mouth turns up at the corners—but just a little. "Take good care of it," she tells me, her voice no-nonsense. "And..." She's lifting up her leather saddle—which doesn't look like any saddle I've ever seen (if anything, it reminds me of something I saw once on a horse at a Renaissance Festival...), but she pauses before placing it on Zilla's back. "If you see the bear again," she begins, turning back to me and holding up her hand. Her amber eyes flash dangerously. "You do not go near her—do you understand? Do not let her near you." Her jaw hardens. "She is a very dangerous beast. You must avoid her at all costs."

I open and shut my mouth. The bear hadn't seemed dangerous to me. She'd seemed the exact opposite of dangerous, actually: peaceful. Kind, even. I want to ask her what she's talking about, but at that moment, Zilla snorts, lifting her massive head and widening her nostrils as she looks out towards the woods. Attis glances toward the trees, too, and shakes her head. "Be ready to go in a moment," she tells me, reaching under the horse's belly and grabbing one of the dangling leather straps of the saddle. "And stay close by. These woods are not safe."

I take a deep breath and grimace. I can't stay close by. I have to pee.

This is going to be so awkward.

I draw in another deep breath and wrap my arms around myself, trying to consider my options. I don't exactly want to step one tree away and do my business where the woman can very well hear it and probably see me (I'm shy, okay?). But Attis looks like she's serious about me actually sticking close by. I glance at the trees surrounding us miserably and clear my throat.

"Uh...where can I go to...you know?" I ask her, waving my hand in a small circle and hoping desperately that she knows what I'm talking about and that I don't have to spell it out.

She looks bemused as she cinches the saddle to her horse. "Are you really so modest?"

"Hey, now," I mutter, going as red as a beet. "It's not necessarily *modesty* that compels me to avoid peeing in front of a stranger," I tell her, placing my hands on my hips. I don't add that I also don't want to pee in front of someone so damn attractive, but I'm certainly thinking it.

I *definitely* fell on my head.

"Behind a tree, if you must," she sighs, shaking her head and chuckling a little.

I march behind the nearest big tree and fumble with the ties at the waistband of my pajama bottoms. And then I do my business in the most clumsy way possible. It's not exactly the most comfortable pee of my life, but finally it's over, and I'm wondering what sort of leaves I should use, or if the leaves here are members of some lethal plant species, much like the random plant that jammed a thorn through the center of my hand yesterday. At the last minute, I simply pray that the leaf belongs to a nice, gentle plant species. I stand up, tie my pants and don't feel so much relieved as embarrassed.

And that's when I hear the mewing.

It's impossible, what I'm hearing. But I'm instantly and instinctively on high-alert, because if there's one thing in the world I know, it's my cat's mew.

It's *Wonder.* And I can hear her. And she's mewing for me.

This is her patented (and highly piteous) "I've not eaten in a thousand years, why are you trying to kill me by starvation, you terrible mom?" mew, which she uses on me about five minutes after she's eaten and wants more food.

Oh, my God, I realize, a cold sweat breaking over my skin.

I can hear my cat.

My cat, who's supposed to be *an entire world away.*

"Wonder?!" I call out to her, standing very still and trying to still my heart (which is beating so quickly, it's almost all I can hear) unsuccessfully. "Wonder?" I try again, a little softer.

There's another mew, but this time, I can hear where it's coming from.

The knoll that I fell down last night. The knoll that is covered in bushes with poisonous thorns that can, apparently, kill you.

That's where her mew is coming from.

I don't have time to think. I only have time to react.

In that moment, nothing else matters—nothing

else in the world, except for saving my cat.

I bolt through the clearing that I woke up in, past the fire that Attis put out. I bolt past the surprised woman tacking up her horse and past the surprised horse. I race past everything, the fear coiling in my throat like something poisonous.

There's another mew at the top of the knoll, and I hit the steep slop running. Pure adrenaline pours through me, propelling me up that hill when, really, I'm not the athletic type. My feet slip on the scree, and I fall forward, my palms sustaining a new nasty brush burn that I immediately ignore, because in a moment of climbing hand over hand, I'm at the top of the knoll...

And I'm staring straight ahead, at a patch of briers.

"Briers" is a stretch. These are bushes that are *as tall as I am;* some of them actually tower over me. These bushes are blood red, which is utterly creepy, but not nearly as creepy as the fact that each branch sports a ton of wicked-looking, clustered thorns that are longer than my hand.

In the cold, drab, gray day, the tips of the thorns closest to me actually *glisten.* Like they're waiting to pierce me through.

"Wonder?" I yell out, and then I see movement. Just a little movement. It's hard to spy anything through the sea of branches that faces me, but then I see...

Wonder. She's practically prancing in her self-satisfied way across the ground, her tail up in a question mark as she slides herself through loops and tangles of the branches effortlessly.

And doesn't touch them at all.

She saunters through the last few feet of the branches, and then she sits down in front of me, glancing up with her slow blink as she begins to purr.

There's not a scratch on her.

I fall to my knees, scoop my stupid, wonderful, brave cat up into my arms, and I squeeze her so hard as I begin to cry that she makes a little squeak in the middle of her purring, but then she goes right back to that purring as she rubs the side of her face against my chin.

Attis is somehow, impossibly, beside me in an instant, staring down at me and my cat with a look that I'm not sure is wonder or bewilderment, or is perhaps a bit of both.

"What just happened?" she asks, glancing from Wonder back to the thorn bushes.

"She's *here*," I breathe, brushing my chin across the top of my blissfully purring cat's head. "How did she get here?" I stand, still holding Wonder, and together Attis and I look out beneath the tall pine trees at the mess of tangled thorns.

"I...don't know," says Attis carefully, placing her hands on her hips. She glances down again at me, raising one brow artfully. "It is well documented, of course, that all cats are magical creatures who can slip into other worlds whenever they wish."

"That's the first thing that's made sense to me all day," I tell her, and then I actually chuckle. I glance out at the thorns again, my eyes wide as I sober. "But...do you think that maybe the portal opened?"

Attis shakes her head and sighs for a long

moment. "Even if it was open, Josie, there's no way that we could ever get to it. Not through those. But rest your mind: I don't believe the portal opened. I checked last night, and there was nothing there. If your cat has followed you here, it's much more possible that she did so under her own enchantments, and it had nothing to do with the portal."

I glance down at my cat, who blinks slowly at me and then—again—makes the mew sound that details how hungry she is, and how wet food had *better* be coming posthaste if I know what's good for me.

"Um," I grimace, glancing up at Attis. "Do you have any...uh...meat?"

Her brow remains up, but Attis chuckles a little, too. "For the little puss? Perhaps."

I carry Wonder back down to the encampment, and Attis produces a few dried meat stick-type...things from one of her packs, and Wonder chews on them like she's died and gone to kitty heaven. Which is good enough for me.

When Wonder is done—and I've stopped wondering (ha!) how she could possibly have gotten here—Attis and Zilla are all suited up and ready to move out.

I open up the cannibal werewolf coat (I'll never be able to think of it as anything else) and scoop my cat up in my arms. She protests, but sleepily, since she's full of meat, and lets me place her not-insubstantial bulk into the coat and against me, buttoning the coat back up. As I turn to take in the fully tacked Zilla and the patiently waiting Attis, Wonder begins to purr again against me.

I have my crazy cat with me, and that's kind of wonderful.

I wander over to Attis and motion toward the trees. "Ready to go?" I ask her.

Attis regards me with an unknowable expression, and then, as smoothly as if she's bowing, Attis kneels to the ground on one knee in front of me and cups her hands together, glancing up at me with her warm amber eyes.

I stare at her for a long moment. She can't be serious.

"Well?" she asks, her voice a low growl.

"Uh...you want me to get up on that thing?" I ask her, staring up at the saddle and chewing my lip. "I'm not really much of a horse...uh, woman."

Attis stares at me, perplexed. "How else do you suppose that we will reach Arktos City before either of us are old and gray? I will walk, and you will ride her," she says simply, as if it's the most obvious thing in the world. "We must travel many miles, and judging by the state of your boots..." She raises an eyebrow as she stares pointedly at my feet and their fuzzy slippers, "I must insist that I walk and you ride. Zilla will take care of you—she is a good beast."

I glance up at the towering horse, feeling my heart thud unpleasantly inside of me. I'm, of course, remembering the single time that I ever sat on a horse. The Grand Canyon trip with my college friends. We were signed up for a trail ride, and they put me on a big black-and-white horse named Buck.

It was kind of an appropriate name, since that's all he was capable of doing.

I'd sailed through the air and sustained a broken wrist. And that was the extent of my horseback adventure.

Zilla is glancing around her shoulder at me now, her ears slicked back. I'm fairly certain that my unhappy feelings about the situation are mutual. Under my coat, Wonder gives an unpleasant growl. I don't think she's thrilled about this, either.

"Josie," says Attis then, with a very long sigh. Her hands are still cupped together, and she's still kneeling, but she's staring up at me with narrowed eyes now. "We really do not have all day."

I shake my head, hold Wonder a little tighter. "Your horse is enormous, I'm afraid of heights, I'm fairly certain she wants me dead..."

Attis closes her eyes and opens them, fixing a smile that's obviously not genuine on her face. She growls out the words, trying to keep her tone light— and failing. "You *will* ride Zilla, and you *will* mount her right now. We have much ground to cover, and this area is not safe. Not with the Ursa being seen here."

"Ursa?" I ask her, but she shakes her head, pins me with her gaze.

"Mount," she growls. "Now." And then, with maddening sarcasm, she says, in a low, hard voice, "Milady."

On any normal day, I don't enjoy being told what to do. When I'm cold and hungry and holding my miraculous-God-knows-how-she-got-here cat and should really be at a board meeting trying to save my radio station, but am, instead, on another *world*...well.

Then I really, *really* don't enjoy being told

what to do.

"No," I tell her, my voice cold and absolutely dead serious. "I can walk. At least for a long while," I tell her, gesturing down to my slippers with their rubber soles. "I'm going to *walk*," I tell her, but then I see the storm building behind her eyes.

The horse glances around her shoulder, as if she finds this interaction vastly amusing.

"You can mount into the saddle, or I can tie you to the saddle," says Attis mildly, her voice in a low, controlled growl. "Which is it?"

I stand firm, rising to my full height, one hand on my hips, another hand holding my cat tightly to me, a little like the weapon I know she can be.

"I'd like to see you try," I tell her, voice even, measured and utterly deadly.

All day long, I deal with crank callers and people who yell a lot at the radio station. I have absolutely no budget, and—somehow—I have to cobble together one hell of a good radio program every damn day. I'm used to dealing with extremely hard situations and turning them into good ones, taking limited resources and making something wonderful out of them.

I'm used to dealing with people who think they're tough and better than me. And I'm used to talking circles around them.

There is not a single part of me that doubts that Attis is considering tying me to that saddle in that moment as she regards me with her warm amber eyes that have suddenly gone cold. She's taller than me, a hell of a lot stronger than me... She could absolutely do it if she really wants to.

But as our eyes lock, as power sizzles in the line of sight between our gazes, I watch a profound—if tiny—shift come over her.

She's amused by me, I realize, as she stands up smoothly, as she turns away, her amber eyes flashing brightly. She places one booted foot in the left stirrup, and then she vaults easily up and onto the back of the towering horse.

"Suit yourself," she tells me, her voice almost chuckling at the end of those words. "But by the end of this day, Josie, mark me well...you'll know that you should have taken me up on my offer."

"I highly doubt it," I mutter, glancing at Zilla, who's snaking her head around, trying to nip at my hands with her gigantic, horsey teeth.

So, together, the four of us start out, like we're in some damn Hobbit movie, Attis on Zilla striding with very long legs quickly forward into the woods, and me, trying to walk just as quickly to keep up, holding my fat cat in front of me like I'm some pillow-stuffed Santa.

I have no idea what I'm in for, and, yeah—that fact is kind of scary (actually, utterly terrifying, if I really think about it). I have no idea where we're going other than a vague notion that it's a city. I have no idea what I'm doing here, on this world, or even really how I got here. I have no idea what's going to happen to me, to us.

But as we walk together into the woods, as I glance up at that gorgeous woman astride that massive, monstrous horse, I have to be perfectly honest:

This is kind of exciting, too.

Chapter 5: The Ex-Knight

In about an hour of trekking through really woodsy forest, I know without a shadow of a doubt that I should have taken Attis up on her offer to ride the damn horse.

But I'm a stubborn lady. And there's no way that I'm going to let her know that she was right.

Me and my stupid pride.

"So!" I say, with as much cheerfulness as I can muster. Attis glances down at me from up on Zilla, her brow raised. "What do you...uh...do? For a living."

Attis glances forward again, tightening the reins of her horse. Zilla reacts by tossing her head, and Attis loosens her grip. "I'm a mercenary," she says mildly, clearing her throat.

"Huh," I say, because I fell asleep when my last girlfriend tried to show me *Lord of the Rings*, and "mercenary" sounds fantasy-Hobbits-boring to me. I have no idea what a mercenary *really* does, only what the word's sort of evolved into (i.e. "that guy is *such* a *mercenary*"). "So, what does that mean?" I ask her.

Attis raises her china and tightens her jaw. "I protect people."

"That's awfully altruistic of you," I tell her, frowning. "How do you make a living doing that?"

"I protect people for a *price*," she tells me, one brow raised.

"Oh." I shift the weight of my cat to my other arm. She keeps on purring. Good God, it's like she's enjoying this, and—knowing Wonder—she probably is.

"So, how did you become a mercenary?" I ask Attis, because if I don't ask her something, I'm going to keep concentrating on how much my damn feet hurt.

"It's what becomes of ex-knights," Attis says, looking forward, clenching her jaw.

"Whoa, whoa," I tell her quickly, almost speechless, but working through that pretty fast. "You're an ex-*knight*?" I ask her, bewildered. "What does that even *mean*?"

Attis glances sidelong at me, knocking her knuckles against the breast plate of her armor. "I was once a knight," she says, the words sharp, "and I am one no longer."

"That's it, really?" I ask her, tripping over a root and muttering a curse to myself under my breath. "What happened? Who were you a knight for?" Secretly thinking: *God, that's so damn hot. An actual knight.*

Again, I'm not the swords and sorcery type, but a woman—a woman I find unbearably attractive—just told me she was once a *knight*. Armor, jousting... I mean, that's all I know about knights, but regardless:

That's *ridiculously* hot.

Attis shrugs elegantly, sitting back in her seat in the saddle. Zilla slows down and stops on a dime, and I run into the horse's hindquarters. Thankfully, Zilla has the presence of mind to *not* kick my brains in, but I can tell she thought about it for a second, lifting up her back left hoof and then placing it down on the ground again firmly, with a muffled sigh.

Attis leaps down from her horse's back in one smooth motion and stretches her shoulders, massaging the back of her neck with a gloved hand. "It was a long time ago," she tells me gruffly. "Many years. I was a knight in Arktos City, for the queen." She shrugs and shakes her head. "And I am a knight no longer. There's really not that much more to tell."

It's obvious that this is Attis' way of shutting down the discussion, but I can't help but be curious. There are a million questions clouding my head, the first and foremost being *why did you stop being a knight?*, but it's so obvious that she doesn't want to talk about it that I'm not sure how to proceed.

"Do you...miss it?" I ask her. She glances at me in surprise. My right hand is completely asleep, and I shift Wonder's bulk back over to my left arm. "I'm a disc jockey," I tell her, then frown, because I have absolutely no idea how to explain that to her, and I'm fairly certain she's not going to know what a disc jockey is. "Um..." I bite my lip. "It's...a person who announces a radio show. A radio show is... There's this little box that plays music," I tell her, trying to think of the simplest explanation. "And I announce on it. Anyway," I say, breezing past that, because Attis looks perplexed, "I lost my job yesterday," I tell her, taking a deep breath. "And I was going to fight to have it back, do anything to get it back." I bite my lip again. "But I don't think I'm going to get that chance now. And to think that I'm not going to be able to do what I love most...I can't imagine that future." I glance up at her. "I'm going to miss it a lot. And I just wonder if you do."

She looks down at me in surprise, both of her brows arched. She runs a gloved hand through her hair. I'm doing my best not to stare at her, but the sun's started to come out from behind the clouds, and when she does that, runs her fingers through her hair...the redness in the strands catches the light, and they seem to shimmer.

Normally, I promise, I'm not like this. I don't fall for every gorgeous woman who walks in front of me. Who could live like that? But there's just something about this one...like the fact that I fell through into another world, and she was there to catch me.

And, you know, to rip a poisonous thorn out of my hand and heal the wound with magic. Little stuff like that is bound to turn anyone's head.

But she can also be a tremendous jerk, so I'm doing my best to reserve judgment. And trying my hardest not to stare at her *too* much.

"I'm sorry for your loss. But, no," she says finally, quietly, until I almost forget what I asked her in the first place. "I don't miss it." She turns away from me and opens up one of the packs lashed behind the saddle. "Are you thirsty?"

"Very," I mutter, my voice cracking. She pulls a sort of leather pouch from the pack and undoes the stopper, and then she holds it out to me.

"Drink. Then we must move on. I want to make it to the Silver Pony by day's end."

"Do I want to know what the Silver Pony is?" I ask her, leaning against a tree and wincing a little. I don't want to look down at my feet, because I'm fairly certain the cheap rubber has worn away from the bottom of the right slipper, and both of my feet are soaked already. It's not going to be a pretty picture...

I think I have blisters on my blisters.

"The Silver Pony is a tavern," says Attis, and then she takes one smooth step forward and—without any warning at all—lifts me up easily, one arm around my shoulders and one arm under the backs of my knees.

"What are you doing?" I ask her calmly, as she carries me like a naughty toddler over to her horse. I hold tightly onto Wonder, who's woken up inside of my coat and isn't pleased about how she's being jostled around.

"You must ride, Josie," Attis says, setting me down on the ground beside the horse. She moves her hands and grips me firmly at my waist now, and I'm doing my best not to blush, but I know I'm still blushing, anyway. Then, in one fluid motion, she lifts me up and seats me sidesaddle on top of Zilla.

"Straddle her," says Attis, gesturing for me to lift my one leg up over the horse's neck. I sigh, far too tired to argue, and do exactly that.

Attis picks up my left foot and gently removes the slipper with a slowness that almost seems (just a little) sexy...until I gasp from the cold air that rushes onto my foot and the pain that blossoms so immediately there: it feels like my foot is on fire.

I was wrong about the blisters. The bottom of my foot, as Attis turns it gently up, is one single bloody mass.

Me and my damn pride.

I wince as Attis turns my ankle slowly in her hand, and then she sighs for a long moment. "Close your eyes," she tells me tiredly, and, again, I do as she says, because I'm still far too tired (and now too much in pain) to argue.

I'm not certain what she's about to do, but just as before, there's a golden pulse of light behind my eyelids, and when I open my eyes...Attis is still holding onto my foot tenderly, with long, gloved fingers, but the bloody mass that my foot had become?

The blood and wound are gone.

My foot is healed.

Attis lets go of my foot, flexing her fingers as she moves around Zilla's side, to my right foot, but I shake my head before she can touch it. "Attis, don't—didn't you say that healing me would make you exhausted?" I ask her, but she shakes her head, lifting up my foot in her hand, cupping my heel with her palm.

"If your wounds aren't healed, you draw attention to us with the blood. There are many predators out here that can scent the blood and come after us. You must not be so foolish," she says, but it's not in a chiding way. She speaks so gently, and when she glances up at me, her brows are knit together, and her warm, amber eyes are glittering. She looks down to my foot, drawing off the slipper as slowly as she can. I hiss and bite my lip, and then she's lifting my foot in her hands, curling her fingers around my ankle with a tenderness that cuts me to my core.

"Close your eyes," she whispers, and I do...but I also leave my right eye open just a tiny crack.

And when Attis bends her head toward my foot, I can see strange, pulsing lines of white light begin to curve up from the muddy ground where she stands. The lines spiral around her body, feeding down her arms, over the armor and her gloves, and into my foot.

The lines, like living, glowing rope, pulse and then shine brightly. And disappear immediately, along with the burning pain in the bottom of my foot. Attis lets me go gently, leaning against Zilla now.

"Is the cat all right?" she growls in a low voice. In shock, I pat Wonder's rump through the coat.

"She's fine," I tell her. "Are *you* all right?" I ask Attis, but she nods, not looking up at me, only staring straight ahead, into the woods.

"Never better," she huffs, pushing off from Zilla gently. She looks a lot paler than she did a moment ago, but she stands steadily, wetting her lips with her pink tongue. I know I'm blushing, so I stare fixedly at Zilla's neck in front of me.

"All right, then," says Attis, in a weary tone. "Forward. Zilla will simply follow me, but take care that the reins stay over her neck and don't fall to the ground. If she gets her hoof caught in the reins, she could hurt herself."

I gather the reins in my hand that isn't holding Wonder, and glance down at the ground. And swallow.

The ground is really, *really* far away.

"So, you protect people?" I squeak, trying (and failing) to maintain a normal speaking voice. I can ride a horse, surely... I've ridden the bus, and that's just as high up as riding this horse. Though, admittedly, with much more stable footing. And plush seats.

"I do a lot of things," says Attis, pushing aside a low pine branch so that Zilla can move between two trees. "Yes, I protect people, but I also do all sorts of odd jobs that you'd need muscle and a sword for."

"Do you like what you do?" I ask her, just for something to occupy my mind, so I can stop imagining this horse bucking and sending me flying into the air.

Attis doesn't respond for a long moment, and I wonder if she heard me, or if this is a touchy subject, but she clears her throat and says, "Sometimes. Sometimes I do." She glances up at me again. "What about you? Will you be able to return to being a...what was it?"

"Radio show host," I tell her, wrinkling my nose. "I don't know if I'll be able to get my old job back. And there are only so many radio stations in Boston...and I kind of burned a bridge at one of them..." I realize I'm rattling on, so I shake my head. "So, no, I don't know if I'll be able to get my job back. But I hope I can. It's all I've ever really wanted to do. And I love doing it."

"That's good," says Attis companionably. She reaches out and unthinkingly pats my thigh. I freeze under that friendly and almost intimate gesture, but that's all it was: friendly. Hell, she might have been aiming for Zilla's neck, to pat her horse.

Attis strides on ahead, pushing a fallen branch out of the way so that Zilla can move through this part of the woods, and I reach down, placing my hand over the spot on my thigh that Attis just touched.

She's really unlike any woman I've ever met.

We travel for hours, and by the time the trees are beginning to thin out and the light is beginning to dim in the sky, my legs are on fire, they're so cramped, and I wonder if I'll ever be able to walk like a normal person again. Now I know why people in old western movies walked with their feet so wide apart: they rode horses.

"I don't think I'm ever going to be able to dismount," I tell Attis, when we exit the thick trees and actually reach something that looks like a dirt road. The long, curving expanse of earth is worn smooth from hoof prints that I can make out in its dust. Attis turns right onto the road, between the dense trees, and Zilla follows obediently, her head down.

"You're just tender because you're not used to riding," says Attis, glancing up at me with warm, twinkling amber eyes. "I remember when I went into knighthood. I didn't own my own horse before that, so I'd never spent much time in the saddle. I had blisters on the insides of my thighs for a moon! But those were good times," she says fondly, reaching up and patting Zilla's shoulder. "It was long before you, old girl," she says, her voice soft.

"That sounds wonderful," I tell her sarcastically, but then I'm chuckling, too. "Will I be able to walk normally ever again, you think?"

Attis winks at me, and then I realize that I'm warm again—and probably blushing. Again. Damn.

"Perhaps," she tells me. "You'll be able to test your legs in only a short while. We're almost at the Silver Pony."

We're in the middle of nowhere, so I have no idea if a "short while" is going to be, truly, a short while. But it is. In a matter of moments, we round a corner in the road, and then there it is.

The tavern.

I've seen *Harry Potter*. I may not be a fantasy nerd, but at least I know what a tavern-type-place should look like from the outside, and this is it. It's a two-story building, surprisingly (I'm not sure why that surprises me, but for some reason, I thought people here might live in one-story hovels), and it looks like something you might see on a British period movie, all stucco and cross-beams, with a thatched roof and a hitching post out front and a big, sprawling stable in the back. There's an old, tired-looking gray horse tied to the hitching post with a piece of rope, and there are lights on in the bottom part of the building, visible through the diamond-paned glass. But other than that (and the murmur of voices coming from within the building), there doesn't seem to be any life around.

Swinging above the door is a peeling, aged sign that shows a rearing white horse. "The Silver Pony" is written in blocky letters beneath.

The words are written in *English*, I realize, startled.

"Hey, how is it that I can understand you?

Why do we speak the same language?" I ask Attis then, surprised. I honestly hadn't thought about it before (there'd been too much else on my mind, but still...). "And how can I *read* that sign?"

Attis shrugs, holding up her hands to me as we pause in front of the tavern. "*That's* what concerns you?" she chides gently, her mouth turning up at the corners. "Not that you've embarked on a quest to a city on a world different from your own with a perfect stranger? But that you can understand her when she speaks?"

"I just think it's weird," I tell her, feeling my blush intensify as her hands go around my waist. Then, again, as if I weigh nothing more than a feather, she lifts me down from the saddle and sets me easily on the ground. Wonder grumbles unhappily from beneath my coat (she was so deeply asleep that she was actually *snoring*), but as I glance up at Attis, as my heart skips a beat, I don't feel any concern for the fact that I'm on this "quest" with a "stranger."

Okay, admittedly, this isn't exactly how I thought today would go. I hoped that I'd be able to knock some sense into those board members' heads and save the radio station (cue the triumphant music in my head) and get my job and everyone else's jobs back. Instead, I'm on another world with a woman wearing armor, and we're on a *quest.*

I can feel my gaze travel down Attis' body for the umpteenth time today, and I stop myself just in time.

But then, in the grand scheme of things, today's not going *terribly* either.

Attis loops Zilla's reins once around the hitching post and then takes Zilla's big, horsey chin in her hands. Attis stares eye to eye with her mare.

"Do not disturb this poor old fellow here. Do you understand?" she says softly, glancing over at the other old, gray horse, who, now that I look at him, is at the very end of his tether, leaning in fear away from Zilla.

Zilla snorts and paws her hoof but then hangs her head as if to say, "Sure, sure." But she glances one wicked, glittering eye at the other horse when Attis turns her back.

Attis pushes open the tavern door, a massive, wooden thing that looks like it should belong on the front of a church. Immediately, the relative quiet of the night is washed away as the riot of warmth and sound from the tavern rolls out to meet us.

My first impression is that there must be a big brawl going on. That's the only thing that could account for the decibels of yelling assaulting my ears, as Attis holds the door open for me and I step into the building. But as my eyes adjust to the dim light of the sprawling room I now find myself in, I realize that there's no big bar fight going on at all...

It's just that the big main room of the tavern is full of very drunk people, and they're all yelling at each other, trying to be heard over the *other* very drunk people.

In short: it's happy chaos.

The dim light brightening the room is coming from the old, wooden candelabras overhead, hanging from the ceiling by rusted chains and filled with dripping candles. Though there are several candelabras, the candles aren't bright enough to accurately light up the room below, and I'm kind of okay with that. There appears to be sawdust (or something very much like sawdust) on the floor, but that's about as close as I'm going to look at the floor...which appears to be pretty damn dirty. The heavy wooden tables scattered around the room are surrounded, elbow to elbow, with all sorts of people. There are big, burly guys in armor, small guys in armor, women in armor... Lots of other people in medieval-looking garb, too. But the minute I caught sight of that table clustered with armored women, I kind of stopped paying attention to everything else.

As does Attis.

"Kell!" she booms, and the tallest woman at the table, the woman with cascading, super-curly blonde hair, stiffens, straightens, and turns with a massive wooden mug (filled with beer, I'm presuming) in her hand.

The minute she sees Attis, her lips curl up into such a wide smile that she dazzles me. God, she's gorgeous. Again, you'd have to be into her type. Her face looks hardened and aggressive, but when she sees Attis, she softens so that you can see what lies beneath that powerful exterior—a lot of compassion. And, you know, passion, in general.

"Attis, it's *you!*" the blonde woman crows, and then she's vaulting over a table of particularly short, squat men in pointy hats (I'll have to ask Attis if there's such a thing as gnomes here in Agrotera, because they remind me, more than anything else, of garden gnomes. And if gnomes actually *do* exist here...I'm not really going to be surprised).

The woman clears the beard-y, pointy-hatted men to then race across the space between us and wrap Attis in such a tight embrace that, for half a moment?

Makes me completely jealous.

Wow, where did *that* come from? But I can't deny it—the jealousy reared up, almost immediately, shaking its ugly, green-eyed head.

Okay, it's pretty obvious that Attis and this woman, Kell, know each other fairly well. It doesn't mean they were lovers (for God's sake, *I don't know if Attis is gay;* it's all just wishful thinking, at this point), and I have to remind myself, for the umpteen millionth time, that *it doesn't matter if Attis is gay or not.* She's from another *world*, and the chances of a relationship starting between us are nil. If there's even a possibility that she's gay, or just likes the ladies. And then, of course, there's the possibility that, even if she is *attracted* to women, she might not be attracted to me, or even unattached. Honestly, I shouldn't be concerned at *all* about the fact that she's hugging another woman so, *so* tightly.

Still, my cheeks are flushed, and there's not a damn thing I can do about that. So I avert my gaze and avoid looking at the two of them embracing, instead turning my attention to the table populated with possible-gnomes.

"Good gods, it's been awhile now, hasn't it?" asks Kell, backing away to hold Attis out at arm's length, gazing at her warmly. Kell has piercing blue eyes, is about as tall as Attis, and together...the two women standing side by side look pretty formidable. They're both in armor, though Kell's is very different from the stuff Attis wears, with her full-body armor. Kell's armor, even though it's miserably cold out, consists of leather pants, a leather skirt, and a leather bra covered in metal plates. There are leather bits all over her, but her stomach is entirely bare, and the only coverings on her arms are occasional straps of leather and metal bands.

I wonder if she's freezing, but she doesn't look at all uncomfortable as she turns from Attis toward me, her blue eyes flashing knowingly. She smirks, her full mouth *curving* knowingly. "And who is this beautiful companion of yours?" she practically purrs, as she sweeps a low bow to me, rising in one fluid motion and taking up my free hand—the one not holding Wonder beneath the coat. She leans forward and slowly, sensually, kisses the back of my hand with warm, full lips.

"This," says Attis, her mouth curling up at the corners in bemusement, "is Josie. I'm taking her to Arktos City."

"Lady Josie," says Kell, her voice dropping to a deep, velvety growl as she pins me to the spot with her flashing blue eyes. "Where did you *find* her, Attis? It has been so long since I saw one so fair—"

Attis folds her arms in front of her, raising a single brow at me as her smile deepens. "I don't believe your sweet words will work on this one, Kell," she says, her head to the side. I glance at Attis with wide eyes. What's *that* supposed to mean?

Also, wow...Kell was *definitely* hitting on me. I have a lot of reactions to that fact slamming into me all at once, but I don't have time to consider them, because Attis is shaking her head. She hooks an armored arm through Kell's naked elbow and chuckles as she draws the woman aside, leaning toward her. "It's been a long time, old friend... Let's dine together." Attis' smile deepens into a Cheshire Cat grin. "You can flirt later."

"Oh, you spoil my fun," says Kell, practically pouting as she drops my hand from her long fingers and straightens, sighing.

"Your fun will not be spoiled, I assure you," says Attis with indulgence as she wraps an arm tightly around Kell's shoulders and squeezes. Her voice drops low as she flicks her gaze to the side: "I'm thinking you're going to get that bar maid who keeps making wide eyes at you into bed before the night's done."

Kell flicks her piercing blue gaze toward said bar maid, who's hanging out behind the bar and leaning on it with her pretty, plump elbows. The bar maid looks young, maybe in her late teens or early twenties, with a big, curly mop of red hair that cascades over her shoulders and down and over breasts that are straining against her bodice. She looks like she should be on the front cover of a straight romance novel.

But the stare she's giving Kell is anything *but* straight. If such a thing happened in real life, cartoon hearts would be circling that bar maid's head as she stares at Kell and sighs happily, putting her chin in her hands, and—I kid you not—actually batting her eyelashes.

"You'll not be lonely tonight, my friend, I guarantee it," says Attis wryly, as she squeezes Kell's shoulder again. "But before you go to bed," she tells her with a wink, "let us catch up. How long has it been, truly?"

Kell tears her glittering gaze from the bar maid and grins at Attis. "Oh, half a year, I think? Really, what could you have possibly been doing to keep so busy?"

"Well, with winter coming, the mercenary business is certainly picking up," says Attis, with a shake of her head. Kell wraps an arm around Attis' shoulders, and speaking in low tones, together the two march around the "gnome" table and toward the back booth, where the other women warriors are clustered.

I shift Wonder's weight under the now too-hot coat and follow them. My cat, as expected, makes a little yowling sound and starts to root her way to the top neck hole of the coat, demanding to be let out of her stuffy prison. I'm also not too happy about carrying around a large, hot cat inside of a large, hot room, so I glance around, making certain there are no dogs in the vicinity, and I let her down on the floor.

You might think that's not very responsible of me, or very safe for my cat. But I promise you: Wonder can hold her own against practically anything in this, or any other, universe. I pity the poor creature who would try to touch her if she doesn't want to be touched.

Predictably, Wonder makes a beeline toward the roaring fire at the far end of the room. Soon, my little gray beast is purring in a perfect circle of cat, her tail resting on top of her nose as she sleeps on the warm stones in front of the fire, just out of reach of the little sparks of the blaze.

As I approach the table, my eyes widen as I

take in the cluster of knightly women. These are all such *strong* women, every one of them; that fact is obvious. Each woman stands with feet wide apart, or sits lounging against the booth as if she doesn't have a care in the world. And each wears armor. Several women have similar armor to Attis, but most of the armor types are different. Attis' armor is more traditional, I think: it makes me think of the Knights of the Round Table, "standard" armor. But at the table, there are women wearing armor made of linked loops of metal, armor made of something copper-colored, and one woman's armor is actually encrusted with gems. Which you'd think would be pretty, or at the very least sparkly, but she just looks uncomfortable in it, leaning as far back as she can as she perches on the edge of the bench with a pinched expression.

So, yes, they're warrior women, but as confidant and strong and armor-wearing as all these women are, they're also—unquestionably—one hundred percent drunk.

Still, it'd be difficult to determine that fact if they weren't all singing together rather off-key—something about swords.

"Hello, ladies," says Attis warmly, and the warrior women rise, embracing her with bellowed greetings of happiness. This far into the tavern, it feels a little like being at a rock concert. Everyone's yelling so loudly to be heard, but they're all so cheerful about it, too, that it's warming to witness, if not hear.

"This is my traveling companion, Josie," says Attis, still wearing a warm smile, her arms around several women, and their arms around her shoulders. She manages to gesture to me, and while everyone else is yelling "hello!", I'm actually *picked up* by the woman to my left, a shorter woman than the others (God, there's someone here who's actually *my height*), who sports close-cropped sandy blonde hair, an upturned nose and a scar slicing her face from her chin to just above her brown right eye. She's wearing armor similar to Attis', and while the others are holding their liquor pretty well, she...isn't.

"Lovely to meet ya, Josie!" the woman yells in my ear, with breath that smells of beer and lemons. "I'm Alinor! What you be doin' with our Attis?"

"Traveling with her to Arktos City!" I yell back at her. Or at least try to yell. She's still squeezing me tightly, and it's a little difficult to breathe at the moment.

"That's good!" she bellows back to me and finally relinquishes me to lift up her mug of beer again in a toast. "To Attis!" She brandishes the mug into the air, sloshing beer down its sides. "It's good to have you back, however long we have you for!"

The other warrior women cheer loudly, and each lifts up their glasses or mugs, the bar maid rushing over to give a mug of sweet-smelling beer to both me and Attis. I lift my mug, too, as Attis chuckles and raises hers high.

"It's good to be among friends," she shouts, and the mugs crash together in a violent toast, droplets (and waves) of beer flying in all directions and spraying pretty much everyone. Not that they notice. They're cheering loudly and embracing one another, and Attis, with a wide smile, sips at her beer and glances at me over the head of Alinor. In that moment, Attis' warm, amber eyes are the softest I've ever seen them.

This might be the first time I've seen Attis truly happy, I realize.

Admittedly, I've only known Attis for a short time, but in that time, she's struck me as a relatively closed-off person. She's guarded—that much is obvious, and she does smile, it's true...but there's so much hardness to her face, her mannerisms, every expression and action. This is the first time I've seen her softened, and she seems, in this moment, vulnerable enough to relax around these, her friends. I don't know how these women know her, but I'm assuming that they were all knights together once.

And however they know each other, the fact of the matter is that Attis seems very happy here with them.

And I *love* seeing her happy. I sip at the sweet beer and surreptitiously glance at her face, feeling my own cheeks flush a little.

"Is the ale good?" Attis asks me, moving smoothly around Alinor so that she's the one standing next to me now. She peers down at my mug with a furrowed brow. "Do you like this? Would you like something else to drink, perhaps?"

I begin to shake my head, tell her the beer's perfect, but then Alinor is offering another toast into the air, her mug sloshing so much beer out of it that I wonder if there'll be any left for her to drink after she toasts. I didn't hear the beginning of the toast because her words are a little more slurred right now, but I think they had something to do with quests, adventures, and comrades. Attis chuckles, leaning down close to me as she wraps an arm around my shoulders.

Instantly, every inch of my body is on high alert, a *zing* of closeness (and, admittedly, the booze hitting my empty stomach) causing my cheeks to warm, and the nether regions of my body to turn on in a less than subtle way. But she's not drawing me close for an embrace, as she did with the other women; she's trying to tell me something.

"Can I leave you with them for just a minute? I need to take care of Zilla," she murmurs into my ear, holding her warm, amber gaze on mine.

Her mouth is so close to my mouth, because she had to lean toward me to be heard. Her lips almost brush against my ear as her warm breath moves over the skin of my neck; I shiver a little. My heart is thundering in me, and, *wow,* did the beer hit my empty stomach hard. I promise, I'm not this much of a lightweight, but as I stand there, trying to quell the shiver that moves through my bones, I'm hyper-aware of how close Attis is, and the fact that I can't help but want to kiss her.

I have to be honest with myself: I want that—I want *her*—fiercely.

"Sure. You go take care of Zilla. I'm fine here," I manage to tell her, and Attis nods twice, setting her mug down on the table and turning to squeeze past the press of other warrior women as she makes her way toward the front door.

"So, Josie," says Kell almost immediately, the moment Attis is out of earshot. Kell's glittering blue gaze pins me from across the table as she leans forward, her shoulders curled toward me, eyes narrowed. "How do you know our Attis?" she asks me. Before I can respond, her gaze is raking me up and down again, her mouth tugging at the corners into a sly, predatory grin. "You...don't look like you're from around here."

"I'm...not...from around here," I tell her, taking another sip of the beer. Its warmth washes down my throat as I realize that my head is starting to get pleasantly fuzzy. "I'm from Earth," I tell her, after clearing my throat.

Alinor throws her arm around my waist and squeezes me against her side, pressing my body against her pointy metal bits. I grimace a little, but she's smiling so hugely, I do my best to push off her without offending her. "Well, wherever you come from, it's good you're with our Attis now," she shouts into my face. "She looks happier than I've seen her since Hera was killed."

Kell's dazzling blue eyes are now pinning down Alinor, but she's three women away from her, and while it's obvious that Kell wants Alinor to stop talking, drunken Alinor, oblivious to Kell's angry face, keeps on talking.

"I never thought she'd recover from that, really. None of us did. It's a right good thing, you being here, Josie. Have you bedded her yet?"

I was in the middle of swallowing a mouthful of beer, but I actually spit a little of it out as I snort through my nose at her remark. I cough hard, trying to get the beer out of my windpipe, and Alinor smacks me so roughly on my back that I actually hear my ribs creaking a little. She pounds my back with her wide, armored hand, trying to "help."

"Bedded?" is the first word I actually manage to say, my voice low and gravelly as I wheeze around the beer in my lungs.

"*Alinor*," Kell snarls, and I glance at Kell, surprised. Her eyes are now a dangerous, cold blue, and she's leaning forward on the table, her hackles up, her palms pressed to the table's surface. "This is not yours to speak of," she hisses, but Alinor simply shrugs.

"You know as well as I do that a nice bedding would do Attis a world of good. It'd get her mind off her troubles, that's for certain," says Alinor, with a shake of her head. "Anyway, 'scuse me," she slurs, pushing off from the table and staggering toward a far back door—what I assume leads toward an approximation of a restroom.

Kell is suddenly in the space that Alinor vacated, moving seamlessly, like a dancer, around the women. If Alinor's drunk, Kell's not even tipsy. Or maybe she's this graceful even when tipsy; it's impossible to tell. Kell leans toward me and clears her throat. "Forgive her. She always says whatever's on her mind," Kell tells me, but her expression is icy as she gazes at me now. "But that really does beggar the question, Josie: why *are* you traveling with Attis?"

"I...came from another world," I tell her, shrugging helplessly. "I mean, Attis found me when I came through from another world. Or...I found Attis. I mean, I *fell* on Attis." Great. The beer is making me extra honest. Fantastic. "So I couldn't find a way to get back home, and Attis says that someone might be able to help me return. Someone who lives in Arktos City. And since she was going there, anyway, she said I could come along."

"Attis asked you to accompany her on her journey. And she asked for no gold for this service?" asks Kell, her brows raised as she stares hard at me.

"Well...I mean, the subject of money has never come up," I tell her miserably. I hadn't thought about it, really, but what if Attis *is* doing this for money? What if, at the end of this journey, once we reach Arktos City, she wants me to pony up funds that I don't have and don't have any sort of access to? God, that'd be terrible.

"There must be something she wants from you," Kell persists. Her face darkens. "How long have you known Attis?"

"Since last night," I tell her.

"Then you know her not at all," says Kell, her voice low and dangerous as she leans even closer to me, her blue eyes dazzlingly dark. "Once, Attis was good. Oh, she's good still," she says with a small shrug, "but much of what made her good, her generosity, her kindness...it's been hidden away. It was hidden away a long time ago." Her voice is a low growl, and she shakes her head. "There must be a reason that she has you with her, is taking you with her on this journey. She isn't altruistic, Josie. There's a reason she's helping you. Be aware of that. You'll repay her, one way or another."

I gaze at Kell, feeling my heart break into a million pieces and not really understanding why. What's wrong with me? The beer is obviously making me more emotional, but there shouldn't be a reason in the world that I should care that Attis wants something from me.

"I tell you this not to startle you," says Kell, her hand at my elbow suddenly. I glance up at her face and notice that her lips have curled into a soft smile. "I tell you this only so that you know. I agree, yes—Attis looks a happier than when last I saw her. But there's nothing and no one, I feel, that will ever make Attis truly happy again. When her lover died, she took Attis' happiness with her."

The warmth floods my face, and, piecing the few mentions together, I understand several things all at once:

Attis had a lover. This lover was a woman.

That's...great. It means that Attis, at the very least, is attracted to women.

But the woman Attis loved died. And though it was a long time ago, Attis still loves her and will never stop loving her...

I take a deep breath, feel my insides begin to cave in. My head's swimming as I consider this twist.

It shouldn't hurt so much. But it does.

Attis mourns a woman who's gone, but her ghost remains.

I feel so much in this moment: deep sorrow that she's been so sad for so long. And, yes, I also have that selfish, painful, punch-to-the-gut feeling of knowing that I'm never going to have a shot with Attis.

My head is reeling, and suddenly the room is too small, too stuffy, and everyone's standing much too close. I feel stifled. I really, really need some air.

"Uh...is there a place to...um... Is there a

lady's powder room?" I ask Kell, using the most antiquated language I can possibly think of for "bathroom." Kell's brows go up, but then she's turning and indicating the corridor that Alinor went down and is now returning in, stumbling over the floor and chuckling to herself as she tugs at the leather straps along the side of her armored chest piece.

I set my empty mug down on the table and move as quickly as I can toward that darkened corridor. I follow the long hallway, one hand on the wall to steady myself, and then I find a door in front of me that leads not to a room but outdoors.

There's a small courtyard that leads off in one direction to the stables, and in the dim twilight, I'm able to make out a lean-to that's obviously an outhouse.

As much as I was hoping (and realizing it was probably impossible) for the tavern to have indoor plumbing, I am resigned to this fate. I shut the door behind me as I step into the outhouse, locking it with the small wooden lock. To my surprise, it actually doesn't smell terrible in here; it's sweet-smelling, actually, the scent of herbs and sawdust and ash the only things I notice. But then, I'm not really paying that much attention to the way the building smells. I lean against the wall, and I wrap my arms around myself as I try, desperately, and with a muzzy head, to make sense of all of everything that's happened.

Kell told me that there's absolutely no way that Attis would be taking me to Arktos City "just because." Kell knows Attis much better than me, that much is obvious, so when she tells me Attis must want something from me, it's probably true. There's also the fact that Attis has been deeply hurt, so deeply hurt that she's never, according to Kell, going to recover.

Yes, it's more painful than I even want to admit that I'm never going to have a chance with Attis. But all of the pain in Attis' features...I understand it now. I understand where it's coming from.

I know nothing about the story, but I can piece it together a little. Alinor said that Hera was killed, didn't she? I press my palm to my forehead and take a few slow breaths. Okay. I need to remove emotion and attraction out of this and get to the root of the matter.

Which is this:

This was never anything more than Attis allowing me to accompany her to Arktos City. She's allowing me to accompany her to, basically, prevent me from dying. Which, you know, is pretty kind of her, so if she really does want something when we reach Arktos City, I'll do my best to get it for her, even if it's gold she wants. Sure. I can get gold. I can figure that out. Maybe I can sell my Scooby Doo shirt for big bucks once we reach the city. Ha. I press the heel of my hand against my dry eyes and try to calm the ache in my heart.

Everything else? The dead lover? Attis and all of my attraction to her? I've got to let that go. Attis' past is not my business, and—frankly...neither is Attis' future.

I take another deep, slow breath and let it out, curling my hands into fists. I don't know why I was so attracted to Attis, but I *was*, and it's perfectly fine that I'm attracted to her. But there can be nothing else. Attis is in mourning, and there's no possibility that anything can ever happen between us.

And that's okay, you know? She's from another world. I'm from earth. It could never work.

Obviously.

I have myself so convinced that when I reach up to tuck a strand of hair behind my ear, I'm surprised when my hand encounters a warm wetness on my cheek. I take my hand back stiffly, wipe the tear off on the arm of my werewolf coat.

This is ridiculous. I'm being ridiculous.

I square my shoulders, put on a hard smile and wrap my coat tightly around me as I exit the outhouse.

I've done much harder things than this in my life. Walking my sister's casket down the aisle was the hardest thing I've ever done.

But this, I must admit, feels a little like that as I enter the tavern again, as I walk slowly down the dark corridor back toward the tavern proper and the table full of laughing warrior women. The warmth of the tavern does nothing to ease the coldness in my heart, the ache there, the deep shooting pain that I'm doing my best to ignore. I glance into the tavern, and I pause in my stride for a moment, taking in the scene.

Attis is back from taking care of Zilla, and she's in the midst of a deep conversation with Kell, who has her arm around Attis' shoulder and is whispering in her ear.

Attis is a little taller than Kell, and is bent

toward Kell. The dark, deep red of her hair, the straightness of it, is actually melding a little with Kell's large, curly mane. If they weren't wearing armor, if they weren't standing in a dimly lit tavern next to a table of possible-gnomes, they'd look like two friends at any bar in the world, deep in conversation.

I continue down the corridor, shoving down any feelings I have. When Attis sees me striding toward them, her amber gaze flicks to me but then back to the floor, her jaw tightens, and she nods once, sharply, to Kell. They move away from each other, and Kell's eyes dart to me, her mouth turning up at the corners...but the smile does not meet her eyes.

"Are you very hungry?" Attis asks me when I get back to the table. I stand beside her, and I'm surprised to feel Attis' gloved hand come to the small of my back. She had leaned toward me and murmured the words into my ear as Kell moved away from us, heading back with a jaunty swagger toward the bar and the smiling bar maid, who leans forward so far when she sees Kell approaching that she's almost lying on the counter.

"I am hungry," I tell her Attis tiredly, not glancing up at her. "But I'm also pretty beat from today. Where are we sleeping tonight?"

Attis looks surprised for a moment, but she shrugs quickly. "Of course, of course... I'm used to the travel, but you aren't. I apologize," she says, much more formally than she's been talking to me on this trip so far. I take a deep breath, steel myself again.

Attis straightens her shoulders, indicates the

Forever and a Knight

staircase along the wall that leads up to a second level, and—I'm assuming—rooms you can rent. "We'll be staying here tonight. The tavern owner, Shannon, is setting up a room for us right now."

"Okay," I tell her, nodding as I wrap my arms around me again, trying to absorb the warmth of the tavern. Trying to warm the coldness seeping into my heart.

"There's something you should know," says Kell then, clearing her throat and leaning close to Attis. "The wolves are on the prowl again," she whispers to her friend.

Attis' brows rise; her mouth turns into an instant grimace. "The wolves? The *same* wolves?" she whispers.

That's when the scream happens.

✂

Chapter 6: The Ghost

The scream is loud, so absolute and enormous, that instantly, and as one, every single person falls silent in the tavern, and we all, as one, turn to search out where the scream was coming from: up on the balcony.

It's...a ghost.

That's really the only way I can describe what I'm seeing. Standing tall and straight on the hand railing of the upper balcony is a white mist, vaguely person-shaped (woman-shaped, really, with a dress and flowing white hair, if you squint), and she's perfectly see-through. She's standing like a ballerina, balanced on that top railing, her arms widespread as if she's about to embrace someone, her white, see-through, wispy hair blowing backward in a nonexistent wind, the skirt of her dress blowing backward, too.

The ghost (or whatever the hell it is) opens her mouth, her mouth that's *black* on the inside. She opens that mouth wide, like a ghost would in a horror movie...and then...it screams again.

The first time, I could imagine the sound was a human scream, but this time...this time it's obvious that the sound being uttered isn't exactly human.

When I say *exactly* human, I mean that it's the kind of sound a human would probably make under extreme duress, something I've—thankfully—never heard in real life, aside from news clips. But it's also a deeply animal sound, a guttural, spine-tingling roar of emotion, of terror, rolled into one deeply chilling maul of a scream that washes over the tavern, going on and on and on until my ears feel raw.

Everyone remains silent as we stare up at this ghost-type-thing.

And then that ghost simply...jumps.

She jumps off the railing that she was standing on, and she falls through the air as quickly as if gravity is attached to her see-through form as much as it's attached to ours. But she comes up short, then, and she's dangling in the air in front of us, as if she's dangling from a rope tied to the balcony.

As we watch, she twirls in the air, hanging there, I realize, as if she just hung herself.

I stare in horror—and the specter vanishes.

"Bloody hell," shouts a booming voice, and then a woman, an actual flesh and blood woman, comes to the railing and squints down at the tavern.

She's a large woman, and she looks like she smiles a lot, judging from the lines on her face—but she's certainly not smiling now. She frowns down at the people gathered in the tavern, and she shakes her head, wisps of graying hair dislodging from beneath the tight white cap she's wearing.

"Sorry 'bout that, everyone," she shouts, rubbing her red hands on her apron as if she's drying them. "Don't you fret about that. How about a round of free ale for all!"

A bright cheer comes from the gathered tavern people, and immediately the silence is overtaken by the happy, boisterous yelling from the patrons. The woman pushes off from the railing and bustles her way down the stairs into the tavern, making a beeline, I realize, for our table, as she reaches us.

"You're knights, right? Can any o' you please help me?" she asks quietly when she reaches us, shaking her head as she leans forward, dropping her voice to a conspirator's whisper. "This be the fifth time in as many days that ol' Mag hurled herself from the rafters, and it's really been puttin' people off their porridge, if'n you know what I mean, to see a woman kill herself during supper each day."

"That was really a ghost?" I'm asking before I realize that the words are out of my mouth.

"Shannon," murmurs Attis, leaning toward the woman—the tavern owner. "What happened? Who is she?"

Shannon screws up her face and shakes her head, lips pursed. She shrugs her wide shoulders. "Bit o' bad business, that was. Ol' Mag, as you know, was my grandmother. But she killed herself right after she had me Ma. Mag had a fever, and it addled her brains, poor dear. She hung herself right from that railing, well...exactly as you just saw it. Her ghost been seen every once in a while, but it's a rare occurrence since we keep giving her cream and gold coins to appease her, placing the offerings by the fire every moon, just as we were told to do by the old witch what lives in the Stick Woods. And, so far, the last time ol' Mag's been seen was when I was a younger lass. But now..." She shakes her head again. "She's been appearin' off and on for about a year, but it's only been about once a month, and if I give a round o' free drinks, nobody much talks about it. But now five times in a row, every day. She be actin' up mightily, and I don't know why, and I can't be havin' my tavern overrun by spirits during the dinner hour— it's bad for business." She huffs her cheeks and spreads her hands to us. "I know you knights have the magic for this. Can ye help me?"

"*We* actually don't have the magic to help you," says Kell, flicking her glittering blue gaze to Attis. "But Attis does. She's a mercenary, and I'm sure she'd be glad to offer her services to you, to help you get rid of the specter."

Attis is glaring daggers at Kell, but her gaze softens when she looks to Shannon again, Shannon with her hopeful face and her hands clasped in front of her expansive chest. Attis clears her throat. "I've not done a ghost removal in....uh...a good, long while," Attis says, holding up a hand, "but it can be done. Still, I must warn you, it seems that the ghost has resided here for many years, so she's quite entranced in this place, and it will be much harder to remove her—"

"Don't be wheedlin' me for more money with the difficulties and such. Name your price, mercenary," Shannon tells her, eyes narrowed.

"Room and board," says Attis calmly, "for me and my friend and my horse for tonight."

"That be all, truly?" asks Shannon, narrowing one eye at Attis until it's just a slit.

"Yes, madame," says Attis, straightening her

shoulders and lifting her chin. "But you must also give me any small thing I require for the spell to remove the ghost. It does require a few...odd ingredients, and you must get them for me quickly and with no fuss."

"Done and done," says Shannon with a wide smile, throwing her arms wide and then ducking forward and wrapping Attis in a tight, squeezing embrace before Attis can react. "Thank you for helping me!" she crows, releasing Attis and taking a quick step back, then barking to the bar maid: "Lanna! Do you have that room ready for our guests of honor?"

"Geez, Ma, Hannah's doin' it," says the bar maid, glancing angrily at her mother. Lanna the bar maid is currently doing her best to flirt the leather pants off of Kell, who is doing her best to flirt the skirts off of Lanna. They're leaning toward each other, elbows on the bar between them, each wearing charming, wide smiles, their faces close enough to one another to kiss...until Lanna screeched at her mother, that is. Kell pushed off from the bar and ducked her head with a small laugh when Lanna yelled across the room.

"Oh, so right you are," says Shannon, patting the white cap on her head. "If'n Hannah's doin' it, that means the room should now be ready for you...if you want to be gettin' on preparations for the removal of the spook," she tells Attis hopefully.

"Yes, of course," says Attis, glancing at her friends clustered around the table with a wistful glance.

"Not just yet, Attis. Stay awhile more. It's

been too long, and we still must catch up," says Kell, striding over and reaching out between them. She places her hand on top of Attis' arm. A meaningful look passes between them, though I can't make out what it is.

"I can go up to the room, actually," I tell her, jerking my thumb toward the stairs as a lump forms in my throat. "I'm just really tired. I need to get off my feet," I tell Attis quickly, as she frowns at me.

"But of course. Our room is the third door down on the left," says Attis, indicating the upper level.

I don't wait to say anything else or see if she has anything more to tell me. I walk over to the roaring fireplace, picking my way around the other boisterous tables and the people laughing, singing or—upon one table—arm wrestling. When I reach Wonder, fast asleep in front of the fire, I pick her up quickly (she's as hot as a loaf of bread just pulled from an oven, so I probably saved her from becoming medium rare). I carry her protesting, fuzzy bulk up the narrow staircase and then down the hallway, the noise of the tavern lessening the further down the hall I get.

The door opens beneath my hand as I lay my palm flat against it, so I worry that there's no lock on the door, but as I step inside, I am relieved to find that there's a lock, similar to the lock that was on the outhouse. So I secure the door before I drop Wonder to the floor and take a deep breath, surveying the tiny room with unseeing eyes.

I sigh, utterly disgusted with myself, as I push off from the door. The ache is so sharp in my heart, and all I can think is: what the hell is wrong with me? This is stupid, *ridiculous.*

I'm not in some romance novel; this is life. And life doesn't give you a gorgeous warrior woman you're desperately attracted to on another world...usually, and it *certainly* doesn't give you a *relationship* with said gorgeous warrior woman. That's not how *life* works.

And I've known that and been perfectly okay with that fact my entire existence. I found and fell in love with women the "normal" way: at bars, at restaurants, at the gym. And I did fall in love with those women, though it scares me that I never felt as strongly about any of the women I slept with, dated for so long, the way that I feel about Attis.

The way I feel about Attis...

I bite my lip hard and shake my head, glancing around the room again as I try to stop thinking. The room itself is very small, with wood paneling that the seventies would have been proud of, a rough wood floor, and roughly hewn bed frames. There are two beds, though they're more narrow than twin beds, but that's okay—there are two of them, and that will alleviate any awkwardness that might have been created by having to share a bed.

Oh, God, who am I kidding? There would have been no awkwardness. At this point, I'm reacting to Attis like a hormonal teenager would. I probably would have thrown myself on her the minute she slid into a bed we shared and tried to make out with her.

Dammit, seriously, I'm driving myself crazy. I run my hand through my hair, biting at my lip again and sinking down on the closest bed to the door. Wonder jumps up next to me and begins to knead the blanket with half-closed eyes, purring louder than a tiger growls as she blinks sleepily at me.

"This has been a really weird day, babe," I tell my cat, rubbing gently behind her ears as I get lost in thought again. Wonder turns and affectionately sinks her fangs into my hand, but I keep petting her, and she removes her mouth. It's just like old times.

Except it's not like old times at all. I just saw the ghost of a woman hang herself off the beam of a tavern in another world.

Yeah. Really not like old times at all.

The door to the room begins to open, but then the lock catches it, and I rise quickly as a soft knock comes at the door.

"Josie?" asks a low voice. Attis.

"Sorry," I tell her, crossing to the door and throwing back the lock. I open the door for her, but she doesn't cross the threshold, only places her arm at shoulder height on the door frame and leans against it, watching me for a long moment with her glittering, amber eyes, and such an intense expression that I'm instantly weak in the knees.

Thoroughly disgusted with myself, I try to straighten, try to lift my chin and not give a damn that her intense, smoldering expression does anything to me. I return her gaze, and I hold it with the same strength that I used when I got the job at the radio station, the same strength that I used when I debated Deb for a prime-time slot for my radio show.

I've got strength in spades, and Attis doesn't have to affect me if I don't let her.

She sighs for a long moment, her frown making her lips downturn. "Did...my friends say anything to you? Were they rude?" she asks me quietly. I stare at her with wide eyes; then my instincts kick back into gear, and my mouth starts talking before my brain catches up.

"No, no, nothing at all. They were great," I tell her, pasting on the big smile that I always wear when I'm announcing the good news on the radio— not the bad stories, but the type of stories that you'd smile at, like the one about a puppy being rescued from a burning building. I take a deep breath, let my radio personality take over. "So, what are you going to do to get rid of that ghost?"

That's when Attis pushes off from the door frame and steps inside of the room, shutting the door quietly behind her.

"Ah, yes," she says with a small grimace. "Sadly, I'm not exactly certain how to remove the ghost, but then...I'm sure I can figure it out."

I stare at her for a long moment, mouth open. "For real? You don't know what to do?" I fold my arms tightly in front of me with a frown. "Then why the hell did you say you could do it, if you don't know how?"

Attis glances at me with one brow raised, her lips downturning at the corners into a deep frown. "Josie, it's not that I can't *do* it," she tells me sharply. "It's that I've not tried. Those are two very different things. I'm sure I can do it. And, anyway, that's what a mercenary *does*. You take a job so that you can put food in your belly and have an occasional soft place to rest your head. Most of the jobs I've taken, other than exterminating large beasts or ferrying noble folk from one place to another, I'd certainly not done before, but I simply had to figure out for myself."

"But...but..." I spread my hands. "I mean, this is a getting rid of a *ghost*. Like, an honest-to-goodness *ghost*. Even the Ghostbusters had problems getting rid of honest-to-goodness ghosts," I tell her, and when her eyebrow rises higher, I realize that I don't want to have to explain what the Ghostbusters are, or what movies are... I shake my head. "I just don't think it's as easy as, say, killing a cannibal werewolf," I tell her, gesturing to my coat.

"Killing a cannibal werewolf, as you so succinctly put it," she tells me with eyes that are beginning to flash, "was hardly a moment of apple picking."

I actually laugh at that, the humor surprises me so much. Her intensity is gone, and she's chuckling a little, too.

"I mean, how do you even go about *beginning* to get rid of a ghost?" I ask her. Then I lower my voice, "It's actually a ghost, right?" I gesture down to my Scooby Doo shirt, visible under the open coat. "I mean, it could be someone *pretending* to be a ghost, couldn't it? And—"

"Why would anyone do anything so preposterous as pretending to be a ghost?" she asks me, eyes wide, and I realize it's a genuine question.

"Uh...lots of reasons," I begin, remembering all of my favorite episodes of *Scooby Doo*, but then I fall silent. I am being far too dorky. "Okay," I tell her, rocking back on my heels. "Are you going to do, like, a ghost exorcism or something?"

"You keep using words," she says, her mouth twitching at the corners as she tries to suppress a smile, "whose meaning I can only guess at. But this one, in particular, has me quite stumped."

"*Exorcism* equals getting rid of ghosts. Banishing them," I tell her with a small smile.

"Exorcism. That's a much more succinct way of putting it. I like it. I may have to start using that word," she says, and then she gives me a small, quick wink. If I wasn't holding her gaze, I never would have noticed it.

And, again, whether I want it to or not, my heart begins to beat just a bit faster inside of my chest, even as I try to take deep, even breaths, even as I command my heart to steady. I think about anything, everything else: I think about hot dogs on the street corners of Boston, and how now—when there's absolutely no way in this world I can get one—I'm craving a damn hot dog so badly that I can't stand it. I think about the radio station, and I wonder what Carly did when I didn't show up to the meeting. I think about...

Attis. And how she's close enough to kiss, her beautiful mouth turning into a slow, soft smile as she stares down at me, her amber eyes warm and soft.

"Are you thirsty?" I blurt out, and then I take a step backward, my hand going to the roughly made ceramic pitcher of water that stands on a small table in the corner of the room.

"Not particularly," she tells me, her eyes amused as she glances around the room, her gloved fingers going to the leather bands at her sides that keep the armor tightly pressed against her body. She begins to undo the leather thongs. "Which bed do you prefer?"

"It doesn't matter to me," I tell her, realizing that she's about to start undressing. Sure, I saw her naked this morning, and that memory will be burned in my mind and heart forever.

I turn away from her, swallowing hard.

Good God, when did I become such a *prude?* I go to the gym; I'm in the locker room, and when I'm in the locker room, yeah, I look at the ladies, but I'm never a blushing idiot about it. I like to think I'm pretty damn suave and stealth about it, actually. My last girlfriend was a woman I asked out in the locker room, and though we only lasted for a few weeks, I was charismatic and my usual charming, sarcastic self when I talked her up, even though she was just wearing a sports bra and a thong.

But now here's Attis. And Attis apparently turns me into a tongue-tied, red-faced idiot. And she's the one woman that I really *don't* want to be a tongue-tied, red-faced idiot around.

The leather thongs at her sides fall away as she unties them with deft fingers, and then she's lifting the chest piece and back piece of her armor up and over her head, letting it *thud* gently onto its side on the bed.

I saw Attis put this armor on this morning, but watching her take it off is even more intriguing and captivating and *utterly sexy*, if you could believe that. I purposefully turn away again (my gaze keeps being pulled back to her like a gravity, and I have to concentrate on *not* concentrating on her), and I sink down onto the edge of the other bed, which Wonder now leaps onto, too, kneading the blanket on this one to make it acceptable for her to sit upon. I pat her head absentmindedly, scratching under her chin as I sit up straighter, stiffening. I just heard the leather and metal skirt that Attis is wearing hit the floor.

"Are you really so modest, Josie?" asks Attis again, her words low. I can hear the smile in her voice. I bristle, but then I grit my jaw, shake my head.

"No," I tell her, the word sounding a hell of a lot more petulant than I wanted it to sound. "Of course I'm not," I continue, rising and turning to face her, crossing my arms as she stands there in her leather pants and shirt, her hip jutted to one side and angling toward me. She places her hands on her hips, lifts her chin defiantly.

"Right," she tells me, and then a smile tugs at the corners of her mouth again as she reaches down, curls her fingers around the hem of her shirt, and smoothly pulls the fabric over her head.

"So. Kell," I say hoarsely, desperate for a change of subject to turn this situation around, so that it starts to have some semblance of normalcy—despite the half-naked woman rummaging around in her pack.

I try not to stare at her like some hormonal teenager who never gets laid. "Kell," I repeat, licking my dry lips when she flicks her gaze my way. "How do you two, uh, know each other?" I stare purposefully at Attis, and I probably look really intense right now as I try very, very hard not to stare at her chest. I hold her gaze like an unhinged person, desperately taking deep, calming breaths.

I probably look like I'm hyperventilating.

"We used to be knights together, she and I," says Attis, pulling a black shirt out of the pack. She turns it in her hands, the fabric sliding over her long fingers like silk. "We went through the training together to become knights, and because of that, we're very close. It was difficult, the training." She shakes out the shirt and then pulls it on over her head, tugging it down over her chest and smooth stomach. This shirt is much more form-fitting than the poet's shirt she was wearing before, the fabric taut over the muscles of her arms.

"Is Kell still a knight?" I ask, before I realize that that might be a pretty insensitive thing to say, but Attis simply nods, pulling her hair through the neck hole of the shirt so that it brushes the tops of her shoulders again. Her hair shimmers in the candlelight, the deep red of it shot through with strands of gold.

"Yes. Most of the women at the table you just met are my comrades, and they're still knights. There are a few who have taken the mercenary path, like myself. But mostly, they're knights." She glances up at me now, tugging her shirt down as her warm, amber eyes narrow. "I must ask, Josie—did Alinor proposition you?"

Wow, that question came from left field. "Alinor?" My mouth is still too dry. "No," I say, leaning away from her as I uncross my arms and bury my hands in my coat pockets. I should probably take the coat off, but it's not as if this room is warm. There's a small fire in the fireplace in the corner, and when I say "small fire," I mean *small fire.* I'll probably wake up tomorrow morning with a frost-bit nose.

Attis takes a step toward me, but then she pauses as if she's run into a wall. I glance up at her just as a look flashes across her face; I'm not able to interpret it before she frowns. "If Alinor *had* propositioned you," Attis says, one brow raised artfully, "what might you have said?"

I frown as I look at her. This is a...pretty odd line of questioning, one I really wasn't prepared for. But then, I'm used to dealing with this kind of stuff, right? The radio show never goes quite as planned, and it's always (*always*) best to simply be honest. "Alinor's nice and all," I say quickly, my heart thrumming against my ribs as I hold Attis' gaze. "But...she's not my type."

Attis sighs for a small moment; then she shakes her head, tilting away from me. "Ah," she says.

"Ah?" I persist, because there's a turning in my stomach, and for some reason, I really want to know why she's asking me this. I feel, for a moment, that I gave the wrong answer.

"She's a good knight, Alinor," says Attis, avoiding my gaze as she gently places the chest piece and back piece of her armor on the floor, leaning them up against the wall.

"I'm sure," I say quietly, utterly mystified. "Attis," I say then, pushing through the discomfort as I take a deep breath, "why do you ask?"

She faces, chin raised, gaze unwavering.

"Do you like women, Josie?" asks Attis, pinning me down with her flashing amber eyes.

O...kay. That cut to the chase.

"Yes," I tell her with a shrug. "I do."

I've always been perfectly open about who and what I am. And considering that Kell hit on me down in the tavern, and apparently Alinor is into the ladies, too, *and* that Attis was once lovers with a woman named Hera...I'm fairly certain that, blessedly, lesbianism is kind of a thing here, too.

But when I tell Attis "yes," something crosses her face again.

And then she crosses the room.

That wasn't the reaction I'd been expecting, especially considering that Kell kind of just gave me a stern talking to about Attis' deceased lover and how Attis really doesn't have time in her life right now for anything related to attraction. But Attis is standing in front of me now, her amber eyes darkening as she gazes down at me.

Her lips are parted, and she's gazing at my mouth...which makes every single inch of my body start to tingle, like electricity crackling over my skin. But as I stare up at Attis, as I feel the warmth of her body so close to mine begin to warm me, too, I remember what Kell said, and the memory into me like an enormous, frozen wave of water: *There must be a reason that she has you with her. She isn't altruistic, Josie.*

God, it hurts to even think about it, but I have to. What if the reason I'm here with Attis now is only because I'm some sort of traveling *booty call*?

What if Attis is letting me go with her to Arktos City so that she has someone she can *do* whenever she feels like it?

As Attis stands over me, as she bends her beautiful head toward mine, her dark red hair sweeping over her shoulder in a soft *shush* of sound, my breathing quickens, my heart beating so fast, the blood roaring through my veins, that I'm starting to feel a little lightheaded.

Okay...so what *if* Attis wants me around for a traveling booty call? Would that really be so bad? I mean, it's not as if I'm a stranger to the concept. After I broke up with Alexandra that one time, we were friends with benefits for, like, an entire year. And, let me be perfectly honest with you, that was pretty damn spectacular. We were both too busy, at the time, for a relationship, and we were pretty good friends, and, hell, we were attracted to one another. So, we thought, why not? And it really worked for us, until Alexandra decided to enter the dating pool again. And then we stopped our amorous relations with absolutely no hard feelings.

So, I know I can do this; I know that I can have sex with a woman without necessarily entering a relationship with her. I could probably do it, no problem, is that's what Attis wanted.

But...*I* don't want it, I realize.

I don't want "friends with benefits." I don't want sex without attachment, as amazing as it would probably be. I don't want lack of feelings, lack of emotion and emotional investment and commitment...

Not with Attis.

I want...something else entirely.

Wow. I didn't realize what I wanted until right this moment, right as Attis bends down toward me, right as I realize that we're about to kiss, her warm, full lips close enough to taste if I just lean forward, just a little.

I want something more, something so deeply impossible that I've tried not to think about it so much that it hurts to try to push it out of my head now.

I want to have a shot with Attis.

Like, a real shot. Like, a falling-in-love shot, a relationship, a shot at all of those great, getting-to-know-you firsts of dating, of learning the intimate dance of sharing your personal space, your hopes, your dreams, your body, your heart with someone else.

I want a shot at something we have absolutely no chance of ever having.

And anything else would be heartbreaking, knowing how I feel about Attis. I've finally allowed the severity of my feelings for her to come crashing down at me, even as she holds me in that gorgeous, intense gaze, as she leans toward me with her warmth, with her gravity pulling me toward her. I'm incapable of stopping this.

But I have to stop this.

I've never felt this way in my entire life. I thought I had—twice. I thought I'd fallen in love two times before now, but this lifting in my heart, this intensity and pull and gravity...I've never felt *this* before, not ever.

I've just met Attis, and from the very first moment I saw her, I knew. There was something between us that I've tried to deny, have tried to deny for about twenty-four hours straight, and there's no use denying it.

I'm attracted to Attis.

I want Attis.

And we're from two different worlds; having each other is impossible.

But as she bends her head toward me, as I feel the enormity of my pull toward her fill my heart and body, I wonder if I could torture myself with one small kiss. Yeah. Maybe one small kiss would be enough to hold me over, would be enough to take back with me when I return to my world.

I know I'm talking myself into something that's going to hurt, so much, when I kiss her, when she kisses me, and then it has to stop. But for a heartbeat, I'm halfway there to convincing myself that the pain will be worth it, the pain of never being able to have this woman I'm falling for so completely...

We're about to kiss, we're about to, so close that it's almost a kiss already...

And that's when the scream comes again.

Attis growls deep in her throat as she turns away from me, staring at the shut-and-locked door with dangerously flashing eyes. The scream, the long, lingering, hair-on-the-back-of-your-neck-raising scream, came from directly out in the hallway, just beyond that shut-and-locked door.

Attis moves swiftly, throws the lock again and pulls the door open with a rough yank.

The ghost is there, standing in front of our door in the hallway—well, not really *standing* so much as hovering in midair. She's walking slowly, agonizingly slowly, floating about a foot or so off the ground, as she's pulled toward the balcony down the hall. She's making her slow parade down the hallway toward the railing...and the recreation of her death, I assume.

Again.

"Looping twice in a night? That's...odd," says Attis quietly. Then she glances back at me, something flickering across her gaze as she shakes her head, turns and strides out into the hallway, following the ghost.

I chase after her, shutting the door behind us, locking Wonder in the room.

The ghost moves so slowly that we make an odd sort of procession as Attis and I follow her down the hall. We take a step about every thirty seconds. I feel like I'm in a *Scooby Doo* episode, tiptoeing around as we try to find the guy in the werewolf suit. I peer around Attis' shoulder at the ghost.

"It's rather odd," says Attis, then, voice husky as she whispers to me over her shoulder. Her voice is so low, the loud, raucous laughter down in the tavern makes it next to impossible for me to pick out her words, but I lean forward, listen closely. "Granted, I'm not well-versed in specters," mutters Attis, narrowing her amber gaze in front of her, "but what little I know of them...they're usually spotted only once each night, and never more than once in a single evening. There must be something that's disturbing her spirit enough to make her go through this again, to awaken her from her spectral slumber, so soon after she just recreated her demise. Something is disturbing her enough to wake her."

"So, it's like in *Poltergeist*," I say, then realize that, of course, she's going to have no idea what I'm talking about. "There's this...movie..." I say, charging right past the word "movie." "Anyway, it's about a family who moves into a new house. But you don't know that this new house was built on an old burial ground, and the spirits of the people buried there were disturbed by the fact that houses were being built on top of their graves. So they start haunting the family."

"That's a common enough occurrence," says Attis mildly, taking another step.

And I, of course, bristle.

Remember, I'm an eternal skeptic. That's why I always loved *Scooby Doo* so much. The "ghosts" and "werewolves" and all of the other "monsters" on the show always turn out to just be people in disguise. It's really, really difficult for me to accept all of this, *any* of this, even though it's right in front of my nose.

No part of me ever believed in ghosts or anything otherworldly. I mean, how could I? I'm the type of person who needs proof, and science can't prove that paranormal stuff, and the television shows and popular movies about hauntings or alien sightings or, you know, whatever else you can lump into that category make it all sound so far-flung. Ridiculous and impossible.

Just call me Scully. I don't want to believe, and I've *never* wanted to believe.

And now here I am, in another world.

This sort of thing is bound to turn anyone's worldview upside-down.

I'm doing my best to keep an open mind about everything, approaching it all from a radio-show-host, journalistic-type perspective. From that angle, I can almost accept (without driving myself crazy) that this has happened, that somehow, magically, I ended up in another world without any rational explanation, and...I just have to roll with it. I am rolling with it, as best as I'm able. If I want to survive in this situation, I've got to *not* be that raving person who falls to pieces and keeps crying about the hot dog she can't have because it's a whole *world* away.

And now I'm tiptoeing behind a knight stalking a ghost. Who just told me that the scenario in the movie *Poltergeist* is kind of common.

Apparently, that's my hard limit of acceptance.

"Really?" I find myself saying with a thick coating of sarcasm, but at that moment, the ghost, not having paid attention to anyone or anything beforehand...suddenly stops on a dime.

The ghost, hovering in midair with her hair and skirts blown back in an invisible wind, turns.

I find myself pinned to the spot. I'm not afraid, I realize distantly, as the ghost holds my gaze with burning black eyes.

I *should* be afraid as she stares to the very deepest part of me, her mouth open, her mouth that, remember, is totally *black* on the inside. She opens her mouth, her black hole of a mouth, into a hideous, round "o." If this were a horror movie, I'm at that moment where I'm probably supposed to die a grisly death, murdered by a vengeful ghost.

But as I stare at her and as she stares at me, that's...all that happens. We stare at one another for a long, long moment.

And then the ghost winks out and disappears, like a television flicked off, as if she were never there at all.

"Interesting," is what Attis says, folding her arms in front of her. She stares at the spot the ghost recently vacated, and then she turns and glances at me with one raised eyebrow, sighing out with a slight shake of her head.

"What?" I ask her, biting my lip as I wrap my arms tightly around my middle, suddenly feeling more than a little odd.

Kind of like I just saw a ghost.

"You look like you just saw a ghost," says Attis at that moment, her mouth turning up at the corners as her lips slide into a warm smile. Then she's chuckling to herself.

"Great. Nice," I tell her, but I'm laughing a little, too, voice weak. "That was...crazy. What just happened..." I trail off and glance up at her. "So, now what?"

"Well," says Attis, peering over the railing down at the bar area. "Shannon said she'd bring up dinner for the both of us soon." She raises a single brow and puts her head to the side as she considers me. "And I think I have an idea for the ghost removal... I mean, *exorcism.*"

"You do?" I ask her, as we head back to the room.

"It's common enough lore that if we can get the specter to break her usual pattern, she might be freed," says Attis, her eyes narrowed as she shuts the door behind us. "Just now, did you note how—when she turned and looked at you, which had not been part of her pattern before, she simply floated to the railing, stood on the railing and then leaped—that the ghost flickered and went out, like a guttering candle flame?

It's odd, I feel, that she would look to you in particular. You don't have any magical power or talent that I'm aware of, but it was you that she looked to. My guess is that she was attracted to you because you come from another world, and she sensed that about you," says Attis mildly, sitting down on her bed and leaning back on her hands as she glances at me with a small smile. "So, Josie, the question is: will you be bait for me?"

"How so?" I ask her, brows furrowing as I frown. I pick up Wonder, who affectionately bites my hand, still purring, and I run my hand over her head again and again, still feeling muddled and kind of wonky.

Attis gets up smoothly, striding over to the far window. She pulls back the curtains and reveals diamond-paned glass that appears to open by a latch on the bottom edge. She undoes the latch and shoves against the window. It creaks and groans and finally gives beneath her pushing. Attis peers out, glancing down.

"Oh, it's not far," she says confidently. Mystified, I move to stand next to her, peering out.

Uh...yeah. It's a two-story drop to the ground, where there just happens to be a very, very small pile of hay. I stare at her. What the hell is she up to?

"You could make that jump, right?" asks Attis, turning to me with one brow raised.

I just realized how close she is. Granted, I'm still holding my cat, my cat who is very affectionately (and robustly) chewing on my hand, as she purrs loudly between us. But still... We're so close, Attis and I. Again, I could kiss her.

But I *can't* kiss her. What a terrible idea that would be.

Just as terrible as *jumping out this window*.

"Why the hell would you want me to make that jump?" I ask her, almost conversationally.

"Because," says Attis, tapping her finger on the window frame, "if you're able to get the ghost to follow you out the window, you'll not only break her pattern, but once the pattern is broken, her hold on this place will be no longer. It will allow her spirit to fly freely again, and to go to the land of the dead, rather than be trapped in this constant loop of death and despair. If her pattern is broken, if she can leave this house, you've freed her soul. You could help her, Josie," says Attis softly, leaning closer to me, her mouth in a small, soft line.

How can I refuse?

How can I refuse her?

"Sure," is what I tell her. I paste on a fake smile, and I squeeze my cat so hard she lets out a little squeak. "It's just...a little jump."

And it'd be just a little kiss.

I squash the thought as much as I can.

Which is not enough.

Chapter 7: The Leap

After dinner, we sit, each of us on our beds, and consider our options.

"We can't guarantee when the ghost will reappear. I'm assuming she'll come back again this night, though," says Attis thoughtfully, wrapping her long fingers around the warm mug of coffee as she leans back against the roughly hewn headboard. "So, we simply wait," she tells me, crossing her legs and glancing sidelong at me.

"I'm so tired," I tell her, wrapped in the blanket I pulled off the bed and still wearing my cannibal werewolf coat. The warmth of Wonder pressing on my stomach, of the blanket and the coat and the larger fire (Attis built it up, thankfully), with the delicious shepherd's pie digesting in my stomach...it's all too much. Especially after the day we had. I'm so tired, in fact, that I'm beginning to fall asleep sitting up.

"Then sleep, Josie," says Attis softly, gazing at me with warm eyes. "I'll wake you when it's time."

"Okay. Just...hurl myself out the window when I have the ghost's attention, right?" I mumble sleepily, finally lying down on the bed on my side, curling toward the fire.

"Right," Attis says with a small chuckle. "Just make sure to—"

But whatever else she says after that is lost on me, since I fall asleep immediately.

ॐ

It's a common enough dream: I have it at least once a month. It's so familiar and well-worn that I know every last part of it, am aware enough during it that I know I'm dreaming, but still...I don't wake myself up. I don't do anything else but let myself dream it.

This is my favorite dream.

It's my favorite, because it's the last thing that connects me to her.

My sister Ellie and I are at her apartment—about a month before the accident that took Ellie's life. The event that I dream about actually did happen; I remember it, remember that afternoon as one of the last memories of my sister, but the dream always deviates a little from what really happened that day, as dreams about real-life experiences tend to do.

Ellie sits on her bulky red couch, blowing on her favorite mug filled with steaming green tea. She glances up at me with twinkling blue eyes as she wiggles her toes in her pink bunny slippers, and then she winks at me with such exaggeration, I find myself laughing.

"You *like* her," says Ellie then, all knowingly, her brows up and triumph clearly on her face, as if she just solved the greatest mystery of our generation.

I stare at her in surprise. "Like who?" I ask.

"Oh, really, you're going to play dumb?" she says, rising easily and plunking the mug of tea on the coffee table. She shakes her head so hard that her long, chestnut ponytail flops over her shoulders energetically. "Come on, Josie—let's cut to the chase. You like this knight chick. You actually like her a *lot*."

Even in the dream, I can begin to feel my blood pounding much quicker through me. "Ellie," I begin, but she shakes her head, takes another step toward me, folding her arms in front of her, over her favorite pair of cat pajamas, a detail I always notice in the dream.

Ellie always had this way about her... She called it "being psychic," but I teased her that this was code for "being a total meddler." Ellie's "being psychic" included that time she "intuitively knew" that Brandy from her yoga class and me would totally hit it off. Brandy and I *did* hit it off, but that's beside the point; there wasn't anything psychic about my big sister setting me up on a date with a woman she knew I'd find attractive. It's just what Ellie *did*. She meddled in my life, and she helped me out as only a big sister could.

She's wearing that exact same mischievous, meddlesome expression now as she did then, when she set me up with Brandy.

But it's a little more pronounced. She looks more than a little triumphant.

"Spill," says Ellie, leaning her elbows on her kitchen counter as she waggles an eyebrow at me.

"Have you guys kissed yet?"

"God, Ellie, no," I tell her with a long sigh. I lean back against her sink, shrug. "I *can't*, okay? Just drop it. I'm attracted to Attis, yeah, but there's nothing I can do about it."

"What are you *talking* about?" asks Ellie, flopping the top half of her body on the counter in an exaggerated movement of frustration. "Josie, seriously, you're on *another world.* Do you think this happens everyday? This is a moment in your life that you could never have predicted, and you're with this super hot warrior chick... I mean, why aren't you throwing yourself at her, if you're that damn attracted to her?"

"Because, first off, I've never *thrown myself* at anyone in my entire life," I tell her archly, tapping my toe on her black-and-white linoleum. "I mean, seriously, what do you take me for? I'm a hell of a lot cooler than that."

"There's such a thing as being cooler than a penguin, and how often do you think penguins get some? Don't be *that* cool; you'll shoot yourself in the foot," she says, shaking her head as her eyes twinkle at me. "Okay, so don't throw yourself at her, but seduce the hell out of her, pour on the charm, and, *damn,* would you just make a move already? It's so obvious that she's into you, and you're being so stoic about it that it practically hurts to watch," says Ellie, brows high.

"So what if she's into me?" I ask her, using the same logic that you always have in dreams: of course, somehow, Ellie knows all this, knows that I'm attracted to Attis and that Attis is attracted to me. I accept the fact that I'm, somehow, speaking to my dead sister—because this is a dream. And anything's possible here.

Ellie stands, then, her teasing expression gone as she skirts the counter quickly and meets me in her kitchen. She stands in front of me, and she grips my shoulders tightly with her hands, shaking me a little as her brows furrow, as her bright blue eyes turn stormy.

"Josie, you've got to wake up, sweetheart," she says, all laughter and smiles gone, replaced, instead, by a deep grimace. "This is so important. You've got to act on your feelings, or you're going to regret it for the rest of your life, I promise you. Stop talking yourself out of everything wonderful in your life, baby. You deserve to be happy."

I stare at her, my eyes filling with tears as I take a deep breath, as I feel the world falling away from beneath me.

My sister hugs me tightly, just the way she used to, when she was trying to convince me that life was really okay, that things turned out for good people.

She's hugging me just like she used to before she was taken away from me.

Ellie steps back, shaking her head, her eyes wide. What's strange is that, behind her, I see something big and silver move, but it's so blurry because everything's becoming fogged up; I can't quite make out what it is.

It reminds me of something. Of a big silver animal...

"Josie," Ellie tells me with urgency. "You've

got to wake up—"

αβ

"Josie? Wake up—"

I open my eyes and take a deep breath.

The ghost is hovering over my bed.

"Josie...it's all right. Don't be afraid," says Attis smoothly, her voice soft and warm and reassuring, even as this ghost, a see-through woman with black eyes and a black mouth that's unhinging, as if she wants to take a bite out of my soul, hovers over me.

Technically, I should be utterly terrified. But, again, for some strange reason, I'm not afraid at all as I stare up into this ghost's black eyes. I listen to Attis' voice, to the calm strength of it. Her voice is all I can really hear.

"All right, Josie," says Attis easily now. She's sitting on her bed, I realize, the mug of coffee probably gone cold in her hands. "You're going to have to get up, get out of the bed," she says, every word smooth and easy. "Can you do that for me?"

"I think so," I whisper, unsure. My cat isn't curled up on me anymore... I wonder where she's gotten to (though she can't have gone far; the room's pretty small). I sit up slowly, and the ghost rises a little into the air above me.

"All right," says Attis, standing and striding quickly toward the door. "Josie, I'm going to go outside. You must keep the ghost's attention, keep her from going back to the hallway and throwing herself off the balcony. The window is open. When you hear me calling you from outside, you jump out the window. And I'll catch you."

For a moment, I think she's joking, and I chuckle a little nervously. But when I flick my gaze to Attis, she's already through the door and gone.

Uh...great. She *was* serious.

I stare up at the ghost, and the ghost stares down at me. It doesn't really make sense *scientifically* that she notices me and not anyone else. I'm fairly certain that I'm not physically or mentally any different from everyone else here, on this world. Just because I come from a different world shouldn't make me *different*, but then, I have to keep reminding myself that it's not like there are scientific principles governing ghosts. So if Attis tells me the ghost is interested in me because I'm from another world, there's a chance that she's right.

I take a deep breath and stare up at the ghost.

Am I really going to leap out the window of a second-story building and hope that I can land in a very small pile of hay? Or, more impossibly yet, in Attis' arms?

The ghost stares down at me with unblinking black eyes.

God...I hope I can do it. I don't really like the look she's giving me right about now.

The ghost opens her mouth; her expression goes just a bit darker and nastier. Yeah, that's not really a good sign...

And that's when Attis' voice comes through the window from outside. "Josie? I'm ready! Jump!"

Suddenly I'm up and out of the bed like it's on fire. I try to hold the gaze of the ghost as I stumble backward, toward the window, fumbling with my hands behind me, reaching for the windowsill. My fingers close around the cold wood of the sill. And that's when it hits me that I'm *about to jump out a window.*

"And you're going to catch me, right, Attis?" I shout down to her, keeping the ghost pinned in my sights.

"Absolutely!" Attis calls up to me.

I can't be sure, but it sounds like she's smiling.

God, it's cold outside, I realize, as I put a leg over the windowsill into the night. I hold the gaze of the ghost, and then I put my other leg over the windowsill, too, so I'm just sitting there suspended in midair, my legs dangling out into nothingness.

This might, possibly, be the stupidest thing I've ever done.

The ghost begins to come towards me now, reaching her arms out to me as she hovers forward.

"Jump now, Josie!"

And, unbelievably, impossibly...

I leap.

One summer, our family went camping up in Maine. It wasn't something we'd ever done before, the whole big family vacation, and we never did it again...but that one week in August was one of the happiest of my life.

It was a few months before Ellie's accident. I was twenty and in college, and she was out of college and happy, and we basked in the knowledge that we thought we had our whole lives in front of us. Everything from that week is gold-tinged in my memory, even though the trip wasn't perfect. It rained almost constantly. Our cabin was next to another cabin full of drunk frat boys. And there was the infamous Raccoon Incident.

But still...I remember it as perfect, golden.

And no moment was more perfect than the afternoon Ellie and I went swimming together in the ocean. The afternoon we dove off the cliff together.

There are a lot of cliff faces in Maine, and we were camped practically on the edge of one. It was an impossibly far leap into the water, though— really—it probably wasn't all that far. In my memory, it was as tall as a five-story building, but if I went back there now, I'd probably be disappointed to realize that it was only about twenty feet. Time makes you remember things differently sometimes, turns that tiny incident into something massive, shining...

But it doesn't matter how high that cliff face was. Because I remember that, when my sister and I leaped together, hand in hand, running as fast as we could across the grass leading up to the drop-off and then suddenly surging through the air together...

I remember that it felt like flying.

And I remember that now, because it's just like then, that long-ago moment, gone forever now.

But I remember.

For this single, absurd moment, as I hang suspended in the air, as the expression of the ghost changes behind me, her face growing ugly and contorted and angry as she races toward me, following me out the window...it feels, again, just like I'm flying.

But it's only for the briefest of moments, that

feeling, that weightlessness, that surge of euphoria as I muse that this must be what birds feel like. But that feeling fades almost immediately, followed by pure adrenaline, and then by pure fear, fear coursing through me so quickly that I catch my breath.

I'm not flying. I'm *falling*. I close my eyes, brace for impact.

I hit her so fast, so hard, the breath should be knocked from me. But it isn't.

Because Attis catches me. Easily.

Somehow, impossibly, *she catches me*.

I'm pillowed in midair by strong arms, one arm under the backs of my knees, the other around my shoulders and chest. I should hurt—I hit her with such force, such impact—but I don't hurt. Nothing hurts, actually.

Attis holds me in her warmth, and I stare up at her face with wide, stunned eyes. I catch my breath, my heartbeat roaring through me as she holds my gaze; her mouth turns up at the corners softly.

She's smiling down at me. And then, as one, we both look up into the air, at the window I just fell from.

The ghost is hovering in midair far above us. She's hovering like she's flying, and she actually probably is. She turns over slowly, her skirt billowing out behind her, her hair floating all around her, like she's suspended in water, and then she looks up at the moon, at the distant, silver curve far, far above.

She doesn't flicker out and disappear, like before.

Slowly, softly, she looks up at the moon...and

then she simply begins to...dissolve.

That's the only way I can explain it. It's like her toes and the hem of her dress begin to turn into sparkling glitter. The dissolution, the transformation from ghost into shimmering particles, moves up through the ghost's body, and then she's entirely made of that shimmering dust...

For a long moment, nothing happens. She shimmers far above us. But then a soft wind begins to blow, the chill breeze brushing past Attis and I and swirling into the air.

And the dust that used to be the ghost blows away into nothingness.

Attis sighs, her shoulders dropping slowly as the tension leaves her. I glance up at her, and, of course, my heart skips a beat.

Her eyes are soft and warm as she gazes up at the moon; her mouth is a soft, sweet curve. She looks at peace, staring at the stars spread above us.

"We did it," she says then, gently.

I stare up at Attis, at her—in that moment—vulnerable, open face, and I know what's happening, and I have to admit it again to myself, what's happening, and that I'm completely incapable of stopping it:

I'm falling in love with her.

I could (sort of) ignore it before. I could ignore it, and I think I might have been able to continue ignoring it. But it took this, it took her *catching* me as I fell, it took this moment of openness, of her face softening, for me to realize that I can't stop the progression of feeling, this unfurling in my heart. I'm powerless against it.

I'm falling in love with her.

Attis glances down at me now, and she sighs again. She gazes at me almost wistfully, but then she shakes herself out of it, and she sets me down gently, my feet finally touching the ground.

I stand, wobbly, for a long moment as we both gaze up at the sky.

"Did that really do it? How do we know that it worked? I mean, is the ghost really gone?" I ask Attis, holding my coat (the coat that I'm still wearing, that I didn't even take off to sleep) close around myself.

"She's at peace now. She's moved on," says Attis, voice low.

Her words were suddenly cold, and I glance up at her, surprised. Whatever made her open, made her vulnerable before, is gone now completely. She's closed off again.

It's like a punch in the gut to see how cool her face has become. What happened? I rub at my arms, suddenly very self-conscious.

She's at peace now. She's moved on.

Something, I realize, that Attis has not done.

"Come on... Let's get some rest," she tells me wearily, turning away from me and not looking at me as, together, we begin to walk toward the entrance to the tavern.

My arms are wrapped tightly around myself, and even though I'm very cold, even though I spent the entire day outside and there's no place I'd rather be but warm in that bed...I know that I need a moment to myself.

"You...go on," I tell Attis quietly. She turns

back, surprised, but her face is still closed off, still hardened to me. I shake my head, feeling my heart ache. "You go back to bed. I'll be up in a minute. I just need some...fresh air..."

She holds my gaze for a long moment before she nods slowly. "All right. But realize we have a long day tomorrow." She doesn't say anything more, simply turns and walks toward the front of the building.

I turn, and I look back up at the sky, at the sliver of moon, and I finally notice...

The millions and millions of stars.

Okay, admittedly, I'm not an outdoorsy-type person, but I can still appreciate the sheer, mind-blowing beauty of nature.

And I don't think I've ever seen anything so beautiful. I certainly have never seen this many stars before in my life.

Well. One other time I did. One other time I saw the heavens so bright and beautiful that it broke my heart with its jaw-dropping majesty.

During the camping trip in Maine.

I take a deep breath and cast about for something to sit on so I can look at the sky comfortably. There's a well in the center of this courtyard (a different courtyard than the outhouse area), so I go and I sit on the lip of the well, the stones cold underneath me, and I look up and up.

There are so many stars overhead that the sky practically glows white. A strip of nebulous galaxy arches across the sky, and I'm able to make out individual bits of pink and purple galaxy, because it's so dark here, with no artificial lighting to pollute the skies, that the stars aren't hidden at all. There's a riot of colors in the galaxy, a riot of colors surrounding the stars, and it takes my breath away.

It reminds me so much of that camping trip that my heart actually hurts. I remember staring up at the constellations with my sister, laughing like we were kids as we snuggled deep in our sleeping bags around the dying campfire, our faces upturned to the skies, just like mine is now.

I wish Ellie were here. Ellie would know what to do; she'd say the perfect thing to soothe me, the perfect thing that I needed to hear...

I remember the dream suddenly, and the ache in my heart intensifies. I actually reach up and place a hand over my heart, pressing down, trying to lessen the pain. It doesn't work.

I'm perfectly aware that dreams are only a muddling of images sent from our subconscious. There's nothing *magical* about a dream, nothing otherworldly, but didn't it seem strange that the only reoccurring dream I have, the one I've had so many times since she died.... Isn't it strange that, for the first time ever...the dream was different?

I don't remember much from the dream other than my sister's insistence and urgency. I remember her taking my shoulders in her hands, shaking me gently. I remember her laughing, but I don't remember about what. She wanted me to do something, wanted me to do that thing with such urgency that I still feel the urgency now, though I don't remember what she wanted me to do...

But I have to remember that it was only a dream, a dream filled with things that I wanted to hear, so my subconscious simply manufactured them for me.

I rub at my eyes with a cold hand. I just need to get home. I need to get out of this world, this world that's so different from my own, this world that makes no real sense to me.

I need to get home, and everything will make sense again.

I stare up at the stars, feeling far, far beneath them, feeling cold and sad and small. I sit on the edge of the well and try to keep my heart from hurting.

And fail.

Chapter 8: The Feather

I wake up to the smell of coffee and the warmth of a roaring fire. I sit up in bed, moving aside the purring, happy bulk of my cat from her place, curled up on top of my stomach.

Attis stands at the foot of the bed, dressed only in a nightshirt that reaches the tops of her thighs. She's bent forward at the waist, washing her face in the chipped basin on the small table by the wall, dipping her hands into the water and bringing them up to her cheeks, brushing the water over her closed eyes, her nose, her soft mouth...

My breath hitches in my throat, and I purposefully look away, swinging my feet over the edge of the bed and stretching overhead exaggeratedly.

"Ah, you're awake!" Attis says warmly, and I glance back at her, relieved that she looks much softer than when we last saw each other last night. She looks bright eyed and energetic, how the morning always makes me feel, too. "Are you ready to go, Josie?" she asks me, picking up the rough scrap of cloth from beside the bowl and patting her face dry. "We've got quite a ways to go today," she says, rubbing the cloth over the back of her neck and running a wet hand through her dark red hair. She shakes her head, and the hair spills over her shoulders as she arches her head back, her creamy white neck drawing my gaze like a gravity. She sets the cloth beside the bowl and regards me. "Are you very sore?"

I try to stand and then topple backward onto the bed, wincing. "Oh, my God, that's harsh," I mutter, massaging my thighs. I'm the kind of sore that a first trip to the gym in twelve months with an absurdly pushy trainer would make you, times ten. I grimace, wincing, and glance back at her. "Tell me this stops after, you know, a thousand hours in the saddle? I feel like I'll never walk again," I tell her dramatically, curling into the fetal position on the bed.

"Oh, not so many as that," she says, and then she crosses the space between us. Smoothly, like she does this sort of thing all the time, she kneels down on one knee in front of me, curling her warm fingers around my hands and drawing me up into a seated position again at the edge of the bed.

"What are you—" I begin, already feeling my cheeks warm, but then there's no helping it...

Attis places her hands around my hips and draws me forward with one smooth motion, so that my legs are dangling off the bed again. She leans forward, and then the front of her body is pressed against my knees, and she places the palms of her hands on the tops of my thighs.

I take a deep breath, feeling the warmth of her waken my entire body in one surging jolt of electricity.

Her hands are placed on my thighs in the smoothest, most non-awkward way possible, and I can either answer that smooth, non-awkwardness with my own smooth, non-awkwardness *or* I can totally blush and stammer and make an idiot of myself.

I'm never an idiot in front of women, I remind myself. I've got this. I can do this. I draw in another deep breath and try to paste a look on my face of calm curiosity and indifference.

I...probably just look unhinged again.

What the hell is it about Attis that reduces me to this? That reduces me to a blushing idiot incapable of normal behavior?

It's because you like her so damn much, comes the agitating thought from the back of my head.

"So," I tell her, reaching into my radio show host brain and letting it run on auto-pilot. "Do you always wake up your traveling companions this way?" I ask her teasingly.

Attis flicks her gaze from my leopard-print thighs to focus on my face.

"No," she says, and that single word is deep and husky, and that single syllable undoes me.

I can feel the blush explode across my cheeks, and I take a single, quivering breath in.

"I need to ease your pain," she says, suddenly all business as she closes her eyes and bows her head. "Close your eyes, Josie."

Oh. Easing my pain. Of course. I feel chagrin move through me, but I find myself nodding. "Sure," I tell her.

But I don't close my eyes.

Threads of white light begin to spin up from the rough boards of the floor. They're almost nonexistent, so it's difficult to see them to start; I only notice them because I was looking for them. But, like the last time she healed me, the strands of white light spiraling up begin to grow in diameter and brilliance. They begin to glow so brightly, in fact, as they tendril out of the floor, that it's difficult to look at them. But I do, anyway. I narrow my eyes, squint, and watch as the strands of white light begin to spiral around Attis, growing up and over her body like an ivy plant made of light. They surge quickly down her arms.

And the light dives into me. Where they touch my skin, they...*tickle*.

The strands of light are now glowing so brightly that I can't see anything but brightness. There's one tremendous flash of light, and then nothing.

They've disappeared. Attis opens her eyes, glances up at me with a small smile.

"There. That should be easier now for you." She rises from kneeling and offers her hands down to me.

I swallow and take her hands.

She pulls me up gently, and then I'm standing on legs that were aching so terribly, when I first woke up, that I couldn't fathom making it through the day. And now, of course, there's no pain. Because Attis healed me again.

"Didn't you say that it's hard for you to do that, to heal me?" I ask her, but she shrugs easily, moving away from me, back to the water basin.

"If it helps you make this journey, then it's worth it," she says, her voice mild as she places her hands in the basin of water.

I shift my weight, turn away from her beautiful face bent toward the bowl of water. "Thank you," I murmur.

She flicks her gaze up to me, and her full lips slant at the corners as water travels over her mouth, dripping off her chin. She picks up the piece of cloth, wipes off her skin. "It's my pleasure, Josie," she tells me.

Wonder ruins this perfectly perfect moment by sauntering up to me and complaining, loudly, sitting her fat cat butt down on the floor and staring up at me with narrowed, demanding eyes. The meow she makes is the type of sound that a Halloween cat would spit out, and I sigh, staring down at her. She needs food and a litter box (I'm thinking the stable yard will do) pronto, so I pick her up and make my way out into the hallway.

Kell's leaning against the door frame of the room across the hall from us, wearing a very deep cat-who-ate-the-canary grin. The bar maid from last night is walking backward out of the room, a blanket wrapped around her middle, her clothes in her arms.

She's wearing nothing more than a very satisfied smile.

Kell watches her for a long moment with hooded, darkened eyes. She reaches out, wrapping her arm around the bar maid and drawing the woman close. Kell's already dressed in her armor, and she pressed the woman to her front hard.

My mouth goes dry as Kell kisses the bar

maid so deeply that the bar maid's toes curl beneath the blanket.

"I'll see you soon," says Kell, her voice deep and husky, as the bar maid giggles and begins walking down the hallway. Kell watches the bar maid for a long moment before flicking her gaze to me. She raises a single brow, tilting her head to the side as a sly smile begins to cross her mouth. Kell then glances at the shut door behind me.

"Well?" she asks, folding her arms in front of her.

There can be only one question she's asking.

"Not that it's any of your business," I mutter to her, shifting my complaining cat over to my other arm. "But, no, we didn't do it."

Kell chuckles at that, her blue eyes darkening. "I was talking about the ghost," she says wickedly. "Did you get rid of her?"

A blush spreads across my face, but I don't answer her, only turn and walk down the hallway as Kell's laughter follows me.

&

Attis' great black mare is saddled and ready to go out front of the tavern, so the only thing that takes us awhile to do, after telling Shannon that her establishment is now ghost-free (which she's pretty darn happy about), is to devour some breakfast and say goodbye to all of Attis' old comrades.

They gather, laughing and telling jokes outside, but you can tell that their mood is much more sober than last night. They gaze at Attis with questioning eyes, and when Kell steps forward, a single tear streaks down the woman's cheek.

"Be careful. Remember what I said about the wolves, all right?" she says mysteriously. Attis nods, her jaw clenched tight. "And you must pledge to see us a little more often." Kell and Attis quietly embrace, with a tightness that I envy.

But as Kell's gaze over Attis' shoulder catches mine.

"Take care of her, will you, Josie?" asks Kell, her voice thick with emotion as she steps back, holding the warrior woman out at arm's length to keep Attis' gaze for a moment longer. "You'll do that for me, yes?" she asks me again.

"Yes, of course," I manage, before I'm embraced tightly, too, by an Alinor who *should*, by all laws of biology, be nursing the worst hangover of all time.

But, of course, she isn't. She's actually super perky and bright eyed and bushy tailed, which I would have thought statistically impossible, considering the gallons of booze I'd watched her consume.

Maybe she can hold her liquor better than I thought she could.

"Next time we see each other, maybe I'll take you for a roll in the hay," says Alinor hopefully, squeezing me. Then she's pounding my back as she laughs loudly. "Naw," she says, with a quick shake of her head. "You're not really my type. But it's nice to tease you, lass. You've got a blush that would make a virgin envious."

I laugh. My blush has always been my curse,

and I'm aware of exactly how red I can get—so my choices are either to laugh at her joke or get all prickly. And let's be honest: my belly is currently full of delicious pancakes. I'm not in the mood to be all prickly.

My quick radio mouth saves me. "Oh, don't worry. I have something else that would make a virgin envious," I tell Alinor, with a wink.

And then...shockingly...

She blushes.

"Now, now—let's not start a competition to out-bawdy each other, miladies," says Kell quickly, but her smirk is wide as she hooks an arm around Alinor's neck and drags her away from me. "It's your stunning intellect, am I right, Josie, that makes those virgins blush?" she asks me with a big wink. "Surely it's your intellect. But then again, it might be your enormous br—"

"Brown eyes," says Attis softly.

Whatever Kell says next fades into the background, and I stare at Attis, my heart *literally* skipping a beat.

Her tone was so soft that, had I not been standing right next to her, I wouldn't have heard her words at all. But I did, and for a long moment I'm so shocked by the intensity with which she spoke that I really can't be certain if I heard her right or not, or if my overactive imagination is making me imagine the gorgeous knight I'm traveling with complimenting my brown eyes (which, I promise, are nothing special at all).

But Attis isn't looking at me; she's checking the girth on Zilla's saddle, taking off her armored gloves to slip a single finger between the leather strap and her horse's stomach. She nods once, replacing her gloves, and turns, as if she had said nothing out of the ordinary.

Maybe...maybe I *was* imagining things?

"Be well, friends, until next we meet," says Attis, holding her hand up into the air in a gesture of farewell to the armored women gathered in front of the tavern. The other knights each raise their fists to the air as one.

Kell looks like she's going to say something else...but she doesn't. Her earlier mirth is gone, and she glances at Attis with her brows furrowed.

Attis kneels down beside Zilla, and, unlike yesterday, without a single argument, I step into her hand, holding Wonder tightly in front of me. I vault into the air as she propels me upward, and I settle myself as best as I can into Zilla's saddle while still holding onto Wonder's protesting bulk. Attis undoes Zilla's reins from the hitching post and hands them up to me before turning back to the women, pressing the first two fingers of her hand to her mouth, and then holding out her hand to them.

"Stay safe," she tells them, her voice thick with emotion.

"You, too," Kell says softly, folding her arms in front of her while biting her lip...and flicking her gaze to me.

As Attis, Zilla, Wonder and I stride purposefully down the road, toward the forest we emerged from yesterday, the women shout behind us: not words so much as a specific sound. It's triumphant, that sound, and I can see Attis smiling down below me, as she walks on the ground.

We merge into the forest again, and the trees and underbrush are so thick that, in the matter of a few steps, it's almost impossible to tell that there was ever a road behind us. The trees swallow up any sound, the forest sighing in the wind.

"Today, we must stop for supplies," Attis tells me, tilting her face up to glance at me as she shoulders her way through a thorny bush. With all of her layers of leather and armor, she doesn't seem touched by the thorns, even when her gloved hand holds a particularly nasty branch out of the way of Zilla—Zilla who forges ever forward, her black head down almost sleepily and her stride steady. Attis lets the branch fall behind us and continues on.

"The tavern we stayed at last night is close to the small village of Oakton," says Attis, "and I know there's a smithy there, which Zilla desperately needs, and a goods store. But we must be quick in the village, because we have time to make up. We should have gotten started much earlier this morning if we intend to arrive in Arktos City as the festival begins."

Considering that we rose with the sun, I can't imagine how much earlier she wanted to get this show on the road.

We travel pretty quickly through the woods, Attis striding out ahead of Zilla, and the massive black horse taking large steps across the forest floor to follow her mistress.

I'm sleepy, as I grip my legs tightly around Zilla's round barrel, and as I hold tightly to the reins, but my mind is energized enough to race. For example: "So, you said there's someone in Arktos

City who can help me get home?" I ask Attis. "Who is it?"

"Well, I have a friend named Virago who lives in Arktos City. She's a knight," says Attis, skirting a particularly thorny patch of weeds, the thorns about as long as my hand. "A few moons ago, Virago was dispatched with her group of knights to hunt a beast, and the beast, being particularly nasty and powerful, managed to get itself through a portal into another world—and it dragged Virago with it. She called the world America, though, not Earth, but when she—"

"Wait, I'm from America!" I tell her, my heart beginning to pound.

Attis looks up at me a little funnily. "I thought you said you were from Earth?"

"Well, I'm from Boston, which is in Massachusetts, which is in America, which is on Earth," I explain, ticking the list off my fingers.

"That seems unnecessarily complicated," Attis tells me, her brows up, but she shrugs easily and keeps going. "Well, then, that's very good—Virago did visit your world, after all. So, you see, when she returned from that place, she brought back with her a lovely woman by name of Holly. Since Holly is from your world, there is a very good chance that, even if they can't take you back home, they may know how you can get there."

Virago brought a woman back with her? I raise my eyebrow, and I'm about to continue down that line of questioning (example: are all the lady knights lesbians, because that'd be pretty damn awesome...), but then the thick expanse of trees in front of us opens up suddenly, revealing a meadow, and a little village spreading out in the very middle of it.

The small dirt road that ran in front of the tavern was a massive highway compared to the tiny trail through the grass that leads from the woods toward the sprinkling of houses and buildings here. Attis strides down that faint trail with Zilla close on her heels, and as we get nearer to the structures in the center of the meadow, I don't really notice the houses so much (only that they're one-story tall, pretty small), because I'm mostly paying attention to what's going on in *front* of the houses.

The houses form a circle around a dusty expanse of ground that would, technically, I guess, be the village square. There's a stone well in the center of the square, and gathered in front of that well is a small crowd of people.

A small *yelling* crowd of people.

Attis sighs for a long moment, but she never breaks her lengthening stride as she makes a beeline toward the melee. Zilla follows her mistress willingly (I'm just hanging onto the reins for dear life; I doubt she'd listen to me if I tried to steer her), and as we get closer, and from my heightened vantage point on Zilla's back, I can make out that the crowd forms a circle around two people in particular: a woman and a man.

The man is tall, with a scruffy beard and a floppy hat and the kind of grubby clothes that make you think he's covered in mud, when he isn't really.

The woman, on the other hand, is shorter, though her air of command makes her seem taller than she actually is. She has long, straight black hair that falls over her shoulders and cascades down her back like an inky curtain, and she's wearing a big, poufy red dress which looks quite out of place, considering the rest of the villagers wear dirt-colored clothing.

For some reason, the woman looks witchy to me, but I could never tell you why she gives me that impression. She stands as tall as she can, her hands in fists at her side, and she's shouting as loudly at the man as the man is shouting at her.

They're practically nose to nose, and the crowd is yelling around them, too, weighing in with such helpful expressions as "yeah!" and "tell her!" but even though they're pretty focused, the assembled people still part like the Red Sea for Attis as she strides forward.

The woman and man stop shouting at the exact same moment when they spot Attis. Everyone, actually, falls perfectly silent. So silent that you could hear a horse snort. Which Zilla does, tossing her head and shaking it a little out of boredom, her bit jangling in her mouth as she chews it, stomping her right front hoof hard on the ground.

"Greetings," says Attis conversationally, lifting up her chin. She narrows her eyes, plants her feet hip-width apart and folds her armored arms in front of herself.

The wind chooses that moment to start up a little, blowing Attis' hair and skirting her red cloak along the edges of the dusty ground, puffing it out behind her. It's dramatic, and, as one, the people take a single step back from the proceedings.

"Hello, Attis," says the woman in the red dress, her brow curving upward as she folds her arms in front of herself, too. Her voice has a slight accent that I've never heard before, and her eyes are flashing dangerously.

"Oh, good, knight—you are of the order of Arktos City, and that means you are just. You must settle this," says the man then, spreading his hands. He, too, has the slight accent; it sounds almost a little French, I realize. The man steps toward Attis, his hands open to her. "We have a dispute that must—"

"I am no knight, sir," says Attis quickly. "I am but a humble mercenary, and—"

"Oh, rubbish, Attis," the woman in red snaps, and then she turns again on the man, stabbing him in the chest with her pointed index finger. "And you know very well that there would *be* no dispute, Haggis, if you'd simply pay me what I'm owed—"

"You haven't done the work properly!" the man blusters (I guess his name is Haggis, which I'm pretty sure is also the name of a sheep intestine sausage). He frowns. "And you can't threaten me, witch. I know my rights!"

Did he say...*witch*?

Attis sighs; then she reaches for her sword over her shoulder, on her back. She simply holds the hilt for a long moment, and with her feet hip-width apart, she looks pretty imposing.

"What is the situation here?" Attis asks, her voice booming across the whispering crowd. The voices stop, and many wide eyes train on Attis.

"Well," says an old man who steps forward, sucking on the ends of his handlebar mustache before blowing them out. He clears his throat, shifts his weight on his feet, then continues: "It's like this." He has his thumbs hooked into his belt loops, and he's leaning so far back, it looks like he wants to sit down in a chair that isn't there. "The witch Ilya gave Haggis a potion to cure his daughter's illness. But it didn't work. She wants payment, but Haggis is not about to give payment for nothing. I think that's the heart of the matter, really," he says, blowing out a sigh of air that makes his mustache move outward.

Ilya, the woman in the red dress, sighs for a long moment, her fingers pinching the bridge of her nose before she straightens up to her full height, and bristles. "I did make the potion, you old fool, and when that *idiot* gave it to his daughter, he didn't do it properly." She rounds on Haggis again. "You know that *you* messed it up. And now I haven't the ingredients to remake it, and I *told* you to make certain that she—"

"What is ailing your daughter, sir?" asks Attis succinctly, pinning Haggis in her sights.

The man shakes his head, his gaze downcast. "Well..." he begins, shifting his weight from foot to foot and taking his floppy hat off his head, wringing it in his hands. He's silent for a long moment.

"She's dead," says Ilya, words sharp as she folds her arms in front of her.

I stare at the woman, waiting for the punchline.

And...there isn't any.

She's serious.

The girl's dead, and the potion that Ilya made for her was supposedly going to...bring her back from the dead?

Really?

"Ilya," says Attis sharply, turning to the woman in red. Ilya tilts her chin up defiantly and holds Attis' gaze with flashing eyes.

It's pretty apparent these two women know each other.

"Yes?" Ilya snaps.

"I don't even know where to start," says Attis, fisting her hands. Her eyes are narrowed, and she's snarling. "You know the laws. You know that to bring someone back from the dead is—"

"I know the laws, but if I have the talent, why should they apply to me? I have hurt nothing," says Ilya proudly, raising her voice. "And it's not," she snarls, "like *you're* one to talk."

Something passes over Attis' face, a dark cloud shifting and changing her features almost imperceptibly, but the darkness is gone just as quickly as it came, taking with it all of Attis' fight. She's still standing, feet still hip-width apart, and her arms are folded in front of her again, but she seems subdued somehow, almost caving inward, deflating.

Ilya folds inward a little, too, her shoulders slumping. "I'm sorry, Attis," she says quietly then. "That was a low blow."

Attis shakes her head, running her gloved fingers through her hair. She turns to Haggis. "How long has your daughter been dead, sir?" she asks him, voice soft.

"Two days," the man tells her, voice shaking.

Attis sighs. "As I'm sure you know, two days is a long while. In order for the magic to work, the spell to resurrect her would need to be recreated almost immediately, and you'd have to administer it properly before sunset," she says, flicking her gaze to the sun that's shining through the thick layer of clouds directly overhead.

I shouldn't be surprised that Attis knows about spells. I mean, after all, she healed me with magic (which I'm actually taking pretty well, considering I would have found the very idea of it laughable at best and utter horseshit at worst a mere two days ago, long before I'd seen all of this with my own eyes and was *forced* to believe). But still, I don't think it's normal for a knight-type person to know *that* much about magic. The people surrounding the witch, the man and Attis are looking at Attis with impressed faces, and they're exchanging glances again, lowered voices whispering among themselves.

"What is the ingredient that you're missing to recreate the spell, Ilya?" Attis asks her, turning to the witch.

The witch shakes her head, crosses her arms again almost petulantly, her mouth pursed in a downward curving line. "I can tell you right now to save your breath, Attis: it's impossible, so don't you start making promises like you do," she begins, but Attis stares Ilya down. After a long moment, and a little flustered, Ilya breaks her gaze with Attis and glances down at the ground. She sighs, and begrudgingly, Ilya mutters, "I'd need a phoenix feather."

Attis considers this, glancing at me and then at Zilla, her eyes distant as she reaches out between us and brushes her gloved fingers over Zilla's neck, patting her horse absentmindedly. "And where is the closest phoenix nest?"

Most of the villagers turn and point toward a mountain rising out of the forest, a mountain so tall that its top is lost in the low cloud cover overhead.

"The only way to get a phoenix feather is if you could journey to the nest in time and get it. And you can't; it's half a day's journey. You could never get there and back in time. And the only *other* way to obtain it as quickly as we'd need it," says Ilya impatiently, her voice snappish again, "is if you called the phoenix down from the mountain to battle it. As you can see, there's no way to do this without destroying something," she snaps. "If you battle the phoenix, you might be killed, or the phoenix might be killed. If you don't battle the phoenix, you'll never reach her nest in time to get the feather, and the girl will remain dead."

Attis turns to Ilya, her gaze piercing. "If the feather was obtained, would your spell actually work, Ilya? If you have another phoenix feather, is it capable of resurrecting the girl?"

Ilya shifts back on her heels uncomfortably and averts her gaze. "It will work," she says, her voice softening. "I've done the spell before—and successfully, Attis. I mean, I've actually been successful a few times, since it didn't work...with you..." She looks up at Attis then, and a shadow passes over her face.

...Regret?

What is she talking about?

"Zilla is quite fast," says Attis, patting Zilla's shoulder again, her eyes unfocused, as if she's weighing the options in her head. She seems to reach a decision, and she glances up at me, one brow rising.

"Are you fine to stay here, just for a little while, while I obtain the feather, Josie?" she asks me, voice low.

"Of course," I tell her, because her jaw is set, and I can see in her eyes that she means to do this. Attis reaches up to me then and grips my waist in her hands, pulling me down before I realize that she's even about to do so. Wonder's so mad about the interruption in her sleep pattern that she actually yowls under my coat, causing several of the closest people in the assembled crowd to jump in surprise.

"Sorry," I mutter with a small grimace, trying to calm my cat down. I scratch her head through the cannibal werewolf coat, and she almost immediately goes back to sleep, purring her heart out like an internal combustion engine as she snuggles uncomfortably against my chest.

"Please stay here, Josie," Attis says a little louder, probably to benefit the crowd, "and wait for my return. It shouldn't be too long before I come back, and I'm certain that, in the meantime, Ilya would be more than happy to make you a cup of tea." Her brow is up as she glances at Ilya with an expectant frown. Ilya nods uncomfortably. "I'll return in one hour with the feather," says Attis, her voice booming over the assembled people as she leaps up onto Zilla's back. Without a backward glance, she gathers Zilla's reins in her hands immediately, and the horse bolts toward the forest and the rising mountain, a streak of black across the meadow that disappears into the trees so quickly, I almost couldn't follow her progress with my eyes.

"She'll do it. The knight will make it in time!" says Haggis, his voice so hopeful that it's heartbreaking.

"Well, if anyone can, it's certainly Attis," says Ilya, with a small sigh, as she crosses her arms in front of her. "And you are?" she asks me, her head to the side and her words barbwire sharp as she glares at me.

"I'm Josie," I tell her, holding out a hand to shake. "Josie Beckett."

"Utterly charmed," says Ilya, in the tone that indicates that, no, actually, she's *not* charmed. "All right, then, follow me. If Attis knows that I was anything less than hospitable to you, I will *never* hear the end of it." She rounds on Haggis, who's standing there, happy tears brimming in his eyes. "And *you* had best be prepared for when Attis returns, Haggis. Make certain your daughter's body is prepared to *properly* receive the potion this time."

Ilya's angry tone is lost on Haggis, though, who still holds his floppy hat in his hands, tears streaming down his face as he smiles at the crowd, raising his arms to them as if he's going to embrace all of them at once.

"My *daughter*," he shouts, his voice breaking on the word. "My daughter's going to come *back*! She's going to come back to *life!*"

Ilya practically snarls as she strides past the man, quickly prowling across the dusty village center, toward the house closest to the edge of the forest in front of the mountain. I trot after her.

This house that we're aiming for is the only

one that stands out from the other villagers' shacks. The most glaring and obvious difference is the fact that, while all of the other house colors resemble varying shades of mud, this house...

This house is purple.

"Come on, come on," Ilya tells me huffily, as she sweeps up the two narrow steps to her sagging front porch. It's a very small front porch, and a few of the purple, peeling floorboards are missing—but, heck, her house actually has a front porch.

I'm fairly certain that the reason the rest of the houses are mud-colored is because they're, you know, *made of mud*.

I follow after the witch, mystified, and when Ilya holds her front door open for me, I pause to stare into her house.

But I don't pause long, because there's an actual boot on my behind, and then Ilya is shoving me into the room with her hands on my back. "Don't stand there gaping, Josie Beckett. You're letting out the warm air," she says almost conversationally. So I step into the house, and Ilya is closing the door behind us before I can blink, effectively plunging us into darkness.

But it's not absolutely dark inside; it's just much darker than outdoors, and it takes my eyes a few moments to adjust to the candlelight and firelight in this main room. I brush the dust off of my butt from her boot, and I glance up.

My very first impression is that her house looks like the architectural offspring of an antiques mall and a psychic's parlor. There are thick, colorful rugs piled on top of each other underfoot, and a big black cauldron is bubbling merrily away in the broad stone fireplace at the end of the room. There are Victorian-looking red chairs with plush seats and a worn black table in front of the fire, and on that table, on top of a lace tablecloth, is an honest-to-goodness crystal ball the size of my head.

"Do you want some tea?" asks Ilya, moving past me and in the middle of a mood swing, it seems, as she goes from pretty damn pissy to calm and good-natured in the time it took for me to realize her house smells of incense. Which was immediately.

"Sure. Tea sounds great. Thank you," I tell her, and then I unbutton my coat, glancing around. "Can I let my cat down?" I ask Ilya.

She glances at me, her eyebrows soaring upward when she sees Wonder's fluffy gray head peeking out of the neck of my coat. "Well...I suppose you can," she tells me, her nose wrinkling. "But, so you know, I'm really not much of a cat person. As long as she doesn't harm anything, she can stretch her legs."

It's not as if I can guarantee my normally violent cat won't harm anything, but I choose not to tell Ilya that. I set Wonder on the ground and sink down onto one of the chairs at the table, and Wonder instantly prowls past me, her tail in the air and her nose pointed to the ground, like she's on some secret mission. Which, in her head, she probably is.

"So, you're really traveling with a cat in your coat? Do you enjoy torturing yourself?" asks Ilya, one brow up. She pours water from a bucket into a battered old tea kettle and suspends the bucket over the fireplace on a hook.

"Not really enjoying it so much," I quip, "but she's my cat, so..."

Ilya flicks her glittering gaze at me, narrowing her eyes. "So," she says, lifting her chin and cutting directly to the chase, "how do you know Attis?"

"Oh, you know..." I spin my finger lazily in a circle as I lean forward, setting my elbows on the table. "I just happened to fall on top of her when I came through a portal from my world." I watch Ilya carefully, and if she's surprised by my declaration, she doesn't show it at all as she begins to scoop dried tea into two bright blue mugs with a tarnished silver spoon. "So, how do *you* know Attis?" I ask her, genuinely curious as I lean back in my chair.

"I tried to bring her lover back from the dead," says Ilya quietly, sitting down across from me.

We lock gazes and stare at one another.

"Really?" I whisper, and she smiles a little, setting one of the mugs of dried tea in front of me.

"Yes," she says, but the smile turns wistful, and she glances at the pot of water over the fire. It's just beginning to whistle faintly. "I was friends with Attis, once, long ago. But I failed when I tried to bring back Hera, and we were friends no longer after that. I don't think that Attis has ever been able to bring herself to forgive me."

"What...happened?" I ask.

Ilya flicks her gaze to me, and her eyes suddenly narrow as she smiles slyly. "What are you, exactly, to Attis, Josie? Why should I tell *you*?" she asks, voice arch.

"I'm just a friend," I say smoothly, quickly, but Ilya's eyes narrow further, and her smile deepens.

"'Just a friend,'" she repeats, nodding knowingly and tapping her fingers on top of the lace tablecloth. "Every woman is 'just friends' with Attis—until they're not," she mutters, but then she glances at the fire again. I'm about to ask her what exactly she means by *that*, but I keep my mouth shut, digging into the deepest reserves of my patience as I wait for Ilya to finish the story.

The tea kettle is practically singing now over the fireplace, and Ilya gets up from the table to remove it from the flames with a folded towel. She pours scalding water out of the kettle over the tea leaves in her mug and then over the leaves in mine, the steam rising between us like curving smoke, shrouding her frowning face.

Ilya puts the tea kettle on a stone in front of the fireplace and sits down quickly across from me, her gaze suddenly intense, her voice dropping to a whisper, even though there's no one (that I know of) but Ilya, me and Wonder (who's currently prowling around in another room, and I really hope that I can find her again...) in the house.

"We used to be *really* good friends, Attis and I," says Ilya quietly. "We both lived in Arktos City, me for my training in witchcraft under Madame Samel, she in her training for knighthood to the queen. Attis and I were...together, too," she says slowly. Her gaze falls. "It was for only a short time, but I cared deeply about her. Gods, she was a heartbreaker back then..." Ilya licks her bright red lips and then turns to stare at the fire.

I swallow, pausing to take this in: Ilya and Attis were together. Together-together. I mean, I guess it makes sense to me. Ilya is fiery tempered and attractive, and—for some reason—fire and passion strikes me as Attis' type. But, still...butterflies flutter in my stomach. I tap my foot, clear my throat, my heart filling with trepidation.

I want to hear the rest of the story.

No. I know I *need* to hear it. Now.

"Well, that was a long time ago. Over fifteen cycles of the sun have come and gone since we last trysted," says Ilya, turning her finger and pointing up in the air, I'm assuming to indicate the planet moving around the sun. I'm also assuming a cycle is similar to our year. "When Attis went out in her knighting, going on missions, we grew further apart, though we were still good friends. I took up the job as witch here, in this village," she says, leaning back in her chair and hooking an arm over the back of it. "And that's when Attis fell in love.

"I could never have predicted that she would settle down. I don't think any of her friends could have predicted that. She wasn't a love 'em and leave 'em type," says Ilya quickly. "She cared for each and every woman she was with, but love never crossed her mind. Settling down wasn't possible for her. Or so we thought," says Ilya, sighing. "But then a visiting dignitary from a far isle arrived in Arktos City, a diplomat on behalf of her island to the royal court, and she met Attis there. Her name was Hera," says Ilya, licking her lips again. She looks distant, drawn and pinched. She was jealous of Hera, I realize. It's obvious that Ilya loved Attis deeply, but Attis didn't return that feeling, and then Hera came along and swept Attis off her feet, something Ilya was incapable of doing.

Of course that would hurt.

I didn't like Ilya from the very first moment I met her—she strikes me as pretty bitchy, actually. But while she's still not my favorite person in the universe, at least I understand her a little better now.

"It was love at first sight between Hera and Attis," says Ilya, with a slight layer of disgust over her voice. She grimaces. "They were obviously meant for each other, though, as much as it pained me to admit it. They complemented each other perfectly, and I've never seen Attis happier than that one summer the two of them came together. But that's all it was—a single summer. Attis was deployed with her regiment to help save a village. There was a werewolf clan that was terrorizing that village, and there was danger that they might branch out to further towns. The werewolves were taking children, and they were, well," she shrugs and frowns, "they were eating them."

I finger the lapel of my coat, but I don't say anything, my heart pounding in me.

"So Attis and her troop set out, and they started a great battle with the werewolves. But Hera didn't know that's what Attis was doing. She thought Attis was journeying with her troop, not battling dangerous creatures, so the night before Hera was supposed to leave to go back to her island nation, she set out on a horse to 'surprise' Attis with a good-bye visit. She came to Attis' encampment and found no one there: the knights and the werewolves were in the middle of a skirmish. No one knows exactly what happened, but Attis swears that, when she came upon

Hera's body in the middle of the melee, she saw a great silver bear. But there were only wolves around, you see—"

"Wait, wait—a silver w*hat*?" I ask, jaw dropping.

"A silver bear," Ilya shrugs. "I got all of this secondhand, mind you, and the knight who told me the story has a flare for the dramatics, but she says that, when they found Hera and Attis together, Attis cradling Hera's body, she was saying over and over again 'a silver bear did this,' even though no one else saw this animal," says Ilya, with a small sigh. "But Attis does not lie, and she can handle trauma... I don't think she'd imagine something like that. It was, admittedly, in the middle of a massive, bloody battle, but whether Hera was killed by the wolves or by the silver bear, the fact of the matter remains: Hera was killed."

I stare at her.

The silver bear.

I doubt, highly, that Attis would ever *imagine* anything. So could this bear possibly be the *same* silver bear that I saw? I mean, how many silver bears are there? Maybe they're a pretty common species on this world. What if there are tons of silver bears all over the place?

The silver bear that I saw...it couldn't possibly be the *same* silver bear, could it?

Ilya doesn't notice my discomfort and keeps talking, her words coming out faster now. "Our village is close to where the battle took place," says Ilya, her mouth set in a severe frown. "So, when Attis came across Hera's body, she immediately brought her to me. I'll never forget that night," she says, running her fingers through her long black hair and staring holes into the center of the table's surface. "I'd never seen Attis weep. Ever. Save for that night."

My stomach turns inside of me. I can only imagine what Ilya isn't saying. I can only imagine the moment Ilya went to the door: Attis carrying Hera's body into this very house, Attis carrying Hera exactly like she carried me when she caught me from the leap outside of the tavern. I can imagine Attis weeping, tears tracing silent paths down her face as she sets Hera gently on this table, Attis turning to Ilya, Attis asking, pleading...

"She asked me to save Hera, to bring her back," says Ilya quietly. "And I don't know if you'll believe me," she says, the words soft, "but I did everything in my power to resurrect her. I'd never done the resurrection spell before, and it's one of the most difficult magical endeavors you can undertake. But I did the spell, anyway. And it was incorrect. I was exhausted, and I was nervous, and Attis was unreachable with grief, and..." She bites her lip, slides her thumb over the grain in the wood beneath the black paint on the table. Ilya shakes her head. "So Hera was dead, and Attis... Well. Attis never quite recovered." She flicks her gaze back up to me. "So," she says with a halfhearted sneer, "now you know how I failed her. Now you know the story."

I stare at Ilya for a long moment, emotions warring within me. "I'm sorry, Ilya," I tell her then, quietly, heart hammering in my chest. "The whole situation was impossible. I hope you know that.

Attis asked what she shouldn't have asked of you, and something terrible happened to Attis that shouldn't have happened...but it's not your fault that Hera's dead. People die," I tell her, a lump growing in my throat. "And there's nothing that can stop it, or change it."

When I close my eyes, I see my sister's smiling face; I see the dimples in her cheeks and the mischievous expression she always gave me right before she came up with one of her crazy ideas. I see her laughing, because Ellie laughed a lot. She was the happiest, best person I've ever known, and she's gone now.

Because people die. And there's nothing you can do to bring them back.

I get up suddenly, tears swimming in front of my eyes. I need a moment to myself, I need some fresh air, I need...

"Sit down, Josie," says Ilya quietly. She glances up at me, and the hard lines of her face soften. "There is great pain within you," she says, her head tilted to the side as I do as she says, sitting down and folding my arms as I grit my teeth, jaw hard. "What happened to you?" she asks me.

No one knows about Ellie. Not my co-workers, not my new friends, not my girlfriends, not my lovers. No one knows, because I never say it, because I *can't*.

"I killed her," I tell Ilya.

Ilya's eyebrows arch, but she leans back against the chair, and she listens. She just waits and listens.

Finally, I work up the courage to say:

"We were out drinking," I tell her, lifting my chin, tears streaming down my cheeks as I keep my voice calm and steady, my heart breaking all over again as I unleash the words I always keep locked so tightly inside of me. "I was too young to be drinking, and I'd had one too many. I lied to her and said I could drive. You don't know what that is," I tell her, a sob choking my words. I swallow, keep going. "We have cars on my world. And they're vehicles that are very, very powerful. You should only drive them when you're sober. But I thought I was invincible, because I'd *always* thought I was invincible. So, though Ellie told me that we should take a cab, I said I knew better. And I tried to drive us home. I got us into an accident," I whisper, voice breaking. I close my eyes. "And she died because of me."

Ilya says nothing for a long moment. I sit there, feeling very sad and small, and then I hear a shift of fabric, and Ilya is reaching across the space between us on the table. She reaches out and takes my hand, covering the back of my hand with her own smaller fingers.

"I'm sorry," says Ilya, and when I open my eyes, when I glance at her, I can see the true sympathy and sorrow etched on her face... I know she's being sincere.

We remain that way for a very long moment, before Ilya pulls her hand back, sitting against her chair, her shoulders poker straight as she crosses her legs.

"I don't know why I told you that," I mutter now, shaking my head and wiping the tears from my cheeks. I laugh bitterly. "I never tell that story to anyone."

Ilya shrugs a little, running her thumb along the wood grain on top of the table again. "I have the face of a listener," she smiles grimly, head to the side, but she sighs after a long moment, face sobering. "Look, Josie...take the advice of a stranger. You must stop torturing yourself."

My jaw sets in a hard line again. "I *killed* her, the person I cared most about..." my low voice shakes. "I'm not *torturing* myself with anything. I'm telling the truth. I killed her. If it wasn't for me and my stupid decision, she'd be alive right now. I'm to blame, and I'm never going to stop blaming myself."

Something passes across Ilya's face, and—for a long moment—she gets a faraway look in her eye as she stares over my shoulder, past me, past everything in the room. "She wouldn't have wanted you to, you know," she tells me in a singsong voice. "Your sister wouldn't have wanted you to blame yourself." Her eyes focus, and she stares fiercely at me. "In fact, I think it'd break her heart to know that you haven't forgiven yourself."

I shake my head, my heart aching so much that I can hardly breathe. "You don't know *anything*," I tell her, words sharp, but Ilya holds up a finger.

"Think on my words, if you can, Josie," she tells me, and then she stands, turning away from me. "Attis has returned."

"What?" I repeat, discombobulated as I stand, as I wipe the tears away from my face again.

A knock comes at the front door.

I want to ask Ilya how she knew that Attis had returned. There certainly hadn't been any sounds of arrival. There was nothing, actually, to tell us that she was back, but when Ilya crosses to the door and opens it, Attis is standing there on Ilya's sagging front porch, and in her outstretched, armored palm is a single feather.

And it's on fire.

The fire is small, maybe the height of my hand, and very narrow. As the flames move across the surface of the feather, I realize...the feather isn't burning.

I smooth the front of my coat, and I take a deep, quavering breath as I still the features of my face, will my cheeks to cool after crying. I glance at Attis as I lift my chin, but she's not looking in my direction. Instead, she's holding Ilya's gaze as she extends the feather to her.

"It's done," says Attis tiredly. Ilya hardens her jaw, taking the burning feather from Attis' hand, the burning feather that doesn't burn either one of the women as they touch it.

"You should stay," says Ilya softly, curling her fingers around the feather and then secreting it away into an invisible pocket in her big red skirt. "Stay for the spell, the both of you, and then for dinner. You can sleep here tonight, and—"

"We've already delayed too long," says Attis, shaking her head. "It's kind of you, Ilya," she says, and her words are gentle, "but we must get supplies and continue on our journey. We'll never reach the city in time for the festival if we stay tonight. I'm grateful, though, for your offer," she says haltingly.

And I know that she means it.

"Don't be a stranger," says Ilya, her voice thick with emotion as I button up my coat and am about to go in search of Wonder. Miraculously, my cat appears from around the corner, covered in dust and cobwebs and wearing a very satisfied kitty smile. I scoop her up with a shake of my head and deposit her down the front of my coat; she curls up against me as I hold her tightly to me. She's already whipping out her most contented purr, sleepily blinking her eyes.

"Goodbye, Ilya," says Attis, finally flicking her gaze to me. She straightens a little, indicating my untouched mug of tea with a small frown. "Are you ready, Josie? We can delay a small while if you—"

"No, I'm ready," I tell her, words falsely bright as I tilt up my chin, as I force a smile. "Thanks for the tea, Ilya," I tell the witch and move past her, ready to leave her house.

"Josie, please...heed my words," Ilya murmurs to me, reaching out between us and clutching my arm with strong fingers. "Try to, anyway," she tells me, and she lets me go, her arm dropping to her side, her fingers curled in a fist.

Together, we leave Ilya's house, and Attis steps down off her front porch, gathering Zilla's reins in her hands. Zilla looks a little tired but not terribly so; her head is just lower than usual. Zilla turns companionably enough, walking sedately behind Attis as I follow the both of them across the town's square, toward what I can only assume is the smithy. The guy is busy pumping his large bellows, and in front of him is an anvil and a horse standing in front of the open building, ready for its shoes.

"You came back so soon. Was it hard to get the feather?" I ask Attis, trying (and pretty much failing) to get my mind off of the conversation I just had with Ilya. Attis shrugs, wrapping the reins around her right hand.

"It was fine," she says distractedly. "Standard job, really. There and back again. But we really must be going, Josie. Zilla has a loose shoe, and it should take the smithy a short while to fix it," she says, glancing quickly at me. "And then right back on the road again. But we also need supplies," she says, jerking her thumb down the road, to the only store I can see on the main drag of buildings. The only reason I can tell it's a store is the fact that it has a badly made wooden sign hanging over the front door. "General Goods," it reads, in roughly painted red letters that look almost like a bad spray paint job.

"I can, uh, go get the supplies we need while you get Zilla a new pair of shoes. Or whatever," I say quickly, when Attis raises a single brow and gazes at me in surprise. A quick smile that passes over her mouth before she frowns again, shaking her head.

"We need," she says, holding up a single finger, and then she rattles off a bunch of items in rapid succession, items I have never heard of before, or seen. I mean, some of the things on this shopping list sound fantasy movie-ish, like what Harry Potter would probably buy when he goes shopping. One of the items, one of the only things I recognize, is "a new cooking pot," and that's about it. The rest is perfect Greek—or Elvish—to me.

"Better yet," says Attis, her brow still raised

as the smile passes over her face again, "why don't you stay here with Zilla?" Her smile deepens. "And why don't I go get the supplies?"

"Good. Great!" I tell her, and Attis chuckles a little, passing close to me and pressing Zilla's reins into my hand.

"The smithy will take Zilla next, after this mare," says Attis, indicating the horse in the cross ties in front of the smithy. "Be ready, and wait for her to be finished." And then Attis is gone, striding over the village square toward the store, little puffs of dust kicking up from beneath the soles of her armored boots.

I watch her walk to the store, my mind crowded with a million thoughts, my heart aching with a million feelings as I take in the contours of her body, still visible (with a good dose of imagination and memory) beneath her cape and armor. I feel my cheeks begin to darken, and I sigh, turning to stare off into the distance purposefully, shifting my grumbling cat under my coat as my eyes unfocus, as I take a few, deep breaths.

I gaze into the forest on the other side of the smithy's open shop.

I'm trying to distract myself from sad thoughts of Ellie, and I'm trying not to think about Attis, either, so whenever Ellie or Attis rise up in my mind, I concentrate on a plan to get the radio station back on air. It's an imperfect system: I'm looping on images of my sister's smile, and then I drag the thought of my office at the radio station into my brain. But, of course, brains are tricky things, and *that* thought is followed immediately by the memory of Attis last night—catching me, catching me out of midair, my knight in shining armor.

Literally.

Then I immediately squash *those* thoughts by thinking of the board meeting I missed, trying to formulate strategies for an excuse and a passionate speech I might never be able to give...

After several long moments of hammer striking horseshoe and anvil, I see the silver flash in the woods.

If I wasn't staring at that particular spot between the trees, I never would have noticed it, but it was there—I *saw* it. A bright silver flash shimmered between those two tree trunks, the kind of silver flash that would happen if someone had turned a mirror into the sunshine overhead, beaming the light in my direction.

But, in all likelihood, there's no one out in the woods with a mirror.

My stomach turns inside of me as I lean forward, as I narrow my eyes and try to make out what could possibly be causing that silver flash. I know what it is, know what it is even before I see her bulk moving deeper into the woods, her shadow passing over the trees.

It's the silver bear.

There is absolutely no reason in this universe (or any other) that I have this immediate compulsion to follow the bear. Especially now that I know she may be dangerous.

But this idea, this ridiculously strong idea wells up inside of me that I need to see her. It's so powerful, this feeling, that I've dropped Zilla's reins on the ground before I even realize what I'm doing, my hands falling to my sides as I take a single step forward.

"Hey...uh...can you watch her?" I ask the big smithy, who's hard at work pounding a horseshoe into submission on his anvil. The guy stops his relentless pounding, lifting the hammer as he squints at Zilla and then back at me with a shrug.

"Sure," he rumbles, then goes right back to swinging the hammer over and over again on the red horseshoe against the anvil.

I loop Zilla's reins around the wooden post in front of the smithy's building, and then I'm trotting through the meadow behind the building and moving into the woods again, between the two pine trees that, the minute I step onto the forest floor, swallow the sound of the smithy immediately.

All is quiet.

As I move between the trees, I don't even think about the fact that it might be difficult to find my way back to the village. That I might get lost with a few more steps. It's impossible to orient myself beneath these massive, close trees, but I don't think about that fact at all. I simply head quickly into the woods, practically running as I duck my head under branches and take quick gulps of cold air in my pursuit...

And I find her, the bear, almost immediately.

Because the silver bear is waiting for me.

That's the only way I can make sense of it. I'm hurrying through the thick underbrush beneath the trees, and then, just as quickly, I have to career to a halt. Wonder makes a little dissatisfied sound from her snuggled cave under my coat.

The bear is standing in a natural break in the forest, a clearing that was made from one of the massive pine trees falling. Sunshine streams down from the gaping hole in the crown of trees overhead, filling this tiny glade with light. Even though it's so cold that I can see my breath in front of me, when I stare at the silver bear, I feel warmth emanating off of her, it seems.

The bear is just as big as I remember her, standing with her great silver bulk in the very center of this glade. Her coat is just as shiny as it was the first time I saw her, seeming to glow from within, as if every strand of her fur is luminescent, pulsing with that bright silver glow. She still strikes me as a sort of wise, kind creature, like an herbivore, as she stands there, head pointed toward me as she blinks sleepily, nose wrinkling as she sniffs the air.

I clear my throat. I take a deep breath.

And then I think, "What the hell?" and I whisper, "Um...are you following me? What do you want from me?"

I don't know why I expected the bear to answer, but I realize that I *did* expect a reply.

Good God, this world is doing things to me. I can't believe I thought a *bear* could actually speak to me...

But that's not what the bear does.

The bear doesn't speak, because—of course— she's a bear. But she does take a single, lumbering step forward, toward me, blinking long and slow with her great blue eyes.

And then she unrolls her tongue from inside

her mouth, a little like a giant cow, or, actually, a bit more like the giraffes at the zoo. Her tongue is *long*. I stare, eyes wide, as she unrolls her tongue all the way, comically, and then something falls right off the tip of her tongue, as if her tongue had been holding that in her mouth, carrying it around with her.

I glance down at the ground, at the thing the bear just dropped, but when I look back up at the bear, utterly perplexed...

Of course she's gone.

My blood is rushing through me, and my breath comes in short, small gasps. "What the *hell?*" I mutter angrily. "What the *hell?*" I yell to the woods, to the gigantic, disappeared silver bear.

To my entire situation.

For a long moment, I close my eyes, my hands curled into fists by my sides. I try to convince myself that what just came out of the bear's mouth—like he was dropping off a special delivery at my feet—isn't there. That I'll open my eyes, and there will be nothing on the forest floor...except for maybe a huge bear paw print, or maybe not even that.

But I know that this just happened. I know the bear stood in front of me, her silver bulk shimmering in the bright sunshine, and that she had unrolled her tongue like a cartoon dog.

I know that the bear had somehow, impossibly, been storing something in her mouth, and that she'd dropped it at my feet.

I know because, when I open my eyes...it's still there on the forest floor.

I crouch down on the ground, staring at the thing the bear left me, covered unceremoniously in bear spit.

I stare, and I stare, and I feel the world fall away from me as I continue to stare.

It's my sister's silver locket.

My sister's silver locket *that she was buried in.*

Chapter 9: The Locket

I have no idea what to do. I have no idea how to explain this so that it fits in with my conception of the world. Because it makes no sense at all. *This was the locket my sister was buried in.* It should be deep in the dark ground, far, far away from here. On another world. It should be something that I will never see again.

Just like my sister.

But the locket is here. Somehow. Impossibly.

It's in my hand.

I stare at the necklace for a long moment, tears swimming in front of my eyes as I rub my thumb over the surface of the locket, wiping away the bit of moss it just picked up from being on the ground. The locket is heart-shaped and ornate, as only something made in the eighties would be. It was my sister's favorite piece of jewelry; our parents gave it to her when we were small, and she loved it so much because it was "grown-up," and then when she was *actually* grown up and it was a little tacky (you know, having been made in the eighties and all), she still wore it constantly, still loved it, still never took it off. Even for the gym. Of course she had to be buried wearing it. It was as much a part of her as anything was.

My heart in my throat, I throw the catch of the locket and open it. I don't know what I'm looking for. Further proof, I guess, further proof that this thing is real, that it's really here, that it's really my sister's locket (even though I know it on sight). I'm desperate for something that makes sense. Maybe this isn't really hers. Maybe it's not, I think (even though I know it is). I'm just so confused.

And then I look inside the locket.

And I know for certain.

Because there's the picture of me as a kid with fantastic, eighties hair (a perm and everything, tightly coiled curls around my face like a halo of clouds), right across from a picture of my sister with equally fantastic eighties hair (massive, massive bangs).

This is her locket. It's Ellie's locket.

I look up, tears streaming down my face. But the bear still hasn't reappeared, and, for some reason, I don't think she's going to come back. At least not today.

What the hell *is* this bear? Where the hell did she get this locket?

And what the hell does she want from me?

There are no answers here, on the forest floor. So I rub the rest of the dirt from the locket onto my coat, and then I undo the tiny clasp and, with shaking fingers that make it very, very difficult, I put the locket around my neck.

And I stumble back to the blacksmith and the patiently waiting Zilla, standing there and chewing on her bit, one back hoof cocked in relaxation, like absolutely, positively, nothing has happened.

I'm shaking harder, I realize, as I unloop her reins from the wooden post.

I want to understand. I want to unravel this.

But I don't know how.

ॐ

That night, it's absolutely freezing. It's the kind of cold that makes me worry my nose might fall off from frostbite if I don't keep reaching up and pressing my palm to it.

The sky looks like it's threatening snow, massive clouds scuttling across the starry night sky. But it doesn't snow. The wind blows wickedly between the trees, and the temperature keeps dropping, but at least there's no snow.

Not until we stop and set up camp, of course.

The sky seems to break, and then softly, gently, thick white flakes begin to fall down from the sky and all around us. I stare at the flakes reproachfully, burying my chin in my coat and sighing as Attis unsaddles Zilla.

"I'm sorry, Josie—there's no village for a very long while. At least until tomorrow night. We are out in no man's land, as it were," she says with a shrug, heaving the heavy leather saddle off of Zilla's back. "But I have a tent," she tells me companionably, "and once it's set up, we'll be nice and warm together. Just have a little patience; it'll be done soon enough."

"I'm being patient," I tell her, my teeth chattering. I glance at Attis, who doesn't seem bothered by the cold at all, as she takes off Zilla's bridle, slipping it over the horse's dark head. I shift my weight and roll my aching shoulders back. Damn, my cat is heavy. "Hey, can I help you with anything? I feel lousy, just watching you work by yourself," I tell her, holding tightly to Wonder.

Attis glances at me in surprise, and she's silent for a long moment as she removes the blanket from Zilla's back, too. "It would be a great help, actually, if you could gather wood for a fire. Dry branches, please," she tells me, then digs out a small strip of cloth from one of her packs. With hard, lightning-fast strokes, she begins to scrub Zilla's black back, scraping away the sweat that had built up beneath the saddle blanket.

"Firewood. Sure," I tell her with a grimace. I don't want to bring up the fact that I've gone camping exactly one time in my entire life, and we *bought* firewood from this guy on the side of the road right before we entered the state park.

But, still, gathering firewood... How hard can it be?

Turns out: pretty damn hard.

Because the trees are so enormous, and most of their *branches* are so enormous, whenever a branch falls to the forest floor, it's far too big for a single person to pick up. I'm talking as-round-as-me big. These branches are so large that if anyone was standing beneath them when they fell, they'd very quickly become a pancake. I'd need a massive chainsaw and a lot of energy to tackle any one of these branches, but they're certainly not kindling or ready-made firewood material as is. Even the smaller branches, the "twigs," off of the big branches are as round as my thigh. I can't break any of them, even though I try with a vicious series of kicks to one that looks a tiny bit promising.

It doesn't budge an inch.

Frustrated, I venture further into the woods. It's twilight, but it's still light enough to see by at least a little, light enough to keep myself from walking into trees. Wonder's grumbling under my coat, but I ignore her, then try bouncing her like a baby to see if that quiets her. My arms are as heavy as lead after holding my chubby kitty all day, and Wonder certainly doesn't seem to appreciate the gesture (I'm worried my chest is in danger of puncture wounds), so I stop bouncing her, and then Wonder gives up her struggles for the moment, snuggling tightly against me again.

I'm walking along, trying to keep my eyes peeled for those poisonous thorns I "found" (or, you know, fell on) my first night here (I'm actually sniffing the air a little like a dog, trying to detect the sickly sweet smell that I now associate with them), when I see a large, wide shadow rising out of the gloom between the trees.

"Huh," I mutter, stopping short.

I stare up at the building.

Well, it's not so much a building as what *used* to be a building.

It's a ruin.

I walk a few steps closer, my curiosity getting the better of me. This is the biggest building I've seen so far on this world, a couple of stories taller than the tavern we stayed in last night. There's one tall tower attached to the building itself and rising far above the base structure, and two shorter ones tower on either side of the tall one. None of these towers (or, even, the building itself), has a roof to speak of—the roofs appear to have caved in. There's a wide stone wall erected around the whole building, and I'm pretty sure, actually, as I look at the dilapidated stone walls and shambled towers, that this used to be a castle of some type.

A small castle, reduced to ruins in the middle of the woods.

I stare at the sprawling building in the dark, my breath coming out like smoke in front of me.

There's a story here.

I venture a little closer toward the building when I stiffen, hearing a shuffle of dead leaves moving behind me. My heart in my throat, I turn instantly, really not ready for any more surprises today. I'm, therefore, utterly relieved when I see Attis making her way toward me across the forest floor, walking with assured purpose as she strides toward me.

"I was worried," she says gruffly when she reaches me, not looking me in the eye as she glances past me, a small frown making her full lips curve downward. "Have you found any firewood?" she asks, raising her eyebrows as she glances at the castle and then back to me again, as if massive castle ruins in the woods are no big deal at all.

"What's that?" I ask her, perplexed, as I gesture back toward the castle.

"A castle," she tells me maddeningly, her one brow raising higher. "Now, the firewood, Josie, we really need—"

"I can't find any," I tell her quickly, which—I realize—sounds terrible (I had *one job!*), but Lord knows I did my best to find some, and there's just nothing small enough to burn here in this part of the woods. As I shift Wonder back to my other arm, I have a brief, fleeting moment of panic as I wonder if—because there wasn't any firewood to be found— that we might actually stand a chance of dying from the cold tonight.

This is not a nice, accommodating world full of heaters and thermostats, as much as I wish it was. This is the kind of world where you spend a freezing night in the snow in the woods, and it might be your very last night because of that.

Attis glances around at all of the massive branches that have fallen, over time, and I can see a grimace pass over her face as she realizes that there aren't any twigs or, really, anything that might qualify in a broader sense as kindling.

She sighs for a long moment, then stands a little straighter. "Well, then," she tells me with a small shrug. Attis crosses her arms, plants her feet firmly in the ground and stares ahead at the castle with narrowed eyes. "Perhaps what we're looking for is there."

I turn to look back at the castle, but Attis wastes no time. She lifts her chin and moves past me into the dark, toward the ruins.

"They would, of course, have had wood stocked here once, before the place was abandoned," says Attis over her shoulder, as I trot to catch up with her long-legged stride. "And we might still be in luck. This place, believe it or not, was abandoned only twelve moons ago."

"Really?" I mutter disbelievingly as I follow her into the dark. It looks like it was abandoned a few *hundred* years ago.

"This forest," says Attis, gesturing around us with her armored hand, "has a habit of reclaiming what it wants. This castle used to be an outpost of Arktos City, actually. It's not *really* a castle; it's a small recreation of a castle," she tells me, as she points up to the empty towers overhead, the towers that no longer have roofs because the trees are starting to crowd them out, curving branches around the dilapidated rock like each tree is trying to squeeze life out of the building.

"What was it for?" I ask her, shivering a little.

"This place was built for our Queen Calla when she was very small, as a gift from her mother, Queen Calliope. Her mother loved Calla very much," says Attis with a small smile. "She wanted Calla to have her own kingdom to rule in play, and the child loved the idea of a castle in the woods. So it was built for her. Calla called it Castle Star." Attis points up to the tallest tower. There, in the stonework, I can make out stones placed into the wall of the tower, stones that, even in the dark, seem to glow gently with a soft, blue light. They're placed in the shape of a rough, five-pointed star.

"So why was Castle Star abandoned?" I ask Attis, as I follow her under the large-mouthed front gate of the castle itself. The iron gate that used to hang here in the entry is hanging off to one side, dragged backward on its hinges by vines and thorn bushes, lying useless and rusty on the ground.

"Queen Calla's lover brought her here about a year ago," says Attis, brows up. "And her lover broke her heart here. She told Calla that she was in love with another woman." Attis bites her lip and shakes her head. "So Calla left this place, and she hasn't been back since. And she asked her outpost of guards to leave this place, too. I honestly thought she'd change her mind, send her guards back here, because she used to love it so much. And, besides, it's a good outpost for the northern border of Arktos. But she never came back. And if you don't keep up with the woods, the woods move in," she says, nodding to the wall to our right that's completely covered in ivy. "I loved this place once," Attis tells me, her voice wistful. "But I think it will remain as it is until Queen Calla's future daughter takes over. If she even has a daughter." She shrugs. "I don't think Queen Calla herself will ever come back here again. A heart, once broken, is difficult to heal," she mutters, her jaw suddenly tense.

I glance at Attis in the encroaching dark, Attis who crouches down smoothly on the floor of this main room, running her gloved hand over a mound of matted leaves, pulling them back to peer underneath as she looks for firewood. Her gaze seems far away, and her shoulders are raised, tense.

I want to ask Attis about her lover Hera, but now's the most imperfect time I could come up with to do so. So I don't ask her. I try to calm my struggling, unhappy cat in my coat, and I cast about in this weird, open expanse of a stone room with its shattered, open maws of windows that let in quite a bit of the dying light. I look for a pile of firewood. I wonder what we'll do if there's nothing here to burn.

It's so cold I can't feel most of my feet.

"Here," says Attis then, rising and striding to another pile of ivy. She moves a few strands of the lush, woody green aside, and this reveals a great mound of old firewood logs, neatly cut and stacked in a row. "Good thing, that," says Attis mildly, taking up a large armful of wood and rising. "It might have been fairly cold tonight without this," she says, and I can hear the slight smile in her voice. And when she glances back at me over her shoulder, she actually winks at me. "Now, can you carry some back?" she asks.

I set Wonder on the ground, admonishing her quietly to stick around. I honestly don't know if she'll listen, but if she came for me across worlds, I kind of like to think that she's going to hang around. And she does. My spoiled cat is grumbly for a full minute, licking the fur on her back furiously, like she's super pissed at me, but then she gets up, meows at me loudly for some type of food (I'm assuming—it's her "feed me now or else" meow), and then she sticks close to my feet as I hold my arms out to Attis for the firewood.

"So, I mean, are all the knights like you?" I ask, and when she gazes at me with a raised brow, I realize I didn't really phrase that correctly. "I mean, are all the knights les...women who love women?" I say quickly. "I mean, your queen is, right? Is that, uh...common around here?"

Attis gazes at me with raised brows, like she doesn't even understand the question. "This is

Arktos," she says then, as if that explains everything. She stands smoothly with a very large armload of firewood in front of her. "We only have women knights," she tells me, "though the kingdom does hire male mercenaries for certain campaigns if there aren't enough knights available. But there are usually enough knights. And, yes," she says, her mouth turning up at the corners, "the knights do love their women."

"Is that, like, a thing here? In Arktos?" I press, feeling my jaw begin to drop as she nods. I firmly hold my mouth closed.

"It's our way," she says, with a small shrug. "There are other countries where this is not as common, of course, but in Arktos..." Attis gives me a small smile as she glances my way. "So, what is it like on your world?" she asks me, as we begin to walk back toward the encampment that Attis had started to set up. At least, I *hope* we're headed back to the encampment. The woods are *very* dark now, and though Attis is walking quickly in a specific direction, if it were up to me, I wouldn't have the first idea where Zilla and the packs are.

"It's not like that on my world," I mutter, glancing backward to make certain that Wonder is sticking close to me. Miraculously, she is, bounding after us over the brush and debris on the forest floor, a little like a puppy might. She's such a weird, wonderful cat. "I mean," I clear my throat, "there are lots of women who love women. And men who love men. And people who like both. And lots of other stuff like that," I tell her quickly. "But we...we don't have our own *country*. Though we *do* have

Provincetown and San Francisco," I mutter, but she doesn't seem to hear me, and I don't know if I'd be able to succinctly explain those cities. "So, what's it like?" I ask her, fascinated. She turns to me, surprised, her head to the side. "What's it like to live in a country full of people like you?" I ask her, practically breathless.

It's a *lesbian kingdom*.

This new development kind of takes the cake. What lesbian *wouldn't* love the idea of a lesbian kingdom? I can't stop wondering how awesome it must be...

"I don't really know how to answer that," she tells me, taking a wide step over a fallen branch. "Be careful there," she tells me, and though she's carrying an enormous load of logs, she's able to steady them all in one hand and reach out quickly in the dark, steadying *me* by curling her fingers around my elbow as I stumble over the branch.

"Thanks," I tell her, feeling my cheeks redden in the twilight, thankful for that darkness just now so she can't see.

Attis is silent for a long moment. "Do you miss your world, Josie?" she asks me.

My breath quickens in the dark, and—ahead of us—I can just make out Zilla's shadowy bulk, can hear her snort out in contentment in the dark. I can see the packs and saddle on the ground around a small circle of cleared earth that Attis must have created while she was waiting for me to gather firewood.

As I stare at the beginnings of the camp, I let myself realize that Attis and I are going to share a tent tonight. I mean, obviously we shared a tavern room last night, our beds very close to one another. But, come on. We're going to be sharing a *tent*. That's a whole other ballgame.

There was tension between us last night... She caught me out of midair. I think she was going to kiss me. I'd wanted to kiss her.

So...why didn't I?

Because I'm going home.

Because I *do* miss my world.

I do...don't I?

God, what a stupid, stupid thought. I grit my teeth, immediately angry at myself. Of course I miss my world. Too much information, but come on, I'm not ashamed to admit that I miss an actual toilet. I miss heat and warm water and baths and coffee and those damn hot dogs that seem to be everywhere I look when I'm in Boston and now are an impossible world away.

I miss my job. I miss my friends. I miss...

I take a deep breath, let the firewood drop next to Attis' stack as she kneels down and begins to place dried moss and tiny twigs (that, impossibly, she was able to find) in the center of a circle of pure dirt that she scraped out on the forest floor.

I'm not an outdoorsy person. There's a lot I really despise about riding a horse every damn day, making tiny (if you compare it to driving a car) dents in this long journey we're going on to reach a city and a festival and the mere *possibility* that I'll be able to return to my world.

But here's the thing, the thing I haven't really wanted to think about, not yet... But it's there, glaring and obvious and something that I really *do* have to consider:

What if I *can't* make it back to my world?

What do I do then?

"I do miss home," I tell Attis quietly. I sit down on one of the larger logs and watch as she crouches in front of the tiny tepee of sticks and moss she's created on the circle of earth. I stare as she takes two stones out of a pocket I didn't realize she had in her armor, watch her strike those two stones together, watch the sparks emanating from the stones. The sparks fall on the kindling, twigs and moss, and then there's a tiny pinprick of light in the dark.

And the fire catches.

I watch Attis bending toward the fire, watch her lips purse as she blows gently on the tiny flame. I watch her red hair shining in the light of that flame as she tucks it behind her ear with an armored glove, setting more twigs on top of the slight fire. Her eyes are narrowed in concentration, and I watch her smooth, assured movements as I feel my heart beating a little faster.

"And then sometimes," I say quietly, so quietly there's a chance that Attis might not hear it, "I don't miss it at all."

Her gaze flicks up to me, and in the firelight, her warm, amber eyes seem to glow golden. "Surely this life is quite rough in comparison to the one you led before," she says, averting her gaze as she sets a log on top of the small fire. The fire licks along the wood almost immediately, and in the space of a heartbeat or two, it gives a little roar, and Attis places another log on the hungry, growing flame, feeding it.

"Yeah. But it's not so bad," I tell her,

reaching down and running my fingers along Wonder's fluffy, warm back, holding her against my leg for a long moment until I make absolutely certain that she's not about to saunter into the fire (or, much more likely, saunter past it and have a spark drift up and onto her fur and set *her* on fire). But, of course, my cat is smarter than that. She leans against my leg, purring up a storm, but also glancing out into the woods as if she sees something she really, really has to investigate. Or, you know, kill.

"There are no big animals about," says Attis conversationally, glancing at Wonder. "If you let her go, I'm sure she'll come back to you."

"That's so irresponsible," I mutter, burying my fingers into her fur. "She's the world to me," I tell Attis, and my breath hitches as I feel Wonder purring against me. I glance down at my slowly blinking cat who's proceeding to kneed the forest floor as she purrs louder. "I mean, I can't believe she found me. Across worlds, she found me. If I can't go back home, she can't, either. At least I have her."

Attis glances at me in surprise. I take a deep breath, and then I let Wonder go, setting my hands on my thighs. Immediately that cat saunters out into the forest, her belly close to the ground as she slinks into the darkness, disappearing from sight. I feel my heart rise in my chest with worry, but I've got to believe that she knows what's she's doing. She came to find me across worlds. I'm sure she can hunt some tiny, defenseless prey and remain safe.

That poor tiny, defenseless prey... I grimace, and I'm about to call after her to not murder small animals when Attis reaches across the space between us.

Reaches across the space...and takes my hand in her own.

Her armor is cold against my skin, but it contrasts with the warm leather beneath the plates of metal, the leather that's warmed from her body. Attis holds my gaze with eyes so warm and golden, like honey, that it melts something inside of me.

"I'm sorry you're stuck with me, Josie," she says, her mouth turning up a little at the corners as she smiles softly.

My heart pounding inside of me, I wet my lips. I take a shallow breath.

"I'm not," I tell her.

For half a heartbeat, Attis looks surprised. But, then, something passes over her eyes, and her gaze darkens visibly in the firelight. Her mouth opens, just a little, as her breathing quickens. God, I can't help but stare at that perfect mouth, at the creamy, curving line of her chin and neck, disappearing beneath the silk curtain of her burnished hair. I want to touch her hair, want to run my fingers through it, want to feel how soft it is, how it streams through my fingers like liquid fire.

I want to taste her.

I want to kiss her.

There are a million reasons I shouldn't do this. Yeah, there's certainly a chance (a *big* chance) that I'm not going to be able to make it home. But there's also a chance that I will. And I don't want a one-night stand. I want her. And if I leave this world, I can't have her.

A ghost stands between us, her lover, long

dead, the woman Attis has never stopped mourning. And I understand; God, I understand. I can never stop mourning my sister. I know what it's like, to have that ghost with you, every day, the press of memories that you'll never be able to make, moments you'll never have. I shouldn't kiss Attis, because Hera is not forgotten.

But *I don't want to let this moment pass*. I don't want to let the possibility disappear from me forever. And I feel that it will, if I don't do this, if I don't find that one, last little scrap of courage to lean forward, to press my mouth against hers, and—in that single moment—drink in all that is Attis.

Even though I shouldn't.

I want to. I want to desperately. I ache to kiss her.

So I take a deep breath.

And I dare.

Attis is kneeling on the ground, and I'm sitting on the log next to her, so it's very, very easy to simply lean forward, to lift up my hand tentatively, softly. I let my fingers brush through the bright strands of her hair, the dark, red, flashing mane of it, letting my fingers drift over its softness until my palm is against the curve of her jaw, my cold fingers tracing the sweet warmth of her skin.

My heartbeat is racing through me as her eyes darken further. As her mouth parts again while I lean forward. I cup her cheek and let my fingers slide down to the back of her neck.

As my mouth meets hers.

She's as soft and warm as I imagined. She tastes of mint. Her mouth is hot and yielding against mine as I reach forward and kiss her, and she's yielding for a long moment until she's no longer soft against me.

Because her hands are at my waist then, and my legs are parted, and she's kneeling there, between my legs, her front pressed against my front, her arms wrapped around me so tightly, possessively, assuredly, that I let a little moan escape me because there was such a surge of euphoria and pleasure that roared through me at that moment, I couldn't remain silent. She's kissing me wholeheartedly, her mouth hard against me one moment, soft the next as she tastes me.

My head is spinning, and every inch of my body is alive, alive and sparking, just like the fire dancing behind us as she moves her hands down, curling her fingers around my hips and gripping me tightly to her. She's pressing her hips between my legs, her armor against my coat and my leopard-print bottoms, and there's really not that much between us, I realize, as my center comes alive, tingling, spreading warm desire and need through every inch of me.

But as Attis kisses me, as I lean forward to follow her movements, as I grip her metal chest piece to hold her tighter against me, the top of my coat shifts open.

And the locket falls out of that coat opening, dangling and flashing in the firelight as it hangs around my neck, out in the open.

And Attis pauses almost instantly. She pulls back, sitting on her heels as she breathes hard, staring at the locket with darkened eyes that suddenly narrow.

"What...what is that?" she asks me, her voice gruff and low as she reaches out between us and takes the locket in her hand, turning it. My heart, pounding through me unstoppably, begins to feel a little heavy.

I don't want to tell her, for some reason. Well. No. I know the reason.

This bear killed her lover. Didn't it? And now it's following us.

I didn't want to worry her. But I can't keep this from her.

"Um..." I undo the clasp at the back of my neck with slightly shaking fingers (God, now that it's started, I never wanted it to stop), and then the locket falls into her outstretched palm. "I got it from... I don't know how to tell you this," I mutter, dragging my fingers through my hair in frustration. "The silver bear was in the woods today. When you went to the store, and while I was waiting for the blacksmith. So I...uh. I followed her."

Attis' face hardens in a single instant. It had been so warm, so open, so wanting, and in a single heartbeat, that all fades into obscurity. Her jaw is clenched, her eyes are flashing dangerously, and her wet lips, a few heartbeats ago soft and drinking me in, are now a thin, hard line.

Yeah, the kissing is definitely over.

"Why didn't you tell me this *immediately*?" she growls, standing and striding around to the other side of the fire. I'm instantly cold from her absence, and I wrap my arms around myself, bristling at her tone. "Where, *exactly,* did you get this locket, Josie?" she says, rounding on me, her tone cold and flat.

"The bear gave it to me," I say, standing, too. I curl my shoulders back, an edge to my voice. "It was my sister's. That locket was buried with her when she died, and I don't know how the bear got it, but she did. Somehow. And she gave it to me."

Attis stares at me, her face going through a very quick range of emotions until she settles on fierceness. And fury. "Why didn't you tell me this *immediately*?" she growls again.

"I didn't want to worry you," I interject quickly, but it sounds flat, even to my own ears. "What the hell is this bear, anyway? How the hell did it get a locket that was buried with my dead sister on another *world?*" Emotion roars through me, and I hate that a single, hot tear creeps down my cheek. My hands are shaking in anger as I curl them into fists. "How is this even happening?" I ask her.

Attis stares at me for a long moment before she softens, her shoulders sloping down as she takes a few steps forward. I didn't expect this, but she's wrapping her arms around me tightly.

It scares me how right this feels, as I press my cheek against the cold metal of her shoulder.

I don't want it to feel this right. But it does.

And I can't deny that feeling.

"I don't know, Josie. I only know that bear is evil," she mutters, pressing her chin to the top of my head.

"But I don't... I'm not sure," I tell her, forcing myself to take a step back from her, forcing myself to hold her gaze as the butterflies rush through my stomach. I'm more nervous about this than any crank caller or show gone wrong.

"What if..." I lick my lips, take a deep breath. "What if she's *not* evil? She doesn't seem evil to me. She could have killed me both times she saw me, but she didn't. And now...now she's bringing this locket to me."

"Josie, you must trust me when I say that I know her very, very well," Attis tells me, her eyes narrowing and her mouth returning to its thin, hard line. "And she is pure evil, the kind of evil that can kill without any ramification or consequence. She kills, of course," she continues, bitterly, "without any sort of consequence, because she is a savage animal, and that is what savage animals do best."

Out in the darkness of the forest, a feeble animal scream cuts the night like a knife, trailing off thinly until it is silenced. Wonder. Wonder found her prey.

I shiver, holding the coat tighter around myself, tight against the coldness of the night. And the coldness of Attis.

"Why would she give me this locket? Why would a bear follow us through the woods and happen to have this locket? How is that even *possible?* Nothing *evil* would give me my sister's locket—"

"Do not speak about something you know *nothing* of," Attis snaps, and—almost immediately—I can tell she regrets her words; her mouth closes, her eyes narrow, and she rakes a gloved hand through her hair, turning from me with a long sigh. But the words are already out between us, crackling in the cold, night air, sharp and deadly.

"How could *you* know anything about this bear?" I ask her angrily.

"Because it's the same bear," she snarls at me.

"What are you talking about? The same bear?" I ask, my heart thudding inside of me.

I know the story. But she doesn't know that I know.

Silence descends between us for a long moment. Attis picks up another log and sets it on the fire, where the flames begin to devour it eagerly. She folds her arms in front of her, rocking back on her heels as she shakes her head, steeling her jaw.

"This is the same bear who killed Hera, my lover," says Attis then, heavily.

All of the fight goes out of me, and I suddenly feel the vast emptiness of the night, pressing down on us. The fire is so small in a forest so vast and dark and unknowable. I wrap my arms even tighter around myself, feeling her lover's name invoked between us.

The darkness seems more absolute, somehow, as we turn away from each other.

"I must set up the tent," Attis tells me formally. I nod, sit down on the log again, pressing my hand to my heart as I curve forward, pain flooding through me.

I shouldn't have kissed her. And I should have told her about the bear. But there are so many shoulds and should-nots that I simply can't think about all of them and remain sane.

I glance up at the trees that rise so far away from me, so tall they seem to brush their majestic heads against the sky.

Beneath them, I feel very small.

Even though Attis is just across the clearing, quickly and efficiently rigging up the tent, even though the fire roars in front of me, small, but savagely bright...

I sit in the dark, alone.

Chapter 10: The Decision

We eat a meager dinner of dried meat and fruit and split a biscuit I pocketed from Ilya's table that morning. We eat in silence, the crackling of the fire the only break in the smothering quiet.

Together, we crawl into the tent; together we lie down, as far apart as possible in the relative smallness of the tent allows. I can't tell what she's thinking. I wish I could.

I close my eyes and fall asleep, heart aching.

❧

I'm standing in my office at the radio station. Somehow, there's the odd sensation flooding my body that I shouldn't be here, that being here is impossible, but I shove the feeling away. Why shouldn't I be in my office? It's a weekday morning. I know that as clearly as I know I should be working...but I can't.

Because it's pitch dark here. I'm only able to make out the outline of my desk because there's a small amount of light thrown in from the hallway. It's dark in my office just as it was the day the lights were turned off, the power shut down, the grant pulled.

Wait, the grant was pulled... There technically isn't a radio station anymore, right? I take a few deep breaths, curling and uncurling my fingers slowly.

Something's not right. But I can't quite put my finger on what, exactly, it is that feels so off...

I shouldn't be here, I realize. But I am.

Why am I here?

There is absolute silence, the heavy press of silence that's so muffling and velvet that I know I could hear a pin drop across the building. But no pin drops. Nothing changes. There is darkness and my empty office, my consoles devoid of light, darkened, dead. These machines will never be turned on again.

My breath catches as I reach out and brush my fingertips against my coffee mug on the edge of the desk. "Josie in the Morning!" the mug reads in a plain, boring font the color of the ocean. "LEM 100.5, Public Access Radio" is scrolled underneath my show's name, most of it worn away from repeated washings. I've used this cup as my coffee mug here, at the station, since I started my show.

I pick up the mug in my hand now, curling my fingers around the well-worn handle, turning it slowly in my hand as I stare down at it, perplexed.

Everything feels kind of heavy, like I'm moving through water. My head feels heavy, too, like I've had too much to drink the night before, but...I'm fairly certain I didn't drink last night.

I can't remember anything, don't feel anything other than that nagging thought that things aren't right.

I let my fingers uncurl, let the mug fall to the floor.

It bounces on the carpeting, bounces slowly, each leap prolonged and extended, like the mug is made of rubber. It rolls to a rest next to my desk, and then—as I watch it—the mug fades out and completely disappears.

I lift my gaze, moving so slowly, moving like I'm covered in mud now, like a mudslide has buried me completely. I turn, can hear my breathing in the absolute silence. Turn, my heart beating faster as I look toward the open doorway of my office.

The bear is there.

She's standing in the hallway, the darkened hallway, but it's not dark, because she's there, her fur glowing like a star. She casts light down the dark corridor as she stands peacefully, each paw firmly planted on the drab hallway carpeting, her silver bulk practically touching each wall, even though the hallway is five feet wide, her back brushing against the ceiling. Her nose is lifted toward me as she wrinkles it, sniffing the air.

I stay perfectly still as I watch the bear, as I listen to her sniff the air, listen to my own breathing, my own heartbeat.

The bear stares at me calmly, her bright blue eyes blinking once.

And then she's gone, too, fading away in an instant. She has completely disappeared.

I move out into the corridor, begin walking down the long hall that stretches in front of me like a strange backdrop to a treadmill. I'm not moving very fast or getting very far. The hallway's not *that* long, but I seem to be stuck in the same place, walking, walking, walking, the same drab carpeting stretching out in front of me, the same stupid, generic artwork on the walls depicting pastoral scenes of barns and buildings and cities and people. Over and over the paintings repeat until, finally, I stop.

I put my hand on the door to the right, the door that always led to the janitor's broom closet (I really did have choice office real estate in our building). The door shouldn't be here; I've walked far enough to be a few blocks away, but when I turn, I take in the fact that I'm still outside of my office. So I turn the doorknob to the closet in my hand, put my shoulder to the door because it always stuck, and I push the door open, pushing so hard that my breathing quickens. I strain, planting my feet into the carpeting, *pushing*.

The door finally opens, swinging wide, and instead of an unkempt pile of brooms, mops, vacuums and cleaning products inside that small broom closet, it's the streets of Boston that I see beyond the door.

I know this place, too, this street: it's that nice little section a few blocks from my apartment, full of coffee shops and bookstores and one little pet store.

But as I step through the door, as the door shuts smoothly behind me, I realize there's something wrong.

There's no one out on these streets.

They're empty.

I walk down the city street, down the very center of that street, peering into the cars that sit in the middle of their lanes, completely empty. I walk down the pavement, my heels clicking against the ground the only sound in this silent city; I feel my heart rise in my throat.

"Hello?" I call out, my voice shaking and soft. I clear my throat, try again: "Is there anyone here?" I shout.

But no one answers me. The words I uttered echo down the street and then come back to me, echoing plaintively around me, over and over and over again. *Hello? Is there anyone here?* The words echo louder and louder, until it sounds like they're mocking me.

I begin to run, my hands over my ears to shut out the words I shouted, my heartbeat roaring through me. I look in every car, peer into every store, calling out for someone, anyone.

But there's no one here.

Finally, I stop in front of a department store. The department store window's display is full of mannequins and mirrors, fake, plastic women wearing short dresses and big shades, jutting their pointy elbows toward me as they gather around the one tall mirror, like they're clamoring to look at themselves. I bury my fingers in my hair in frustration, and I crumple to my knees, curving my shoulders forward. Where is everyone?

God, I feel so alone.

"What's the matter?"

I look up, heart in my throat, and I stare at my reflection in the mirror in the department store window. But...I'm not properly reflected in that mirror, it seems.

I'm afraid right now, fear scorching through my veins like fire. But the Josie in that mirror doesn't look afraid at all. She's sneering angrily, snidely. Bitterness exudes from her narrowed eyes, from her frowning mouth.

"What's the matter?" she repeats, lifting her chin and smiling. The smile doesn't reach her eyes. "Why aren't you ridiculously happy? I mean, isn't this exactly what you wanted?"

I lick my dry lips, stare wide-eyed at my reflection. "What are you *talking* about?" I ask her, taking a deep breath as the sob wells up within me; I swallow it down and draw in another deep breath.

"Why aren't you happy?" she repeats snidely. "This is what you've always wanted," she tells me, gesturing to indicate the empty streets and buildings, to indicate a world completely devoid of people. She folds her arms in front of her, lifts her chin defiantly. "You wanted to be alone, so now you've got your wish. Now no one will bother you ever again. Why doesn't that make you happy?" she asks me, shaking her head with an exaggerated frown.

"*What*?" I gasp, pressing my fingers to the store window as the Josie in the mirror sits back on her heels, grinning smugly at me. "You're crazy. This *isn't* what I wanted—" I begin to argue, but the other-me crows, throwing back her head and laughing so loudly and harshly that I flinch.

"You're kidding me," she snarls. "After what you did to your sister? Like you deserve anything better. That's what you've done all this time, isn't it? Pushed everyone away?"

My heart's in my throat, and I find I can't swallow the lump there. I take a deep breath, feel hot tears pouring down my cheeks. "I..." I don't know what else to say.

"Sarcastic Josie. Josie with the awesome radio show, Josie who's got it all together never needs to let anyone in. She's got it all figured out, all by herself," my reflection tells me, her head to the side as she gives me another grotesque frown. "But that wasn't the real reason you didn't let anyone close to you, why you don't have friends? *You know why.* You don't deserve it."

Every word is razor sharp as she snarls at me.

"That's not...that's not true," I tell her weakly, but my tone sounds like I'm lying.

"So, now look," she says, holding out her arms and raising her eyes to the empty buildings surrounding us. "Now you have your perfect, empty world. There's no one to bother you, no one to get close to you. No one to touch you or connect with you. No one at all but you and me. An eternity of being alone. Exactly what you wanted."

I stand up, press my hands to my ears. "I don't want this," I whimper, but my reflection is laughing too hard for me to be heard.

I take a step back from the reflection, and another, and another. I'm standing in the middle of the street, my heart breaking inside of me, because I know she's right. I know I don't deserve anything. I know it's my fault that my sister died; I know I don't deserve anything better than...

Eyes squeezed tightly shut, for a brief, tiny flicker...I think about my sister.

I think about Ellie's smiling face. I think about her laughter. I think about Ellie so hard, that—for a moment—I thought I heard...

"Josie?"

My arms fall to my sides, as—tears pouring down my cheeks—I look up.

And Ellie's there. She's *here.*

She's standing in the center of the street in her favorite cat pajamas. She looks perplexed as she glances around the street at the empty cars and buildings—but then she sees me.

And the way her expression changes, the way she smiles...it lights up the dark world.

"Josie," she says softly, and she holds out her arms. "Josie," she says again, the word soft and sweet as she shakes her head. "Stop this," she tells me. "Stop this right now."

"No," I tell her, the ache unfurling deeper in my heart. "I'm right. I don't deserve anything. I don't deserve happiness. I don't deserve being close to anyone because I'll hurt them, just like I hurt you. I need to be alone. It's what I've always wanted," I tell her, curling my arms around myself and turning to leave. Turning to walk back down the empty streets toward my empty apartment in my empty building in my empty city.

Everything's exactly the way I wanted it to be. My reflection was right. This *is* all I've ever wanted.

"Josie," my sister whispers.

I stop.

Somewhere, far down the street, I see something silver moving, something big, something glowing softly with silver light...

I turn.

Ellie's there, her arms out to me, her jaw set in determination. "No one's to blame for the night I died. Not you. Not me. Not anyone. It was a *mistake*. Do you understand me?" she asks, every word firm and immovable.

"That's a lie," I tell her quietly. "We both know that if I'd never—"

"I'm the one who took my underage sister drinking," says Ellie succinctly, one brow up. "Ted's the guy who gave us the drinks, knowing you were underage. Aaron's the guy who let us leave the party, knowing you were smashed. I let you get behind the wheel of the car, knowing I shouldn't. You've got to stop blaming—"

"No one else was behind that wheel of the car, Ellie. No one but me," I tell her, a sob rising in my throat. "You're *dead* because of *me*."

Ellie crosses the space between us. She curls her fingers around my shoulders, and then, gently, she shakes me three times. "Josie," she tells me, her eyes fiercely burning as she holds my gaze. "You're my little sister, and I love you. I've never stopped loving you. And love is all that's important. Do you understand me?"

I watch her carefully, taking deep breaths, feeling my world fall away from me.

"You don't have to be alone anymore," says Ellie, shaking me gently again. "But *you* have to decide that you don't deserve to be alone. I can't make you believe that. No one can. No one...but you." She takes a step back, holds out her arms, holding them out to the empty street and city. "You can change this, Josie," she whispers.

And then, Ellie disappears.

I glance sidelong at my reflection in the

window. My reflection has her arms crossed, her head to the side. She's watching me with predatory eyes, a cold, calculating gaze that makes me shiver.

"You *know* what you deserve," my reflection tells me in a low growl.

I take another deep breath, my hands curling into fists at my sides.

And then, in that instant, something shifts inside of me. And then I turn around. I walk back the way I came. I put one foot in front of the other, walking down the empty, echoing street.

I close my eyes, lift my chin.

"Hello?" I call, my voice shaking. "Is anyone there?"

"There's no one there!" my reflection shrieks after me. "You're alone because that's what you deserve!"

"Hello?" I call again, my voice louder, stronger. I break out into a trot, my heart pumping behind my ribs as I take deep gulps of warm air. "Is anyone there?"

My boots click against the pavement as I race along the street. Race like I'm flying, the buildings blurring around me as I run.

"Hello?" I call again. I careen to a stop, breathing hard, looking up at the empty buildings, stretching away from me.

There's pure silence, pure, heavy silence, and nothing besides.

"I don't want this!" I shout at the buildings, at the cars, at the city. At a silent Boston. "I don't want to be alone anymore," I yell, closing my eyes tightly and tensing my body.

And then I hold my breath.

And I listen.

Far, far ahead of me down the street moves a shadow, a shadow attached to a glowing, silver hulk of an animal...an animal that trundles slowly through the city. A silver bear.

"Josie?" comes a voice, a voice I recognize.

I glance over my shoulder, my heart in my throat.

And there, standing on the empty streets of Boston, in full armor, her dark red hair blowing in a soft wind, her single brow artfully raised...

Is Attis.

ଔ

"Josie?"

I open my eyes, my breath rushing through me. I'm so cold. Why am I so cold?

Oh. Because I'm in a tent. At night. And it's freezing out.

That's the first thing I realize. But then I open my eyes a little more, and I realize that Attis is there, lying next to me. She's rolled over, actually...

And she's above me, leaning on her elbow on the ground, brows narrowed in concern as she stares down at me. Her warm hands are on my shoulders, and when I look her in the eyes, she sighs with relief.

"You were having a bad dream," she tells me softly.

Yes.

A very bad dream.

And it's over now.

"Attis," I tell her, rising up onto my elbows so that our faces are close. My blood roars through me, from the adrenaline of the dream, from the adrenaline of my decision. For the first time in forever, I'm calmly focused. The bitterness in my heart fades away like smoke. "Attis, I'm sorry—I should have told you about the bear. I should have—" I begin, but then tears are falling down my cheeks, and as she gazes down at me, her face softening, I no longer care about shoulds or should-nots or obligations or responsibilities or different worlds.

All I care about is the fact that, out of all the places in the universe I could have landed, when I fell through an impossible portal...

I landed *here*. On top of *her*. Out of all the people and beings in this whole big universe, she was there. She was there to catch me. And over and over again, since we've met, she's caught me.

Attis has been there. Attis with her warm smile that's hard earned, but—when it happens—it's brighter than a heaven full of stars.

I stare up at her, up into her warm, amber eyes, eyes that are so hard to see in the dark, but eyes that I've memorized. I can make out that she has one brow raised, that she stares down at me, her face softening by degrees.

Her mouth turns up at the corners then, just a little...just a tiny, tiny bit that—if I wasn't looking for that hint of a smile—I never would have seen it.

And I know I have to do this. And that I have to do this now.

So I tilt my head back, and I capture her mouth with a kiss.

For a long moment, it's all sweetness and gentle surrender. Me, surrendering to my need for her, and her surrendering to my kiss, her warm mouth open and inviting as she lets me in. But Attis strikes me as the type of person who never surrenders to anything. She conquers everything, instead.

Just like she conquers me now.

Attis gently curls her arm under my neck and around my shoulders, pulling me tightly to her as her other hand drifts down my body, making me shiver in delight, until she cups her fingers around the curve of my hipbone and tugs me even closer to her. She devours me utterly, her mouth over mine, both of us merging together as she tastes me, as her tongue meets my tongue. Again, I moan against her, because I can't stop that gesture of need, of desire, that roars through me, as my center wakes up instantly, as every inch of my body begins to come alive.

Invisible sparks are dancing over my skin, and, God, I want this. I want her. I don't deserve to be alone. I know that now. I know it like I know that I was meant to come through that portal. That I was meant to meet Attis.

A long time ago, I used to believe in fate, in destiny. That was before Ellie died. After her death, I closed off everything inside of me but the bitterness at myself, my anger at myself. I stopped believing in everything, started to think that anyone who believed in anything was narrow-minded, foolish...kind of stupid.

But I find myself believing in something again. I believe I was meant to meet Attis, believe that fact utterly. Actually, I don't believe it.

I know.

I know I was meant to meet her.

Attis rises to her hands and knees, moving over me in a swift, fluid motion. She shifts over my leg, rising over me, between my legs, her face a tantalizing few inches from my own.

I watch as emotion clouds her eyes. As her jaw clenches. "Josie," she growls softly, gently, then, her eyes darkening with desire as she takes me in, the fact that I'm panting and desperate with want. "I want this," she whispers, dipping low and brushing her lips to the hot skin of my neck, making me arch beneath her. "But," she whispers against my ear, her mouth warm, "I want this to *mean* something."

"Oh, God, Attis," I tell her, wrapping my arms around her and drawing her down to me so that she lies on top of me. I hold her tightly, her cheek pressed against my cheek, her mouth against my mouth, and I draw in a deep breath that ends with a single tear falling from my right eye, trailing down the side of my face. "You don't know..." I take in another deep, aching breath and swallow a sob. "You don't know how *much* this means. Yes, this means something," I whisper to her. She shifts over me, rising up on her hands again as she stares into my eyes intensely. "You don't know," I whisper, reaching up and threading my hand through her hair, letting the silk of it drift over my fingers as I shiver, "how much *you* mean to me."

Attis shuts her eyes, her jaw tightening again as she stays still for a very long moment, still over me, against me, on me. I can see the war that's taking place, shadows of it sweeping over her face as she thinks long and hard for that excruciating heartbeat.

I wait. I hold my breath, my heart rising in me, ready to fall to pieces, ready to break as I wait...hoping...wishing with all my might...

Attis opens her eyes, gazing down at me with such a softening to her jaw, her brow. Her warm, golden eyes soften at the edges, too, and then her gaze darkens as she looks down at me again. "I want to remember this moment forever," she breathes, as she lowers her beautiful face to mine, as she drifts her warm mouth over the curve of my chin, down my neck, making me gasp beneath her as I wrap my fingers in her hair, as I press her against me. "I want to remember everything," she whispers, as her fingers find the hem of my shirt, as her warm fingers find the skin of my stomach beneath the fabric.

I gasp against her as she traces a teasing line up my stomach, around to my side, and then around my right breast. She presses her mouth against me, all warmth and heat and soft aggression as she tastes me, drinking me deep as her hand finds my breast, presses her palm against it, cupping it, teasing my nipple with a fingernail, and then rolling it between her thumb and finger.

It's been such a long time since I've been with anyone...but it's not that. As Attis arches over me, as she touches me, gently at first, and then as I respond with moans and hitches of breath, as she begins to learn the map of my body, I feel it. I feel it unfurling inside of me so clearly, it's almost a physical sensation as I stare up at this beautiful woman, touching me like I'm precious.

I'm falling in love with her.

Attis crouches on her elbow over me, dragging her fingernails down lightly over my stomach, into the waistband of my pants, gently dipping them down to smooth the skin there with such light fingertips that I shiver against her. She tugs my pants down, over my hips with determined movements, pulling me up to sitting as she pulls the shirt up and over my head.

I sit, completely naked in front of her, placing my weight back on my hands as I feel the blush rise. I'm so exposed, so utterly vulnerable as she sits back on her heels between my knees, staring down at me, her eyes seeming to spark with desire in the dark. The sheer exhilaration of feeling so exposed to someone so extraordinary is such a rare, foreign thing, that—for a moment—I want to reach forward and cover my breasts with my arms: it's too much, too raw, too vulnerable. But I take a deep breath; I gather every last bit of courage I possess as her eyes rake over my body, as I sit in front of her, my heart open to her.

Attis makes a growl of pleasure deep in her throat, arranging her legs fluidly into a cross-legged position as she grips my hips and draws me up, onto her lap, my legs hooking around her waist. She pulls me up and onto her.

She's wearing her leather breeches and poet's shirt, still fully clothed, as I straddle her lap, deliciously naked against her. I gasp as her mouth finds my right breast, as she takes my nipple into her mouth, flicking her tongue against it and pressing it against her teeth. I throw back my head as her fingers find my other breast, as it's cupped and teased, her arm folded around my waist and pressing me to her like she's never going to let go.

But then that hand drifts down, down, fingernails dancing over my skin as I arch against her, whimpering, my fingers gripping her shoulders so tightly, I'm surprised my nails aren't drawing blood. Her hand drifts, maddeningly light and caressing, down my middle, over my stomach, and then, then...

God, when her fingers move over the hot skin of my thigh, turning to smooth a thumb over my center, I jolt against her, the roar of pleasure so intense as it pours through me. She flicks her thumb again, over my clit, and I whimper against her, throwing back my head as she drifts a wet trail of kisses up from my breast to my neck, where she nips my skin to redness, her teeth leaving a trail of red, her tongue laving my skin as I press my hips against her hand, desperate for her to touch me more, more, desperate for her fingers to curl up inside of me.

And they do now. She chuckles in a low growl against my throat, and then her fingers are curling up inside of me, and with short, hard strokes, questing harder and further into me. They draw me closer to her, closer to her so that every inch of my skin is pressed against her, so that everything that I am is now merged with her. She seems to know every part of me, what I need and what I want, all mixing into one as she draws a hiss out of me, a cry of desperation. My legs are spread so wide and I am so open to her that, when she lightly bites my neck, then, her other arm wrapped tightly around me, holding me like she'll never let go, her thumb against my clit, and her fingers curving inside of me, it's all too much, too wonderful. Too perfect.

Release spreads through me like an exploding star, all splendor and waves of pleasure as she rocks her hips against mine, her fingers drawing out moment after moment of whimpered cries, of sweet bliss as my orgasm shakes me to my very core. I collapse against her, my head on her shoulder as I try to take deep, quavering breaths, my hands shaking as I reach tentative fingers up to curl around a strand of her silken hair, letting the dark red of it drift over my skin like I'd been imagining. Like I'd been wanting.

I find the strength to raise my head, to capture her mouth in mine again. The kiss is very weak to start as pleasure still pours through me, as her fingers are still inside of me, but then she draws her fingers out with a small chuckle against me, traces a sweet, wet pattern up my thigh, curling her fingers around my thighs, now, as she smiles against me.

"What are you doing?" she whispers warmly, as my mouth drifts down from her mouth, as I taste her neck, tracing the curve of her neck and shoulder with my tongue.

I lean back from her, gazing into her eyes, darkened with desire.

"Claiming you," I whisper, a rush of excitement moving through me.

Attis gazes at me for a long moment, her breath coming faster, her lips parting. "I am yours to do with as you wish," she whispers then, her lips curling up at the corners, her eyes narrowing slyly. "Milady."

A rush of desire pours through me as she tilts her head back, as I kiss over and over again her cream-colored neck, her sweet, hot skin.

Wonder purrs contentedly at the very edge of the tent, dead to the world as Attis and I take back the night.

Chapter 11: The City

The next few days pass in a blur. There's the constant journeying and cold. There's setting up the tent at night with no light to guide us, fingers frozen from a day of frigid temperatures—but the laughter, her company, her smile, her touch...all of it keeps me warm.

It's during these precious days that I find that I love, more than anything, to make Attis laugh. Every night, after we set up camp or reach a tavern, we're together, she and I, exploring and learning every inch of each other's skin, learning the taste and touch, learning our bodies and hearts.

And though, each night, her warm amber eyes are filled with desire for me, though she touches me with a soft gentleness and deep-seated need, and though—each day—the hard lines of her face soften when she looks at me, her mouth turning up at the corners with genuine pleasure...there's still something...off. Something missing.

I know that Attis cares about me, that she cares more about me each day that passes, but I still have this small, terrible, nagging feeling in the back of my head that there's something's wrong.

Honestly, I'm worried that maybe I'm falling faster for her than she's falling for me.

Or that there's one last thing standing between us...one, last thing that, if I could only figure out what it is, I could fix and change everything.

I know that this urgency is growing in me because I feel like I'm running out of time. I've counted the days we've been together, and today marks the seventh day. Though Attis said nothing about arriving at Arktos City when we rose this morning, when we broke camp and started out on our journey, I feel it, just the same.

I feel like we're drawing close to the end of our time together. And the mere thought of that is so heartbreaking that I don't know what to do.

So, this afternoon, I'm bound and determined to get to the root of the matter. To talk to Attis about that thing we've been carefully skirting during our time together: the fact that I'm supposed to be heading back to my world.

I'm on Zilla's back, Wonder pillowed in front of me under the coat (I think that, at this point, she really enjoys being carried several miles each day on horseback like the queen that she is), and Attis strides ahead of us down the narrow animal path in the woods, moving through the branches and holding them aside so that Zilla has clear footing.

It's pretty balmy out, considering how miserably cold it was last night. When I breathe out into the air, my breath doesn't hover like a cloud but dissipates almost immediately. In this world that completely lacks thermometers, I'm using that as an indicator to mean it's currently "not cold enough to kill you." Which is a very good thing.

I take a deep breath, letting it it out slowly into the air, and I screw up my courage to talk about the white elephant in the room, the white elephant that we've both been purposefully ignoring, and I open my mouth, ready to start all of this, when Attis takes a wider step than usual, springing out from the thick underbrush of the forest, and landing deftly on a stone path in the open.

Zilla follows her mistress companionably out onto the path and then pauses, her big, black head butting against Attis' shoulder as she tosses her nose, glancing forward. I blink, eyes suddenly dazzled by how bright it is (it was really quite dark beneath the fir tree canopy in the forest), squinting and placing my hand over my eyes to escape the sunshine. Attis shields her eyes, too, gazing down the road with her chin lifted, her nose scenting the breeze.

And it's an actual road, I realize in shock, as I stare down at the stones. This isn't a dirt path, or even a more compact dirt path masquerading as a road. This is actual *cobblestones*.

Attis chooses that moment to flick her gaze back up to me, her eyes soft at the edges, her mouth turning up, and her warm amber stare golden with affection and triumph as she sweeps her arm in front of her.

"There," she whispers softly, her voice full of emotion. "There is Arktos City. We've arrived."

My gaze follows her hand, and then I clutch tightly to Zilla's saddle, because if I didn't, I'd be in danger of falling off.

The city rises in front of us, and I can honestly say that, though I've lived in Boston, though I've gone to New York City many, many times, which is (arguably) the greatest city on the planet, I've...never quite seen anything like this.

This city is like a painting from a history book come to life. The very first thing I notice is the massive stone wall that looms, thick and imposing, around the outer edge of the city, ending at the very front, where the road leads, with a massive iron gate that now stands open—but I can imagine it being shut at night. The closest thing I can compare this wall to is the type of wall they put up around a prison, but while most outer prison walls that I've seen are ugly and blocky—obviously meant to keep people in—this stone wall has the characteristic, to me, of fine architecture. There are wide, almost Greek key-looking designs made with different-colored stone around the top edge of the wall, and every hundred feet or so, there's a tower with a pointed slate roof.

This city is built on a hill; I can see the stone streets winding their ways gracefully, higher and higher between tall, blocky stone buildings the color of granite and shorter ones the color of sand. These roads lead up to the tallest building at the very center of the city, a sprawling, many-towered castle. This castle is utterly beautiful, with narrow towers made of white stone that flute upward with graceful curves, and golden-colored roofs with bright, many-colored pennants flying from every tower, lines of pennants flapping briskly in the wind in every hue of the rainbow.

There's a small line of people making their

way into the city on the same road we stand on, and sprawling on either side of the iron gate, in front of the city and outside of its walls, are about fifty tents, maybe more. The tents are brightly colored, unlike the drab black tent we're traveling with ("standard issue for knights," Attis told me one night with a laugh), and these tents look like they're all from different places; they're so unique. Honestly, it looks like an encampment is set up in front of the city.

"Gods, I hope we're not too late," sighs Attis, taking in the encampment, too, with a frown. "All of the inns are usually full up for the Festival of Stars, and it starts tonight, so—technically—we're already late if we wanted to find room and board. We might have to rough it out here," she tells me, gesturing to the tents. "But we'll see, yes? It's not the worst thing in the world to camp out, is it?" Attis glances up at me with a small smile. "Do I keep you warm enough?" she asks, the words a low growl as she lifts one brow artfully, placing her palm on Zilla's shoulder and brushing the backs of her fingers against my thigh.

I know I'm already blushing before I feel the warmth spread across my cheeks. "Crap," I mutter, reaching up and touching my very hot skin, but I'm chuckling as I look down at her, breathing out. "Yes," I tell her, my voice low. My hand drops down to my thigh and I reach out to touch her hand as I hold her gaze. "Yes, you do," I whisper.

Attis is smiling as she turns away from me, as she lifts her chin, lengthening her stride. She begins to walk purposefully down the stone street toward the city, but I saw a flicker of something pass over her face before she turned from me. Pain, fleeting pain that she swallowed and silenced.

I need to talk to her about this. Tonight.

I think it's mostly the fact that I could be leaving. But I also think this is about Hera.

I mean, it would make sense. I know that Attis cares about me, and I know that Attis wants to be with me. We're not doing anything that makes her uncomfortable, as we begin this—whatever "this" is—together, but I'm worried that the ghost of Hera is still standing between us. It would be Attis' right, obviously, to never forget her; she loved Hera fiercely and deeply. And there's nothing that I can do if that's the case, if Attis feels guilty for starting something with me, something she had with Hera.

But it makes my heart ache to think about the fact that Attis might be thinking of Hera when she looks at me. Might be comparing me to her, might be thinking about what Hera would have done in a situation, how Hera would have smiled or laughed or touched her.

I take a deep breath as I remember the way that Attis moved over me last night, as her eyes darkened, as she gazed down at me with desire crackling between us... Was Attis wishing it was Hera and not me beneath her?

I rake my hand through my hair, bite my lip, try not to let the fear or worry of that tortured thought twist further into my gut. I don't honestly know if Attis was thinking any of that, and honestly, wouldn't it be her right to think it?

I don't know how many more days I'm going to have with her. I don't know how this will end.

And it's started to make me nervous. Because I *am* falling for Attis; I am falling head over heels in love with her, and it's a progression that I'm powerless to stop.

Right now, I don't know what the next few days will bring, and that mere thought terrifies me. What if I'm whisked back to my world, and I never see her again?

And what if I'm *not*? What if I can't get home? Would I be perfectly happy to stay here, on Agrotera, forever?

I think you would, comes a deep, secret thought. And I think about it for a long moment before I put my attention back on the present, back on Zilla and Attis and Wonder, snuggled tightly against me, and this impossible, beautiful city rising in front of us.

I don't know how many of these moments I have left. And I need to treasure each one. No matter what may come.

But we still have to talk about all of this. And we have to talk soon.

I clear my throat. "So, what's the plan?" I ask Attis, wrapping my fingers in Zilla's reins and mane tightly as the big, black horse lengthens her gait to follow closer behind Attis, Attis who's moving so quickly toward the city, she's almost trotting.

"Well," says Attis, glancing up at the sun, directly above us and shining weaker now through the thin cloud cover. Attis flicks her gaze ahead of us. "We need to get to the city, and then we find my knights, get settled in... We'll speak with Virago then. The festival starts at sundown, so the festivities will begin, but we should be able to find out if you'll be able to return home or not beforehand." Attis glances up at me quickly and then away—if I hadn't been watching her, I wouldn't have seen the worry that passed over her face, quickly covered by the warm smile she flashed up to me.

My heart's thundering in my chest as I grip Zilla's mane tighter, my fingernails curling against my palm so hard it hurts.

So there's no time for that talk. Because I'm going to find out this afternoon if I can go back home or not.

The seemingly unhurried pace of our journey, the many wonderful conversations and the few precious nights we had together suddenly don't seem like enough. Not *nearly* enough.

I'm just learning what makes Attis laugh, just learning what makes her sigh in pleasure and growl in delight. I'm just learning the way her hair falls in the sunlight, flashing a brilliant, transcendent red when she bends down to kiss me, how her hands feel around my waist as her fingers grip me tightly, what her cold, hard armor feels like, pressed against my chest when she draws me to her for an embrace. I'm just learning that, when she's in a particularly good mood, she calls her massive war horse the ridiculous nickname "Zilly," and that she couldn't cook porridge over a fire to save her life (but that I, surprisingly, can). I'm just learning that she hates goodbyes and will never say the word, especially to her friends that she sees so infrequently. She always promises that she'll see them again because she thinks it brings good luck, that to say "goodbye" would court disaster for her and them.

I'm just learning that she misses being a knight so much that she's wondering if she should go back to it.

I'm just learning *her*. And it's like I've lived an entire lifetime in these past few days, but these past few days, by themselves, will *never be enough*. I want a lifetime with her.

And how is it possible that I can get that?

I'm becoming sadder and more frustrated the closer we draw to the city, the towers, its walls and castle looming over us like an impossible fantasy. I try to concentrate on how beautiful it is, on these last few moments of my journey with Attis, but I can't do it: I keep thinking about what we've had and everything we won't get to have, and it's breaking my heart.

I'm halfheartedly trying to carry on a conversation with Attis about the great food she promises is in Arktos City, as I try to figure out what the hell I'm going to do. I didn't want to face this decision yet, if there's even a decision to face. I didn't want to figure this out yet.

I wanted more time. But I don't have it.

"Attis?!"

I blink in surprise at that one shouted word that echoed from behind us, and both Attis and I turn toward the jubilant outcry of her name, the sound of quick, heavy hoof beats against the stone road filling the air.

A knight on horseback is barreling toward us; that's the first thing I notice, the sunlight reflecting off her silver armor and into my eyes, practically blinding me. Then I take in the fact that she's somehow, impossibly, on a *taller* horse than Zilla. This one is gray and dappled and quite pretty, though very large (again, similar in build to a Clydesdale, but gray).

And the knight?

Um. Wow.

She has long black hair streaming behind her in a high ponytail (with, oddly enough, a wolf's tail tied into her hair, the tail streaming out behind her, too). Her armor is bright silver and very flashy; it's better quality than Attis' armor, I can see, though maybe it's just more decorative, prettier. Every piece of the intricate armor has scrollwork on it, and delicate lines and curves that look almost like Celtic knots spiral around each piece of the armor.

The knight barreling down on us has the most piercing ice blue eyes I've ever seen.

And, put succinctly, she's hot as hell.

What the hell do they *feed* these lady knights here, anyway?

She's tall; I can see that even though she's in the saddle, and she's muscular, just as are all of the other knights I've met, but there's something about this one. She has an inordinate amount of grace and poise as she sits in the saddle like she was born to do it. She also has muscular curves that fill out her armor perfectly, her body fitting snugly in the leather beneath the armor as if it was made for her—which it probably was.

She looks so self-assured and regal as she pulls her horse up sharply right in front of us, and then she vaults off her saddle, onto the ground, and—

immediately—has Attis in a tight embrace, her wide grin pulling up full lips as she kisses Attis on the cheek.

Attis grimaces, laughing, rubbing the back of her armored glove over her cheek as she pushes this new knight off her, holding her out at arm's length to take her in, then drawing her back to embrace her tightly.

"Gods, Virago, I've missed you," says Attis, hooking her chin over the knight's shoulder and squeezing her in such a hold that any normal woman's ribs would probably be broken right about now.

Wait.

Virago?

This is the woman who can help me get back home.

I take a deep breath, feeling everything fall away from me.

This is the beginning of the end. It's all over, starting now.

My heart aches so fiercely inside of me, I wonder if it's already broken.

This new knight, Virago, steps back, laughing brightly as she looks Attis up and down with those searing, ice blue eyes. "You're surviving, I see? Gods, I've been so worried about you, friend..." Her voice is low, throaty, velvety...the kind of voice that reaches deep inside of you and warms you. But the merriment leaves this new knight's eyes as she stares hard at Attis. "You've been well?" she asks, voice low as she ducks her head toward Attis, wrapping her hand around Attis' neck and drawing her forward to press her forehead against Attis' forehead, closing her eyes and breathing out.

These are intimate gestures, but it's very clear to me that these two knights have known each other for a great deal of time and are the best of friends. Virago looks up just then, when Attis doesn't speak, when Attis' jaw clenches, and Virago looks past Attis...up at me.

"Gods, where are my manners?" asks Virago hollowly, shaking her head fast and then—like she's not in the middle of a dusty stone road—Virago kneels down smoothly, her hand over her heart as she bows her head to me, her ponytail and wolf tail falling over her shoulder to lie over her chest. "Milady," she says formally, voice low, then glances up at me with sparking blue eyes. "I am Virago of the Royal Knights of Arktos City, capital of Arktos," Virago tells me smoothly, her chin lifted in pride as she smiles up at me. She rises fluidly in a single motion, her smile deepening as she glances at me.

"Virago, my beloved show-off," says Attis fondly, with a soft smile, wrapping her arm around Virago's shoulders and squeezing, "this is Josie Beckett." She gazes up to me, and then she holds my gaze with her unwavering amber eyes. "She is my lover," Attis tells Virago softly.

Virago stiffens and turns to look at Attis with wide blue eyes. "It's true?" she whispers. Attis doesn't look at Virago but keeps looking at me, her amber eyes flickering with something I can't quite place. But Attis smiles softly at Virago's question and nods once.

And then Virago steps back from Attis and whoops with joy so loudly that both horses startle.

Bridget Essex

Virago darts forward and puts her hands around my waist, lifting me down from Zilla's back (much to my cat's lack of amusement, still buried down the front of my coat), like she does this sort of thing all the time. And, judging from her enthusiasm and skill, perhaps she does.

So I'm lifted off of Zilla and set down on the ground, and then Virago is embracing *me* so tightly I'm kind of worried about my ribs snapping. But her enthusiasm is difficult not to catch. When she steps away from me with a huge smile, I can't help but smile up at her, too, as I tuck a loose strand of hair behind my ear and try to calm my startled cat, bouncing her a little beneath the coat.

"I can't believe it... I *can't* believe it, but, gods, I'm so happy for the both of you. Attis, you deserve to be so happy," she says, and then Virago's voice is breaking a little as she looks to Attis, Attis who holds her gaze with soft strength, melancholy flickering over her face.

Wonder takes that moment to struggle a little more beneath the coat, and I shift her weight, bouncing her a little more.

"And you're expecting!" says Virago joyously, throwing her arms wide to take in my coat and my big "stomach." "Ah, but it's a good day," she breathes out in satisfaction.

"Oh, no...no..." I tell Virago with a little laugh as Attis laughs, too, running her gloved fingers through her hair as she raises a single brow and fixes me in her sights. "I'm, uh... I'm carrying my cat," I tell Virago, and when she stares at me, utterly perplexed, I unbutton the first two buttons of the cannibal werewolf coat, and I let Wonder peek her head out at the two knights, her ears flat back and whiskers pushed forward in a determined cat pout.

Virago chuckles in surprise at that but steps forward, scratching the top of Wonder's head gently with the tips of her armored gloves. Surprisingly, Wonder purrs, ducking her head back into my coat as I do up the buttons again, shivering a little as the wind begins to blow a little colder, clouds scuttling over the sun above us.

"I can't believe you were able to settle my dear friend down," says Virago then, her low voice warm as she shakes her head at me, her ice blue eyes soft with affection. She glances at Attis. "I am so, so happy for the both of you, truly," she tells us.

"You are the best of comrades," says Attis, her voice tight as she holds Virago's gaze. "It has been too long, my friend. We have much catching up to do."

"Surely, surely," says Virago, but she says those words in distraction as she cocks her head to the side, glancing me up and down. "But...ah..." She flicks her gaze back up to my face, her eyes narrowing. "Josie, you don't look like you're from around here. Where was it that you said you were from?"

"Um..." I lick my lips, stiffening. This moment marks the true beginning of the end, I realize, and I curl my hands into fists at my sides, wishing I could stop time, just for a moment.

But I can't. I know I can't.

"I'm from Boston," I tell Virago quietly.

And then Virago's bright blue eyes go very

wide, her jaw dropping open as she stares at me.

"We were actually hoping that you could help us, dear friend," Attis tells her quietly, as Virago glances back to her. "I know this is strange," says Attis, holding up her hand as Virago breathes out, shutting her mouth. "It was as much a surprise to me as it is to you," says Attis, one brow up, "but Josie is from another world. And I know that Holly is—"

"*Holly* is from Boston, too," says Virago quickly. "That's where I went when the Beast dragged me through the portal. I went to Earth, to Boston."

Attis clears her throat and leans back on her heels, lifting her chin. She sighs for a long moment as Virago stares at me in wonder. "Virago," Attis says then, folding her arms in front of her. "We were, uh, wondering...is the portal you went through still open? Have you and Holly gone back to Boston since you went back to get her?"

Virago shakes her head. "Not once, I'm afraid. It's very difficult to open the portal, and..." Virago's eyes narrow, and then realization comes over her face. "Wait. You want to go back home, don't you, Josie?" she asks me.

My heart squeezes inside of me as both Attis and Virago watch me closely. I feel so sad and small as my radio brain takes over, starts to talk, while my heart, inside of me, twists in pain. "Yes," I tell her, my voice cracking at the end of that single, painful word.

Virago frowns, rocking back on her heels. "I'm afraid it's not as easy as that, unfortunately. To go through the portal to another world, a world of your *choosing*, is very difficult. When the beast dragged me through the portal, it was a world at random that I was thrust into. When I went through the portal to find Holly, it was another matter entirely to journey to a specific world, and took a concerted amount of effort and magical energy," says Virago, shaking her head. Her jaw tenses. "It took *so much* magic for me to go back through the portal, fall to your Earth and find Holly..." She trails off, shakes her head again. She repeats, "I was, of course, dragged through the portal to your world because of a great beast. I met Holly there, on Earth, and we fell in love." Her face softens so much that it makes my heart skip a beat for a moment. "So, when I returned to this world, I did everything in my power to go back and see Holly. And when I found her again, she came back to Agrotera with me," Virago says, her smile widening. But then she grimaces a little as she looks down at me. "I just want you to know that it will not be easy to get you back to your world, but that I think we can manage it. I'm not certain," she tells me, holding up a hand, "but I do think it's possible. But...what of the two of you? You're lovers, aren't you? I don't..." She glances at Attis and trails off.

Attis breathes out, shrugs. "Go on, old friend," she murmurs, her jaw tight.

"Well. It's just that it will be a *great* deal of work, once we get you back to Earth, to bring you back to Agrotera," Virago tells me gently. "You see, I belong here," Virago says, tapping her hand over her heart, "so the portal accepts me right away and brings me back to my world of origin, which is why I think it will take you back to Earth. But when I brought Holly through, because she is not from this land, it was deeply difficult. She will be able to visit her friends and family on her world possibly a few more times, each time more difficult than the last, until there will come a time that she must remain here with me...forever." Virago cocks her head to the side, looking me up and down. "So you see, you two will have to make a decision..." She glances from me to Attis.

Attis shakes her head, takes a deep breath and stands straighter. "Don't trouble yourself on our account, Virago," she says companionably, curling her fingers over Virago's shoulder and squeezing gently. "Josie traveled with me across our land, seeking this eventuality." Her gaze flicks to me, and she tilts her chin up, her eyes glittering. "Josie belongs on her world. She should be wherever her home is." Attis clears her throat, turns away from me. "Now, the festival begins tonight! We must find a place to stay..."

And, just like that, I know she knows what I'm going to do.

And I know, too.

I have to go home.

My breath catches in my throat as I hold Wonder's warm bulk tightly in front of me, as Attis loops Zilla's reins around her hand and then, shoulder to shoulder, with Virago's horse trailing her, Virago and Attis start down the road again, the road that ends in Arktos City.

I follow a little behind them, but my throat is so tight, I swallow, choking down the sob that wells up inside of me.

I'm being so stupid; the truth of the matter is that I always knew this is where we were headed, that this is what I wanted—or why would I have completed this journey with Attis?

But, seven days ago, of *course* I wanted to go back to my world. I wanted to go back to the life I knew, the life that wasn't exactly happy, wasn't exactly fulfilling, but was the only one I'd ever lived. It was the life I was comfortable with, the life where I pushed everyone away so that I was alone. But I've learned so much here, on Agrotera, and I think I've grown and changed as a person.

I know what I have to do now, and I wish I didn't.

But Attis is right. Even though the past seven days have been more enjoyable than I thought possible, I'm not meant for this kind of life. I don't *belong* here. I belong on my world with all of its convenience and family and memories. I belong with my job (if I still have a chance to get it back). I belong...

You belong with her, comes the deep, secret thought from the bottom of my heart, and I try to ignore it this time. But I can't. I know that thought, that feeling that's currently breaking my heart apart, is right. I *do* belong with her. There's something that's happening between us, something that doesn't happen every day or even once in a lifetime. This is precious and lovely, what's growing between Attis and me, and I'm just going to throw it away?

But I want to go home. *I don't belong here*. Radio is my life, my life's work, and, damn it, I'm good at it. I love doing it. I love my job, and...

Okay, so I didn't love my life before. I loved my job, yes, but my life was actually kind of rotten. I'd worked so hard at the ability to push people away that it had become like second nature back home. I knew no one in my apartment building, knew no one really at work, didn't even like when the barista at my favorite coffee shop learned my name and started using it. I loved anonymity because anonymity meant that it was impossible to grow close to anyone. I'd built up so many walls and defenses that—quite like this city rising in front of us—I was utterly impenetrable.

And then Attis came along, and it's not that she consciously started breaking down my defenses...

It's that I *wanted her to.*

There was something about Attis, something that—from the very start—called to me, answered something in me, completed me. And now I'm just going to throw that all away?

What else am I *supposed* to do?

This isn't home.

And I need to go home.

I swallow another sob, and I steel myself against feeling anything. It's already begun; this path is already set in motion. I'm going home, and, God, it was great while it lasted. But from the moment I fell into this world, I knew this day would come, and— despite knowing better—I started this, anyway. We started this, Attis and I, when we knew that this relationship would be utterly finite and could only grow within the confines of a handful of days and then would have to be halted forever.

But as I follow Virago and Attis, even though

I know all of this logically, even though I realize I must go home, that it was fun while it lasted, but that it's close to being over now...I can feel my heart breaking inside of me, and nothing I can think about, nothing I can feel, can stop it from breaking.

The city rises in front of us, and it's beautiful and impressive. That massive encampment of brightly colored tents pitched in front of the city is magical, and the castle, rising far above us, looks like it comes directly from a medieval painting. I should be in awe right now, in awe that something I could never have believed existed does. I should be in awe that I'm in a world right now where magic isn't just believed in but real, a world where a knight can journey for a phoenix feather, and a witch can construct a spell to bring someone back from the dead.

And all of these miraculous things should fill me with wonder and awe.

But they don't.

Not nearly as much as she does.

Wonder growls beneath my coat, bringing me back to the present as she twists around in her current position and starts to burrow upward, looking for a place to stick her head out of, probably to get a little fresh air in her hot, stuffy prison. I sigh and oblige her, undoing the top two buttons of the coat as she shoves her head out into the cold, blinking muzzily up at me, and then immediately focusing on her surroundings, as if she's trying to sight prey. I can feel her tail flick against my belly.

Virago glances backward at me, and then she grimaces, slowing her pace and coming alongside me, trailing her horse behind her. "I wouldn't do that with your pretty puss, Josie," she says then, one brow up as she shakes her head. "There's been some wolves spotted near about lately, and they can scent defenseless prey very, very well in winter when they're most voracious. It would be best if your puss remained hidden in your coat."

"Wonder's hardly defenseless," I chuckle, but I oblige, pushing my cat's head back down into the coat and doing up the buttons again. But Attis is frowning, glancing back at us, and then she's slowing her pace, too, bringing her and Zilla, led behind her, beside us.

"Wolves, Virago?" she asks, her tone mild, but there's a sharp edge beneath those words.

Virago shrugs, keeping her face carefully neutral. "There's nothing to be alarmed about, old friend. You know very well that predators of many stripes come close to the city in the winter, looking for food. The wall stops them, and they don't dare come close enough to the encampment to cause any trouble. We knights have been on guard patrol around the encampment since it began a couple of days ago," she says with confidence, rolling her shoulders back.

But Attis' face has darkened, and she's frowning as she stares ahead, taking in the tents. "Are you sure?" she persists, glancing back at her friend. "You know as well as I that this encampment is utterly defenseless, full of festivalgoers who aren't prepared for any sort of attack..." She drifts off and swallows, dropping her voice low. "Virago...remember the werewolf clan?"

"The Berserkers? The *cannibals*?" asks Virago, brows up. "Good gods, they're long, long gone. We destroyed them long ago, together," she tells Attis soothingly, shaking her head. "And they were *were*wolves. These predators around the city now are simply wolves, I promise you. Ease your heart, my friend; the wolves will never attack the encampment, let alone a pack of werewolves, long since dead."

Attis shivers a little, glancing up at the clouds scuttling in front of the sun. "Well. They're not *all* dead and gone. Remember what the leader promised us when we cornered him on the cliff face?" She glances at Virago, her face clouding. "He promised *revenge*. That he would, somehow, get revenge on us, and that he would remember us. And then he slipped through our ranks, ran back into the woods—"

Virago shakes her head. "Good gods, no. Those were the emptiest of promises. Remember what we did that day," she says, her mouth in a thin line as she draws her wolf tail over her shoulder and runs a hand over its fur. "You must stop thinking about that day, Attis. That leader was a madman, a rogue wolf with the taste for human blood; it had addled his brains, and there is *no way* that he would be able to round up enough wolves who agreed with him to 'exact revenge.' The ones that he'd been able to convince were his own family and a few other young pups, all aggressive and dangerous because they were maddened by the need for human flesh," she snorts, then takes a deep breath, turning to look at Attis. "In the end, you must remember—they were relatively easily defeated. And that it was a *very* long time ago, that—all of that. Hera would want you to stop remembering," she says then, her voice dropping even lower.

I think that if anyone else in the world had told Attis that thought, she would have become very, very angry. But it was Virago who delivered those words softly, and—as such—Attis takes a deep breath, gazing up at the city wall in front of us as pain passes over her face.

"I know," she says softly. She licks her lips, shakes her head, clenching her hand over her heart into a fist. "But I can never forget."

"I will do my best," says Virago, walking closer to Attis and wrapping an arm around Attis' shoulders companionably, "to *help* you forget, I promise you. We all will," she says firmly, glancing back at me with her brows raised. "Be that as it may," she says, clearing her throat. There was a flicker of worry in Virago's eyes just then; she straightens, taking a deep breath. "We've glimpsed the wolves, and we know they're not *were*." She frowns, "but I will ask that their activities concerning the encampment are fully monitored."

"Thank you, old friend," Attis says quietly, peering up at the thin sunshine with a grimace. "Always better safe than sorry," she mutters.

Virago nods, but then she's smiling again, her concern already in the past. "This is going to be a splendid festival. Holly, for one, is *very* excited. It's her first Festival of Stars, you know."

Attis smiles back at me over her shoulder as Virago puts an arm around her again, and—

together—we approach the city gates.

There are two knights on either side of the open city gates. The gates themselves are about twenty feet across, and the massive iron gate that's usually lowered to close up the city (I'm assuming each night) is raised and dangling in the air above us. It's a little unnerving to walk beneath that thick iron gate with its pointed tips dangling over us, but large iron chains appear to have drawn the gate upward, and it looks pretty safe...I think.

The two lady knights guarding the gate are dressed in armor exactly like Virago's, but perhaps a little less fancy. They're speaking with each person who wants to enter the city, the line of people stretching out from the gate down the road toward us, but when the knights see Virago and Attis, they wave both of the women through with large smiles, and wave me through, too, with polite nods.

"Where are you living now?" Attis asks Virago, as we fold into the press of people on the city streets in front of us. Attis must raise her voice to be heard, but Virago nods, forging through the press of people, her horse trailing out behind her. Before Virago, a small free lane opens, people stepping out of her way with respectful nods, then merging into the sea of bodies behind me when we pass.

"We're living in the bookmaker district now," Virago shouts back. "It's just a little place we share, but Holly loves it. You see, she worked with books back on her world, so it makes her happy to be around so many of them."

"Bookmaker district!" Attis whistles, pausing for a moment so that I can catch up with her. "That's pricey!" she shouts ahead to her friend.

Virago glances back and pauses, too, waiting for us. "It is," says Virago, her smile spreading across her face again and her eyes sparkling. "But Holly is very much worth it."

"To be sure, to be sure," Attis agrees with a soft chuckle. Once I reach her through the press of people, Attis kneels down easily beside Zilla, lacing her fingers together and holding them out to me. "Up you go," she tells me softly, glancing up to me with her warm amber eyes.

I stare down at her, kneeling before me, her dark red hair falling across the side of her cream-colored cheek, amber eyes unwavering as she gazes to the deepest parts of myself, and—again—I want to freeze this moment forever. I want to stop time and stay here, but I know I can't. So I lean forward, and I place my hand on her shoulder, my palm against the cold metal as I curl my fingertips underneath that armored shoulder plate and brush the warm leather on her shoulder. I squeeze gently, memorizing what that warm leather feels like against my skin, what her armor feels like, under my palm.

"Thank you," I whisper to her. She glances up at me in surprise, her golden eyes wide.

"It's nothing," she tells me gruffly, holding my gaze with hers as she holds out her cupped hands to me and nods toward Zilla. "It's quite a ways to the bookmaker district," she tells me, her mouth curling up at the corners. "And I didn't want you to have to walk the whole way."

"That's not what I meant," I tell her, shaking my head as my voice catches, but I realize that here and now is not the best time for this. So I take a deep breath, give her a watery smile, and then I step up gently into her strong, cupped hands. Attis rises, tosses me up onto Zilla's back lightly, and then she's leading Zilla behind her as we follow Virago deeper into the city.

We move through the city streets one after the other as I take in the sights of Arktos City. The buildings rise away from us, not unlike on the streets of Boston, but this is certainly not Boston. The streets here in Arktos City are cobblestone, and there are no sidewalks: people walk with horses and with horses with carts, and there are a few oxen, trundling buggies behind them, all in a joyful, loud press of people and animals going in opposite directions. It's happy chaos.

As we move further into the city, the streets become wider, and the wide expanse is now bordered with brightly colored tents and people selling many different things. There are fruit and vegetables that look similar to ones we have back at home (and then there are ones I've never seen before in my life), pots and pans and clothes and cloth and animals and pottery. There's a blacksmith shop that has swords, knives and horseshoes spread out front on a woven blanket, along with one silver shield leaning against his shop. There's a seamstress shop with two women standing in the window, one twirling around and around in a big, blue gown, the other shifting from side to side with a knowing smirk, showing off closely-tailored pants and a smart suit jacket over a ruffled shirt.

That's when I begin to notice that most of the

people here in the city are women.

There are definitely a couple of men; they're noticeable moving through the press of people simply because there are so few of them. But every single person selling wares or running a shop seems to be female, as far as I can see. As we move further and further into the city, the occasional few men that I've noticed seem to vanish, and there are only women surrounding us now.

Attis calls out to a few people, and they return her greetings with happy smiles and exclamations of greeting and good wishes. The entire atmosphere of the city, it seems, is one of jubilation as preparations are underway for the festival.

Even though we've spent so many days together, I never thought to ask Attis about what the Festival of Stars *is*. There are people now hanging garlands of paper stars from windows above the shops to dangle down the front of their homes, and there are paper stars floating above a lot of the tent shops lining the streets, and tied with string to the shop signs of brick and mortar stores. Originally, I thought they must be balloons, but they're too blocky. When I ride closer to one of the "balloons," that's when I realize they're made of ultra-thin, gauzy paper, and there's a small candle lit inside of each one. I'm not sure how they're floating in the air, but then, that's really the least of the things I should be wondering about here.

"Did you come across the Hellions on your journey to Arktos City?" Virago shouts back to us with a smirk, as we round another street corner of the city. There's an enormous garland of a hundred paper stars dangling out of a window above me, and Zilla is so tall that, as I pass beneath the garland, the paper stars brush against the top of my head. I stare up in wonder.

Attis laughs in surprise. "Oh, gods—is that what we're calling Kell and Alinor's brigade now?"

Virago's laughing, too, as she leads her horse out of the way of a large carriage that trundles past, pulled by two big bay horses. "The name has evolved, I'll give you that, but I think it best describes them now," says Virago, winking back at the two of us.

"We did come across them, yes," Attis tells her, "but they had to stay another day where they were. They were stationed at the Silver Pony on a campaign. But they should be getting to the city tonight, because they were going to push forward, and they could sustain a much quicker pace than us."

"That's wonderful. Oh, Gods, can you really imagine a party without them? I don't think it could be done!" says Virago, shaking her head with a wide smile. "Do you know where you're staying?" she asks Attis now.

Attis grimaces and shakes her head. "I was hoping there'd be room at an inn or tavern—"

"That time has come and gone, I'm afraid," says Virago, glancing back at us with a shake of her head, her brow furrowed in concern. "I'm so sorry, Attis, truly, but what tiny amount of room we had is taken up by Artema and her dog, and—"

"Oh, don't trouble yourself on our account," says Attis easily, with a warm smile. "Josie and I have been making do almost every night in the tent, and we'll continue to do so. We'll find friends among the encampment and pitch there." She holds up a hand when Virago starts to protest. "Truly, Virago, it's fine," she tells her, voice low.

"I feel *terrible*," Virago sighs, casting her eyes heavenward. "I should have told Artema that she'd have to bed out in the encampments. Really, two dogs in our small quarters makes for quite a crowd," she tells us, shaking her head. "But you would have been *so welcome*. I know!" she says, face brightening, "I can sleep with Holly out on the balcony. We'll pitch a small tent there! Oh, we'll be cozy—"

Attis laughs. "I would never hear of it," she tells Virago, shaking her head and gazing at her affectionately. "Truly, Virago, please. We're fine."

"Honestly, I love camping in the tent," I tell Virago now, and I'm surprised that—when I say it—I actually mean it. For the few short days that we've been together, that tent has been the site of a lot of happy memories. Camping in a tent when it's so cold out has its challenges, of course, but I've gotten a little less indoors-y since I've *had* to spend every waking moment outside.

Attis glances up at me in surprise, but her face softens when I smile down at her. She reaches out in the space between us, curls her fingers softly around my calf and squeezes gently.

Warmth floods through me at the intimate, sweet gesture, and the ache in my heart, the ache that I'd been able to ignore a little as I took in the magnificence of the city, roars back to life, pulsing with a bright, unwavering throb through me.

Am I really going to give this up?

Am I really going to give *her* up?

As Attis leads Zilla through the beautiful streets of Arktos City, I realize, again, that I have no idea what to do.

✿

Chapter 12: The Star

When we arrive at the livery stables down the street from Virago and Holly's rooms, Virago steps into the stable and crows with delight.

"It looks like they're already here," she tells us over her shoulder, leading her enormous gray horse down the aisle toward the back of the stable.

"Gods, they are," mutters Attis, leading Zilla up to the entrance of the stable and taking in the large horses lined up at the front, tied to the hitching post at the entrance.

"Who?" I ask.

"The Hellions," says Attis, her mouth twitching into a smirk as she glances up at me. "All right. Down you go," she tells me, then, holding her arms up.

I glance down at her and push myself forward so that I fall the few inches into her arms, my front pressing to her cool armor. Attis' smile deepens as she gazes into my eyes. She leans forward, brushing her lips against my forehead, and then she lowers me gently to the ground.

Attis ties Zilla next to the other horses at the hitching post, all massive ones. Honestly, it seems the bigger the horse, the better choice for a knight.

Virago hands the reins of her mount over to a stable girl, pressing a coin into her hands. "Let's go up," she says excitedly, turning back to us with a wide smile. "And let's begin the party."

"What's the Festival of Stars about?" I ask, as Virago walks back through the stable, and Attis and I turn and make our way back down the street. We stop at the second building, and Virago begins to trot up the creaking, wooden stairs wrapped around the building on the outside.

Attis smiles softly at me; then she hooks an arm around my waist as we begin to climb the stairs together.

"You'll see," she whispers, pressing her mouth against the skin beneath my ear and kissing me warmly there.

I shiver against her as I look up into her bright amber eyes that stare down at me almost wistfully.

We reach the third level of stairs, and I turn to take in the city. This high up, I can see to the next street. The sun is starting to drift toward the far horizon, and the quality of light in the afternoon makes everything look warm and golden below us. Laughter drifts up to us from down below on the cobblestones, and someone across the way, on the same level as us in the opposite building, throws open her diamond-paned windows and begins to toss long strings of paper stars to dangle out the window, down the side of her building. The paper stars almost seem to float in the air as they fall gracefully, their many colors fluttering in the breeze.

"Here we are," says Virago, reaching the third

level of the staircase and stopping at the door. It's a hand-carved, very pretty wooden affair of a door, made of a very dark wood that has, at head height, a stained glass window inlaid into the wood in an enormous diamond pane. The ruby red, sapphire blue and emerald green of the window take my breath away, as the light inside of the rooms shines through to greet us warmly.

Virago opens the door, and the wash of laughter and happy voices comes out to meet us, along with the tantalizing aroma of something that smells like frying onions and pancakes. My stomach immediately growls as Virago ushers both Attis and I indoors, shutting the door behind all of us.

My eyes adjust to the darkness as someone immediately grabs me and hugs me tightly. From the tightness of the hug, I recognize Alinor. Wonder wiggles out from beneath the coat and leaps to the floor, but I'm fairly certain she'll be fine in this joyful chaos.

"Josie!" Alinor crows, then immediately launches herself onto Attis. "Attis!" she shouts loudly, picking up a mug of what appears to be drink from a little table by the door. "Hail and welcome!" she bellows. She downs the contents of the very large mug in a few enormous gulps.

"Hail and welcome, Alinor," Attis chuckles, readjusting her armored shoulder piece that Alinor practically pulled off.

The low-ceilinged rooms are as warm and welcoming as an embrace, and each of these rooms are full of people, of women, I realize, in different styles of armor, along with a few women in dresses, and a few women in pants and suit jackets. I take in the press of people, and my eyes land on a few in particular—a gorgeous, older woman wearing a clinging sky-blue dress, drinking out of a fluted glass. In the corner, there's one very pretty woman with long, curly black hair braided smartly behind her, her face practically obscured by the enormous tri-corner hat on top of her head. Her jacket looks like hand-embroidered brocade, and at the base of her beautiful, earth-colored throat is a mound of creamy lace that flows out of the top of her shirt and down her chest like a waterfall. The women's dresses resemble medieval-style clothing...but not quite. The material of the dresses is brocade or heavy velvet, and there's something almost Victorian about the way their hair is upswept, and the style of their jewelry.

"Virago!" calls a happy voice, and out of the press of people comes a woman with long red hair sweeping over the shoulders of her blood-red gown with a plunging front. Her face is warm and inviting, and her smile is so utterly genuine that it makes me smile, too. This woman dashes forward, and then Virago has her arms around her, is lifting her and twirling her in place with a bright laugh of joy. The woman falls into Virago's arms, and then Virago has her hand at the back of the woman's neck and is drinking her deeply in an intoxicating, passionate kiss.

Wow. It's...*very* passionate.

When they finally break away (to a whoop of amusement from the woman in the brocade jacket), Virago turns to us triumphantly, an arm tightly wrapped around the smaller woman, who leans against her, cheeks flushed, her face bright with happiness.

"Josie, this is Holly," Virago tells us proudly. "Holly is from your world."

"What?" Holly says, her brow furrowing immediately as she glances up at Virago. "Virago, *what*?"

"I'm as surprised as you are, my darling," Virago tells her, her full mouth curling up at the corners with bemusement as she shrugs. "Apparently, Josie came through from Boston. Attis found her in the forest."

"Wow," says Holly, gazing at me with wide eyes. Then she smiles brightly, steps forward and holds out her hand to me. "It's nice to meet you, Josie. God, I have a million questions for you. How did you come through the portal?"

"I don't honestly know," I tell her with an uncomfortable shrug. "I was in my basement, doing laundry—"

"Wait, wait... Do I know you?" asks Holly, her head to the side as she stares at me with wide eyes. "Your voice sounds super familiar—"

I actually laugh out loud at that, and then I smile, raise a single brow as I take a chance and say, "Good *morning*, Boston! This is Josie Beckett with LEM 100.5, Public Access Radio."

"Oh, my *God*, *no way*," says Holly. She darts forward and gives me a huge, tight hug. "Your program is my absolute favorite. I'm kind of a crazy fan girl for you, actually. You interviewed one of my favorite authors! Oh, my *God*, I can't believe you're here, and that I'm finally meeting you...in, you know, kind of the craziest way possible," she says with a little chagrin, as she chuckles and indicates our surroundings with a sweep of her hand.

Alinor races past, pretty deftly for being so drunk, chasing another knight in golden armor who's laughing so hard, she's going to be caught in a second.

"Admittedly, it's a little weird that I'd find the only fan of my show on another world," I tell her with a short laugh, and she's laughing, too. Virago and Attis stare at us, pleasantly perplexed.

"She's from the radio, sweetheart," says Holly, wrapping her arm around Virago and glancing up at her with a wide smile. "Remember, the thing that plays music?"

"Ah," says Virago, her head to the side as she takes me in. "You're the woman who's funny, the one in the morning? I thought I recognized your voice, too."

"I'll take that as a big compliment," I tell her, secretly pretty damn pleased with myself.

"So, what are you doing here?' Holly asks, breaking away from Virago, taking me by the elbow and pulling me gently toward the wide far window that looks down over the street. "Do you want to go back to Earth?" she asks, glancing back at Attis, across the room with one brow raised. "Or did you, you know, find your own knight, too?" she asks, her lips twitching upwards.

"That seems to be kind of a thing, doesn't it?" I ask with a tight chuckle as she winks at Virago across the room.

"Yeah. It's kind of...magical," she says with a

soft sigh; then her face darkens. "Do you want to go home, Josie?" she asks me softly, holding my gaze. "What about... What about you and Attis?"

"You're perceptive," I tell her, head to the side. I raise a brow with a sigh.

"I can see the way you look at her," Holly tells me decisively. "And I'm pretty damn sure that's how I looked at Virago from the very start. There's something about a lady knight, isn't there?" she asks, her lips twitching up at the corners. "So, tell me," she says, leaning back against the wall beside the window. "What do you want?"

The question is so innocent-sounding and kind that I can feel the pain reaching out from my heart, squeezing my insides again. I bite my lip, glance out the window at the packed streets below, the glowing paper stars floating up from the shop signs, the dangling paper stars fluttering out of people's windows.

"I don't know. I thought I wanted to go home, but...everything's changed. I didn't intend to fall in love. But I...did," I tell her quietly. "Still, I feel like I *have* to go home. This world is definitely magical and amazing and just... I mean, it's *amazing*, don't get me wrong," I tell her, opening my palms to her. "But this isn't my home, you know?"

"I know," she says quietly, nodding. "For me, Agrotera, from the very first mention...I knew it was my home. I never felt quite like I belonged in Boston, on Earth, really, as silly as it sounds," she tells me, smiling softly. "But I know you must love it, must love Boston—that much is very easy to understand from your radio show. It seems like your home, the place you're meant to be. You're passionate about the city; that much is clear."

I glance across the room at Attis, who's currently being embraced tightly by Kell, who's also whispering something in her ear. Attis' soft, happy expression recedes as she holds Kell out at arm's length, her eyes narrowing. She shakes her head once, twice, leaning forward and speaking lowly.

"I just don't know what to do," I tell Holly. My stomach clenches as I look to her, leaning against the window so peacefully. Happily, I realize. "Can I...can I ask you something?" I say, stepping close. Holly glances at me with a furrowed brow, but she nods. "What do you know of what happened...with Attis and Hera?"

"Oh, God," she mutters, biting her lip as she shakes her head. "It was terrible. It was over ten years ago now, but Attis has never forgotten. Honestly, today she seems happier than I've ever seen her. I hope you know that," Holly tells me quickly.

"But she's never been able to forget," I tell her, my heart sinking.

"Josie," says Holly gently, pushing off the wall and rubbing my shoulder in sympathy, "these are questions you should be asking Attis. Have you talked to her about this? About Hera?"

"No," I say miserably, taking a deep breath. "I mean, how can I even bring that up? *Is your dead lover coming between us*? That's really not the kind of conversation that—"

"It would be hard to talk about, I understand that," says Holly, crossing her arms in front of her, "but you need to talk to her about it. This is a huge

Bridget Essex

decision you're about to make, whether to go back home or not. I don't know exactly where Attis factors into that decision... I mean, you guys are together, right?"

"Yes," I tell her simply, with a slight shrug. "But I think there's something holding Attis back. I'm falling in love with her," I tell her, surprised that I'd be so vulnerable and open, but Holly has a kind face, the kind of face you tell big, vulnerable things to. And I think that out of all people in the universe, she'd understand about falling in love with a lady knight.

"Listen to me," says Holly then, leaning close to me, her brows furrowed and her eyes bright. "I let Virago go. It was by accident. She was drawn back to her world after the Boston Beast dragged her through—"

I feel the world fall away from me as I stare at her with wide eyes. "*What*?"

"The Boston Beast," she says impatiently, waving her hand. "It's not important. What *is* important is the fact that I realized after she left that I'd made the *biggest mistake of my life*. I'm not telling you what to do, or what I think you should do," she says, holding up her hands to me in a gesture of surrender, "but I'm telling you that whatever decision you make, whether you go through that portal or not, I want to make absolutely certain that you know exactly what you're getting into. It's almost impossible to come and go through the portals; you have to pretty much be decided that this is what you want to do. There are rarely second chances in life," she tells me, her voice pleading. "Just...think about everything. Think about what would make you happiest, and then, good God, do that thing. That's all that matters. Love, really, is the only thing that matters," she says quietly.

"Beloved!" Virago shouts jubilantly across the room, "Cenla has challenged me for your hand! Should I duel to the death, my love? I must defend your honor!"

The brocade-wearing woman shakes her head, laughing and holding up a hand. "I said you were beautiful, Holly, and she thinks this is a challenge! Can I not offer a compliment?"

"Virago, remember that Cenla told us our *curtains* were beautiful, too" says Holly, laughing. "And if you're going to duel, *please* do it outside. Remember what happened last week..."

When Holly looks back to me, her cheeks are pink, and her smile is almost flustered as she tucks a strand of red hair behind her ear. "Knights," she tells me with a laugh.

"She's so smitten with you," I tell her softly. I take a deep gulp of air, and then I speak the truth, even though it sounds terrible: "I wish Attis would look at me the way Virago looks at you."

"Josie," Holly says gently, leaning close to me, her brow furrowed, "she *does*. Attis and Virago are two very different people. I think your worry is clouding what's right there...right in front of you. I mean, I'm one to talk," says Holly, holding up her hands and shaking her head. "But, seriously...you need to speak with Attis about all of this. I think you might be surprised at what she tells you."

"Okay," I whisper with a weak smile,

nodding. "I'll try."

Holly reaches forward, and then she hugs me tightly. "Good luck, Josie," she tells me, her face wholly sincere as she smiles encouragingly.

The sound of breaking glass fills the room, followed by a roar of laughter.

"Oh, Lord," Holly mutters, but she's laughing as she rolls her eyes and mutters something about "knights" again, and then darts away to see what could possibly have just happened. "Virago, my love!" she shouts pointedly above the chaos. "Why don't you be a dear and start the festivities? Why don't you tell us a story?"

A roar of ascent accompanies Holly's words, and then—like a magical spell has come over the crowded room of women—everyone finds a seat and settles down, nursing their drinks as they turn, as one, to take in Virago, standing in the center of the room...standing a little sheepishly over the remains of what looks like it was once a teacup.

"Sorry, beloved. I got carried away with demonstrating the hack and slash dance," says Virago, leaning forward and sweeping up Holly in an arm and a passionate kiss. Virago then bends down easily, crouching as she picks up the pieces of the teacup in one hand and deposits them in a small woven basket by the door.

Attis is suddenly by my side, her pale cheeks warmed, I realize, by a bit of liquor as she presses her mouth fiercely to mine. She tastes like something finer than beer, something a little like grapes. Wine? Attis puts her hands around my waist; then she draws my back against her front as she sits down on one of the plush seats by the window, drawing me down onto her lap. She threads her fingers through mine, then leans her head against my shoulder as I lean back against her.

"Virago is a lovely storyteller," Attis whispers to me, her breath warm and soft against the skin of my neck. I shiver a little, then relax against her as she holds me tightly to her, her arms wrapped around me in a sweet embrace.

Virago clears her throat; then she stands in the center of the room, her feet hip-width apart, bowing her head, and when she looks up at us, her eyes are flashing.

She begins, her eyes bright with an intensity that transports me, and apparently everyone else in the room. "There was once a star," she breathes, raising her hand.

ᘓ

This was the very first star, the very first thing that ever existed, and whether she was a star who became a goddess or whether she was a goddess who became a star, we'll never quite know. Either way, the beautiful goddess shone, bright in an endless sea of darkness, and she was the only thing in existence, or so she thought.

And she was very lonely.

"Is this all there is, this sea of darkness?" she asked herself, one dark day. She shone brighter and brighter, trying to illuminate anything other than the blackness that surrounded her, but there was nothing else to see but the dark. "This cannot be all there is,"

she said to herself. So the goddess rose, burning brighter and fiercer, determined to find something other than herself in this sea of darkness.

She traveled a long, long way, tiring and resting and tiring and resting again. She went on and on forever, trailing light out behind her as she searched for another. But she journeyed in a sea of darkness, and she could not quite be sure if she was going in circles or if she was journeying as far as she thought she was. Had she even moved from her spot in space? She didn't know, but she kept believing, as she went, that there must be something besides her. There must *be.*

Finally, the goddess could go no further. She collapsed, miserable, exhausted, in the sea of darkness, feeling herself sinking into the black. She closed her eyes, felt her brightness dim. She didn't see any point to exist in this lonely place of nothingness if there was nothing else besides her.

And that's when strong hands lifted her chin, when strong hands picked her up from the sea of darkness, embracing her tightly. That's when her heart pressed against another.

The star goddess opened her eyes, and they were immediately filled with tears, for—before her— stood another star goddess, standing tall and strong. This star goddess was lovely, everything the star goddess had been searching for, but it wasn't that that touched her so deeply. It was the fact that, when the star goddess looked into the other's face, she knew now that she was no longer alone. That this perfect creature, by her mere existence, proved that there was something better in the universe than endless darkness and loneliness.

For the other star goddess had come into being at the other end of the universe. And, like the first star goddess, had waited and waited in her sea of darkness, waiting for something to change. Waiting for some reason to be. The sea of darkness was so vast and so wide, and she couldn't imagine that there was anything beside her, but she gathered her courage to her heart, and she set out in the blackness, searching for something else. For she, too, was utterly lonely.

The two goddesses embraced, and the two goddesses kissed, and where their bright, shining hearts touched one another, sparks began to fly, hissing sparks that arced through the endless sea of darkness, transforming the place. Whereas there was just darkness before, velvet blackness that was all-consuming, now there were the two goddesses and the many sparks, and, from there, everything else began to grow.

The two goddesses loved one another fiercely, and from their love, the worlds began to form.

The one star goddess became known as the great silver bear—the Ursa. And from her magnificent, strong heart, she turned the planets around and around until they were done and born. And the other star goddess became known as the great silver seal—the Selkie. And from her magnificent, kind heart, she turned the stars and moons around and around until they were done and born. And both goddesses loved one another so much that all existence came to be through their love.

When they were all said and done, when all

creatures were made and set in their places, the Ursa and the Selkie looked down at their worlds, and they watched the people try to live. But it was hard, in the beginning; life was difficult for everyone and everything, and the people were so cold. They, too, were lost in the dark.

"Let us give them one last gift," the two goddesses said together. "Out of love all things are made, after all." And they kissed, the Ursa and the Selkie. And this kiss—this kiss was so beautiful, so passionate, that the sparks that fell from their lips began to fall through the sky, hurtling toward the ground.

These sparks were stars, falling stars that fell through the heavens, landing at the feet of the people. The people lifted the stars in their hands, turning them this way and that, gazing down at the gift their goddesses had given them.

And those stars were the very first fires. The very first gift of many that the goddesses have given us.

And that night was the very first Festival of Stars, that night that we celebrate this *night, for this is a festival born of love, like all great things.*

慓

My heart is thudding in my chest as Virago finishes the story, sweeping a flourished bow to applause and cheers, the women raising their mugs and glasses to her in a very messy toast (most of them are already *really* drunk).

I stare at Virago, my mouth open, as I think

about that star goddess...

The goddess who was, or so this story says, a silver bear.

"Attis," I begin quietly, turning to glance back at her, but she doesn't seem to hear me. Attis is rising, pressing a kiss to my shoulder as she gently pushes me off of her lap to stand and stretch.

"We've got to get going if we're going to have camp set up by the time the stars begin," Attis tells Virago, stepping forward as she takes the other knight's forearm in her hand, gripping it tightly, as Virago grips hers. "We'll see you tomorrow, though, the both of you, yes?" asks Attis, her head to the side as she flicks her bright gaze from Virago, who stands before her, to Holly, who comes to stand beside Virago. "We'll get this all sorted...tomorrow," says Attis quietly.

We'll get this all sorted. I'm assuming she means...me.

I take a deep breath, my heart thrumming blood through me as I bite my lip nervously. I might be going home tomorrow.

But there's something that's bothering me, and I really need to know... "Virago," I say, stepping forward as other women come and go, clapping the knight on the back for the delivery of her story or telling her she's out of a particular kind of beer (some problems are, apparently, universal). "Virago, that story you just told—it's a great story, by the way," I tell her quickly as she turns, smiling to me. "Um...the silver-bear-goddess-person in the story..."

"The Ursa," Virago supplies easily. "One of our goddesses that we worship here on Agrotera, though she's one of the older ones, to be sure, just as that story is one of the older ones. But it's always good to tell it around the Festival of Stars. My mother told me that story when I was very, very small," she says, her full mouth turning up at the corners as her eyes glitter with unshed tears. "And that was a very long time ago. But I love telling that story because it helps me feel closer to her. Like she's still part of these festivities, even though she's long gone."

"That's...that's lovely," I tell her, taking a deep breath. It *is* lovely, and I feel like a heel for bringing this up now, but I soldier forward. "I just think it's strange, that it's a silver bear in the story. There's another silver bear, right?" I ask her, lifting my brow.

Virago pales a little, glancing at Attis. "Well, yes. There was," she says, lifting her chin. "But—"

"We'll see you tomorrow, the both of you," says Attis, her jaw clenched, and then she has my arm in her grip, and she's pulling me backward, out of the warm, infectiously happy rooms to the cold chill of twilight on the balcony. I hardly have time to scoop up Wonder before we're out in the cold.

I put Wonder under my coat and do up the buttons as I watch Attis, my brows furrowed. Attis shuts the door behind her and shakes her head once, letting out her breath in a long sigh. Her sigh comes out into the air between us like smoke, spiraling upward toward the very first star of the night, peeking out of the deep blue heavens.

"What's wrong?" I ask her, drawing my coat closer to me, feeling the weight of Wonder rest against me. She begins to purr under the warmth of my coat.

"I was the only one," says Attis then, lifting her chin and staring deeply into my eyes. "I was the only one who saw the bear that day." Her jaw is so tense, and she sighs again as she leans forward, running a gloved hand through her hair.

Overhead, a shooting star arcs across the sky, dragging a trail of light across the brilliant blue.

"The only one," I repeat softly. "But...Hera was killed by the bear..."

"When I reached her," Attis says woodenly, "she was dead, lying face down in the shallow water of the river. There was the silver bear standing next to her, in the mud, her head pointed toward Hera. When the bear saw me..." Attis takes another deep breath. "She opened her maw and roared at me. There were wolves everywhere; there was the chaos of battle... She roared, and then she just... She just vanished. Disappeared. I told the knights what happened, after I took Hera to try to be resurrected. They said they'd seen no bear, that it hadn't actually happened. That the extreme trauma of losing Hera meant that I'd seen something that wasn't there. Virago believed me...sort of," says Attis, raising a single brow artfully. "She knows that I'm calm and steady," she says gruffly, "and that I never make things up. That I see what's really there, even when there was no other evidence than the fact that I say I saw the bear. But I've never stopped believing what I know I saw. And then you...you saw the bear. There were bits of fur on your blanket. You *saw* her. And you saw her again."

I take a deep breath, steeling myself as I reach

up, brushing my fingers over the locket lying in the hollow of my throat. "How do you know it was the bear who killed Hera?" I ask her.

"Because I know," Attis tells me quietly.

And then, as I watch in shock, tears spring up in the corners of Attis' eyes.

"I know," she repeats brokenly.

A wash of pain floods through me, and I do the only thing I can do; I step forward, I wrap Attis tightly in my arms, and I hold her to me. Wonder, for once in her life, remains quiet and doesn't protest. "I'm so sorry," I whisper into her ear, and then a great sob wracks Attis, a sob that seems to come from the deepest part of her.

"I was... I was right *there*, and I couldn't save her," says Attis after a long moment of silence. That one sob was the only one she allowed herself. "I was right there," she repeats, her words and eyes haunted, "and I *couldn't save her*."

I hold her tightly, feeling the familiar flare of ache deep inside of me, too.

I take a deep breath.

"One night, when I was twenty," I tell her, taking a step back and holding her gaze, "I had too much to drink. I was driving a car. It's like a carriage, I guess, on your world, but it's powered by a motor. It was powered and steered by me." I take a deep breath, tears leaking out of the corners of my eyes, too. "I'd had too much to drink, but I lied to my sister. I said I was fine to take us back home, but I wasn't fine. I got us into an accident, a bad accident, and my sister...she died. I've spent every day, since that terrible night, blaming myself. And, yes, analytically, it's my fault. But I know now that Ellie wouldn't want me to live every day of my life as some sort of penitence for making a mistake. If you could have saved Hera, you would have. No questions. I know you now," I whisper, holding her gaze. "I know that you're strong and fierce and utterly courageous."

Something flickers over her warm, amber eyes, but I keep going.

"I know you're tremendously loyal. That the people you care about you care about *forever*. I know that, having spent just a few short days with you. You're *extraordinary*, Attis," I tell her, and then I fall silent, blush flushing through my cheeks, my heart pounding a million miles a minute.

Attis watches me as darkness falls around us. Even in the deep, velvet blue of twilight, the gold of her eyes shines as she gazes at me, her face softening. She reaches up and gently brushes her thumb across my cheek, wiping away my tears. Her hand remains, the warm leather of the palm of her glove caressing my skin.

"I've cared for no one since Hera," she says then gruffly, her voice low and shaky, but she continues. "And then you came, Josie. You came, and now..." She trails off, bends toward me, holding my gaze. "And now you're breaking my heart," she whispers.

You're breaking my heart.

I stare up at her, a shiver moving through me as she bends low and brushes her mouth over mine. She kisses me softly, gently, as a single tear rolls down her face, hot and sweet and salty as it falls to our lips and I taste it as I taste her. As she tastes me.

The ache unfurls inside of me, so absolute that I'm consumed by it.

But, just then, there's a flash of light in the sky as Attis straightens, as she looks up. I can't help but gaze up, too, because there's another great flash, so bright you'd think there was a violent thunderstorm, that lightning is blossoming along the edges of the sky and that a deep roll of thunder is about to wash over us, too, but that's not what's happening at all.

Up in the sky, there's *light*. Because there are falling stars, falling stars *everywhere*.

I know that falling stars aren't *actually* stars, but what's really weird is that. as I tilt my head back and look up at the meteorites trailing light behind themselves as they fall toward earth...I really think they *are* stars. Which would, of course, be impossible. But they're so bright, so vivid, in the night sky, those pinpoints of light, growing larger as they descend toward us...

"It's beginning," Attis tells me sadly, her smile soft as she gazes up with me, her arms wrapped tightly around me. My ear is pressed to her chest now, and I can hear the steady, comforting thrum of her heartbeat.

"What is?" I ask her, unable to tear my gaze away from the millions of falling points of light.

Attis sighs and then wraps her arms tighter around me, turning me gently so that my back is pressed to her front. She lowers her head slowly and places her chin on my shoulder, and, together, we watch the falling light.

"The Festival of Stars," she whispers, her

breath warm against my ear, causing me to shiver again as we watch the stars fall.

They *are* stars. I watch these points of light fall, growing a little alarmed as I see how close they're coming to us...but none actually hit us. The glowing spheres of light fall to the ground and touch gently down, bouncing there almost like a rubber ball until they land still against the cobblestones. Attis and I walk down the stairs from Virago and Holly's balcony, and when we reach the ground, I crouch down to stare at the closest glowing orb.

It's about six inches wide and perfectly spherical, this orb, glowing as brightly as if a light bulb were lit inside of it, but I know that's impossible.

They're falling all around us now, sailing gently down to earth and bouncing lightly on the ground with little *whoop* sounds as they finally settle. More and more of them fall, raining down all around us. One brushes against my shoulder, but because it's so light, I can hardly even feel it until I see it bouncing away behind me and realize that's what that soft touch was.

"What *are* they?" I ask Attis, glancing sidelong at her as she crouches down next to me, a small smile tugging up the corners of her lips.

"Stars," she replies maddeningly, one brow up as she reaches down and picks up one of the spheres, the orb settling into the palm of her hand. She reaches forward and holds it out to me. "Don't worry; it won't burn you," she says, her head to the side. Tentatively, I reach out and take it.

There's a very pleasant warmth in my hands as I hold it in front of me. "A star?" I repeat.

"It's just like the story," says Attis, rising smoothly and helping me up, her fingers wrapped gently around my elbow. "These are stars that fall, every Festival of Stars, so that we can have fire throughout the year. They're not really needed now. We know how to make fire," she says, her smile soft, "but still, the stars fall. And you can use them as fire starters, so people take them into their houses and do exactly like...like their mothers did before them, and their mothers before them..."

"This sets fires to things?" I ask her, alarmed, but Attis shakes her head, reaching out and scooping the orb up from my hands.

"Only if you activate them," she tells me, turning the orb in her hand. She flicks her gaze up to me, her eyes soft. "They're a sign that the goddess still watches out for us, still takes care of us."

I keep my mouth shut. I don't claim to know how the universe was created or if there's a higher power or not, but I've never exactly believed in one myself. I'm not going to tell Attis that she's incorrect for believing anything she wants to believe.

And, hell, I don't exactly have an alternative explanation for stars falling from the sky.

"On my world, this isn't what we consider a star," is what I tell her then, taking the orb back from her and staring down at it, turning it this way and that in my hands. "Those are stars," I tell her, pointing up at the stars that are now coming out in the darkening sky, far above us.

Attis stares at me curiously. "This doesn't happen on your world?"

"Yeah, *no*," I tell her, brows up as I let the star

fall from my fingers, bouncing gently on the ground until it rolls to a stop against the stairs that lead up to Virago and Holly's balcony. "You guys are very lucky," I tell her quietly, gazing around at all of the people coming down out of their houses and shops, gathering the stars that landed at their feet. Some women just pile them in their arms; others place them in the fronts of their skirts that they hold out before them. Two women close by us are laughing together, picking up stars and depositing them into baskets as they hold hands. I take a deep breath, gaze down at the stars littering the ground. "You're lucky," I repeat quietly. "This is... This is magical."

Attis smiles at me, but it's a tired smile. "Shall we go?" she asks, gesturing toward the livery stables. "We should be able to make it out of the city much easier than getting into it. There are fewer travelers on the road right now, and we should set up camp before we lose all the light."

I nod, feeling my heart flutter inside of my chest as she turns away from me. For a moment, her profile was etched against the starry sky, and it hurt to look at her, because I want her so fiercely.

I reach down, scoop up one of the stars, and holding its warmth against me, I follow after Attis.

I am hyper aware that this is the last: the last time that we journey together, even though it's so close, the encampment. This is the last time that we spend a night together.

I'm highly aware that this will be the last night for *everything*.

Unless I stay.

Chapter 13: The Parting

We reach the city gate just as they're about to lower it for the evening.

"Sorry we're late, Rexie," says Attis, waving to the knight who's gripping tightly the wooden base the gate's chain is attached to. "Thanks for holding the gate for us," Attis tells Rexie, who grimaces a little, but smiles after she releases the wooden bar, slowly walking it around and around the winch, letting the chain release as we pass beneath it. The iron gate clicks down behind us.

"You're just fashionably late, Attis, my dear," says Rexie. "Why aren't you staying for the big party at the barracks? You know you're always welcome." Rexie leaves the winch to come stand on the other side of the gate, threading her arms through the iron bars to lean comfortably against it. "There's a side door I could let you in. You're...*very* welcome, you know," she tells Attis, waggling her brows high and putting her head to the side suggestively.

And, yeah, the look that this lady knight is giving Attis is a little more than friendly.

"Thank you kindly, but I'm busy tonight," says Attis, looping an arm around my shoulders and drawing me close to her. She presses her warm mouth against my forehead, and Rexie raises her brows, backing away from the gate with a shrug.

"Well, then, suit yourself," she tells us, turning to stride back into the city, the city that's breaking out into music and dance on the streets as the stars are gathered up by countless celebratory women.

Walking down the main road outside of the city, the encampment opening up on either side of the cobblestone street, I see that people out here are scooping up the stars, too. But, honestly, it seems like a more wild party is breaking out beyond the walls. The music out here has more of a distinct drumbeat to it, the kind of beat that gets into your blood, that makes you want to dance. It's primal, and it's starting to thrum through me, mirroring my heartbeat as it quickens.

"Let's find a place to set up the tent," Attis tells me quietly, hooking her arm around my waist and pulling me closer, Zilla walking along companionably behind us. "And then..." Attis tells me, trailing off as she trains her bright, golden eyes on my face. "Do you want to dance?"

I look up at her, at her face, silhouetted by the night sky, illuminated by the hundreds, perhaps thousands of fallen stars littering the ground, glowing sweetly and brightening the night. Attis is quiet as she asks me that question, but there's so much behind her words, so much that she's not saying. Her face is unreadable as she gazes down at me, but...

But...

This is the last night.

I think we both know that.

Unless I stay.

"I'd love to dance," I tell her quietly, reaching across the divide between us and taking her hand in mine, threading my fingers through hers like we fit together, she and I. Attis squeezes my hand gently, and then, leading Zilla along behind us, we turn and continue down the road together.

We find a clear spot close to the road for setting up our camp, and Attis ground ties Zilla, removing her packs off the saddle and then unsaddling her enormous horse. I set Wonder down onto the ground and tell her to stick close, but—of course—she's my cat, and she darts away the moment my back is turned. Again, I remind myself that she came across worlds to find me, so she'll find me again, but it's nerve-wracking having her run all around this enormous encampment. I help Attis pitch the tent (I'm almost becoming a pro at this point), and then Attis is starting our fire, and I'm inside the tent, unrolling my bedroll, setting up our meager living quarters...

But that's when I feel Attis enter the tent behind me. I can feel her presence as she moves soundlessly through the tent flap, and then she ties the flap closed behind her, kneeling in the entrance and breathing steadily.

I know why she's here. I know why she's come, and we have to talk; we have to talk now. Because I need to tell her that I don't know what to do. I need to tell her that I don't know if I should stay or if I should go. That I know I'm not meant for this world...

But that I know I'm meant for *her*.

Why were we born on separate worlds if we fit so perfectly together? It's maddening to me that this is how it should have happened, that I fell for a knight from another world...

But what if we're supposed to be together? What if we're *supposed* to be, in that enormous, cosmic, woo-woo way that I would have rolled my eyes at a mere week ago...but am now finding that I'm starting to believe?

You're breaking my heart, Attis whispered to me. And I feel that ache, because my heart is breaking too, damn it.

I don't want to make this decision, but I have to. It would have been so clear seven days ago. But no. I had to go and fall in love.

Attis shifts behind me—I can hear her moving softly over the ground, and then I feel her hands curling around my waist, pulling me back against her, turning me as her mouth finds me.

No matter what, I don't regret falling in love. I don't regret it for a heartbeat.

We should talk about what's happening. About what will happen tomorrow. We should talk about what's happened between us, how we've changed together. We should talk about the fact that I'm in love with her, and I'm pretty sure she's in love with me. We should talk about that love.

But it would all be wasted words, words that would hurt and make our hearts ache.

And we don't have enough time for that.

So when her mouth finds mine, I welcome her, a single tear leaking out of my right eye, tracing hotly down my cheek as she pushes me down gently on my blanket roll, rising over me like a falling star. When her armor presses against me, I fumble with my fingers at the buckles at her sides and waist, over her arms. I need her more than I need oxygen, more than I've ever needed anything in my entire life.

This is the last time.

Unless I stop this.

I fumble with the leather straps, making a growl of frustration in the back of my throat. The last buckle gives way, and her armor falls to the ground, and then she's there, over me, her pale skin hot and sweet and everything I need as my clothes fall away, too, beneath her careful hands, her careful hands she runs over my skin, knowing every last place that makes me shiver, that makes me gasp with need.

We are together, length to length, curve to curve, heart to heart as she covers me, covers me and tastes me and merges with me utterly.

There's never been a more perfect moment, I know, as my heart aches, as my center aches, and she finds me wet and wanting, smiling against me in her knowing way as she traces a smooth pattern of kisses down my neck, capturing my breasts in a hot and perfect mouth. Everything is moving too fast, and I desperately want to slow it down. I want to slow down the relentless march of time. I want this moment to last forever.

I grip her tightly, wrap my legs around her waist, my arms around her shoulders, lift my chest to her mouth, arching beneath her, offering everything that I am and more, and then turning, turning, twisting beneath her as I climb on top of her, tasting, drinking her in.

And that's when time seems to stop. When I'm straddling her, when I'm rising over her, in her, my fingers wet with her need for me, my beautiful knight utterly open beneath me, open and wanting and holding my gaze with her sparking amber eyes because she can't look away, because holding my gaze makes this more vulnerable and intense...

Because holding my gaze, in this moment, means that she sees to the very core of me.

I stop. I stop, panting, over her, stop everything, and the drumbeat of the night rises around us, the whooping and hollering and exultation of the people in the encampment around us as they celebrate life and a world that would give them fire and stars to fall at their feet.

"I can't do this," I whisper to her. Attis stares up at me, her fingers gripping my arms tightly, her warm palms washing my skin in surety. I take a deep breath as she holds my gaze. "I want to stay," I tell her.

Attis' eyes grow wider in the dark. "You know what that means," she whispers to me, her low voice full of emotion. I watch her face in the darkness of the tent, follow the curves of her cheeks, of her nose, of her chin and jaw and neck. Every last swell and curve of her is perfect to my eyes; every last word she utters is one I want to hear. Her laughter and her intensity and her calm, quiet surety are anchors in my heart.

"I know," I tell her, breathing out.

And then I lick my lips, and I say the truest thing I know: "I want you," I murmur quietly. "I need to stay."

Attis rises up onto her elbows, her mouth an inch from my own as she sighs, her breath ragged. "Say it again," she whispers, her eyes flashing in the dark.

"I want you," I tell her, my blood roaring through me as the truth of those three words becomes so clear. So perfectly clear, like a bright star falling in the night. I don't know why I didn't see it before. I want her. I love her. I need to stay. There is no decision.

I need to stay.

"Josie," she whispers, and her voice cracks on that single word. I love it when she says my name; she speaks those two syllables like my name is the most important and precious word she's ever heard. Like it's a prayer. And when she speaks my name now, her full lips and tongue tasting the word like it's precious to her, I know I made the right decision. I know that I'm meant to do this; I know, I know...

My eyes full of tears, my heart welling with emotion that I've not let spill in so very long, I take a deep breath. The world is spinning beneath me, but it stops for the span of a heartbeat. It stops when I whisper, "I love—"

There's a scream.

It's a breathless, piercing scream, like someone was caught unawares, in surprise, but not like anything terrible is happening. I honestly wouldn't have stopped speaking if the scream hadn't happened so close. But then the scream comes again, almost immediately after that first one, and it no longer sounds surprised. It's high-pitched, that scream, urgent. And, honestly, blood-curdling.

And then there are more screams, one after the other, in a chorus of terror.

And, outside of our tent, I hear a vicious snarl.

Beneath me, Attis stiffens immediately, her body tensing as her skin turns white as a sheet, and she's immediately pulling away from me, sliding out from under me in a seamless motion, sitting up. I ease back in shock as she throws her leather shirt on over her head, threading her arms through the sleeves and her neck through the neck hole, pulling on her pants in one vicious jerk and grabbing up her sword in a single instant. And then she's at the tent flap, undoing the ties and out before I can even blink.

Fumbling, with shaking hands, I try to find my clothes as there are more screams, terrified screams, the kinds of screams I've never heard before in my life, all accompanied by the sounds of animal snarling, the snarls so vicious and otherworldly that every hair on the back of my neck is standing on end.

Honestly, if I didn't know better, I'd say it sounded like a...

"Wolf!" comes a woman's bellow from somewhere close by. "The wolves are attacking! Everyone, up, up! Grab a weapon! Stand your ground! Protect the children and the infirm! Now, *now*!"

The sound of a horn resounds around the encampment, for a brief moment louder than the sounds of the screaming people and the snarling of the wolves as I finally fumble into my coat and my pajama bottoms, hands shaking as I do up the buttons.

I'm out of the tent flap, standing in the middle

of what looks like a war zone. There are shadows of people running everywhere; they're hard to see because there appears to have been a fire started. Hazy smoke hangs in the air, and at the edge of the encampment, it's too unnaturally orange in the sky. I can smell something burning, and it makes me cough, the smoke stinging the back of my throat, my eyes. Women run around me, racing past me, but they're not running in any particular direction. This is panic, pure panic, causing everyone to race every which way, trying to outrun *something*.

I stand perfectly still, holding my breath as my heart thuds against my ribs.

Because there, striding with a predatory gait down the center of the stone road, is a massive wolf.

Its shoulders are as high as my waist, and it prowls with a surety and savage grace that's breathtaking at the exact same time that it's utterly terrifying. I think there's something hardwired in all of us that makes seeing a wolf in the "wild," uncontained and unstoppable, something that reaches back into the deepest instinctual parts of ourselves. Our oldest cavemen ancestors were the ones who survived wolf attacks, the ones who knew to run the moment they saw a wolf...

But as I stare at that wolf, a chilling thought freezes me to my bones. As the wolf prowls down the center of the street, I realize that it reminds me of something. Of someone.

It reminds me of Wonder.

"Wonder?" I call, terror making my word tiny. I try again, belting out her name as I turn away from the wolf. There are so many people running around me, so much smoke and chaos that it's impossible to make out anything but the shadows of running bodies racing past me, the shadow of the wolf as it pauses in its stalking down the street, pauses and lifts its snout, breathing in the chaos and the smoke.

"Wonder!" I call again, holding my coat tightly to me as I take another gulp of air and cough, the smoke stinging my lungs. "Wonder?" I crouch down, try to make out the shapes better in the increasing smoke.

"Josie," comes my name, the word soft and sharp, and then I'm being pulled upright, Attis' fingers curling around my arm so tightly that when I fold into her embrace, the smoke is almost squeezed right out of my lungs. "Josie, the wolves are attacking," she tells me, voice soft and low as she stares down at me with her warm amber eyes that are flashing with something I can't quite place.

"Attis," I tell her, gripping her shoulders, eyes wide with fear, "I can't find Wonder."

Attis glances down the corridor of tents and back to the main road—the main road where the wolf has vanished. Zilla dances in place on her picket next to our tent, swishing her tail, her nose lifted to the wind as she tosses her head over and over again nervously, making low snorts as she paws at the ground.

"Don't worry, I'll find Wonder, but we've got to get you to safety," Attis tells me, her jaw clenched. "I need to help these people, too. There are more knights coming," she says quickly. "I heard the summoning horn. But the knights have to take the back way out; they can't open the gate and risk an attack on the city. So they're not going to get here in time if we don't stand against them."

Attis takes my arm with her warm, reassuring fingers, and then we move toward Zilla's side in the smoke.

"You'll have to ride her bareback. I'm sorry; there's no time to saddle her," Attis tells me, and then she cups her hands and kneels down. I want to argue with her, want to tell her that I have to stay, but I saw the look in her eyes. I saw the past flicker across her face, how finding Hera dead destroyed her. So I step into Attis' hands, my world and mind spinning as the screams continue, as the smoke thickens. She tosses me lightly up onto Zilla's back, and there's a terrifying moment where I think I'm going to fall over Zilla's shoulder onto the other side; her fur is shiny and so smooth that it's hard for me to find purchase on her without a saddle, but I grip my legs around the mare's barrel and weave my fingers into her mane.

"She's a trained warhorse. There is no way that she would let a wolf touch you," says Attis, reaching up to brush her fingers across my face as I lean down to her. She clenches her jaw, takes a deep breath. "Zilla will take you away from here, keep you safe until the knights arrive."

"Attis, I don't want to leave you," I tell her, my heart in my throat.

"You'll be *safe*," she says firmly, gazing up at me with unwavering golden eyes. "I love you, Josie," she tells me then, her voice breaking, and before I can respond, before I can say anything, she smacks Zilla's rump hard. Zilla snorts, dancing sideways, and then bolts through the chaos of the encampment, angling away from the encampment and the castle, her hooves thundering over the ground.

I grip Zilla's barrel as tightly as I can, curl my fingers into her mane and hold on for dear life, adrenaline pouring through me as I slip and slide on her back, scrabbling for purchase and so that I don't go sailing through the air and hit the ground. We're racing through the edge of the encampment, passing falling tents and women holding sword. Fire is spreading through the tents almost as fast as Zilla can run.

Everything passes by in a blur as I cling to Zilla's neck, but then, as we race through a tent corridor, I see someone lying in the center of the aisle of tents, face down, and there, crouching over her, is a wolf...

"Whoa! Whoa!" I yell at Zilla desperately, and—surprising no one more than me—Zilla actually grinds to a halt, her back legs crouching under her as she stops on a dime, tossing her head in the air. Somehow, I manage to sit her abrupt stop, and with noodly legs slipping on her barrel, I make a very quick decision.

"Just...just stay right here, okay?" I tell the horse, my voice cracking from the smoke. I have no idea how I think I'm going to get back up on her, but I don't know what else to do, so I slide off Zilla's back, and then I'm running at the wolf with shaky legs and no plan whatsoever.

"Get away from her!" I scream, picking up the closest thing I can find—a skirt just laying on the ground. The wolf is crouching over the woman, snarl lifting its lips, viciously revealing about a million

320

extremely pointy, extremely long white teeth, and I just have a *skirt,* of all things, to fight this creature with, but I wave the flimsy fabric at the wolf again, shouting as loudly as I can. They're unintelligible noises I'm bellowing, but adrenaline is surging through me, and all I know is that there's a woman on the ground, a hurt woman who needs someone's help—and that someone is going to have to be me.

The wolf takes one step backwards in surprise, the hackles on its back rising even farther as its snarl deepens.

"Are you okay? Hello?" I ask the woman on the ground. I'm worried that if I make the tiniest movement, this apparent staring contest between myself and the wolf will stop, and I'll have technically "blinked," the wolf launching itself at me and burying its jaws in my throat. But I don't have to wait long. The woman lying on the ground lifts her head tentatively, staring at me with wide, terrified eyes.

"Please help me," she whispers.

She's younger than me, with bright red hair and big blue eyes. She's very pretty, I realize, in the back of my head, but what I notice most is the fine white skin of her neck—and how it's torn open, blood pouring out of the wound onto the ground.

Like, a *lot* of blood. Oh, God.

"Zilla? A little help here!" I yell at the top of my lungs.

And, again—surprising no one more than me—Zilla actually listens to me and charges forward, stomping her massive hooves at the wolf as she sits back on her big, horsey haunches and stomps again and again, bugling a neigh that actually sounds kind of terrifying. The wolf flattens its ears in response to Zilla's advances, and when Zilla stomps her huge hooves even closer to its head, the wolf actually bolts away, tail between its legs as Zilla chases after it, her teeth bared, her head snaking, and her ears slicked back, like she's going to kill the wolf herself.

"Come on," I tell the woman, my voice shaking as I help her sit up, pressing the skirt in my hands against her neck to help staunch the flow of blood, the blood that's seeping down her skin, dripping onto her dress. "You need help," I tell her quietly, as Zilla circles back to me, tossing her head and snorting in, what seems to me, at least, an air of triumph and self-satisfaction. "Zilla—come here, girl?" I ask the big, black horse, and she trots over to me, peering down at the woman with wide brown eyes.

"Stand still, okay?" I ask the horse, and then I pull the woman to a semi-standing position with a grunt of effort. All I can think about is what Attis told me, how blood attracts predators, and then what Virago told me, how defenseless things will attract predators, and how there are many, *many* predators around, and how I have to get this woman to safety *right now*.

"I'm going to help you get up on the horse, okay?" I say to the woman, but her head is lolling back—probably from the loss of too much blood. She's losing consciousness. "Shit," I mutter to myself. "*Shit*," I mutter again, glancing around. There's no one in this corridor of tents, though I can hear screaming and yelling coming from very close by. I gulp air, coughing from the smoke. "Zilla, come closer," I tell the horse, the horse who *probably* doesn't understand actual words, my voice catching as I sob out in frustration, the woman falling against me.

But Zilla bows her front legs down, and miraculously, she's a lot lower. "Remind me how many carrots I owe you," I tell the horse, gritting my teeth as I lift the woman up onto Zilla, the woman's stomach pressing against the horse's back, her arms dangling over the other side of Zilla's shoulder.

I'm about to climb up behind her onto Zilla, very, very ready to get the hell out of Dodge, when I stop, a chill racing through me.

I thought I heard...

"Wonder?" I yell out, turning and peering as best as I can through the smoke. I thought I heard a very soft meow. I could have *sworn* I heard it. "Wonder, are you there?" I yell again, taking a deep breath and shielding my eyes from the smoke, frantically trying to find my cat in the chaos.

And, blessedly, miraculously, my beautiful, crazy gray cat darts out from the flap of a tent, her tail so large, and all of the fur on her back standing straight up, that I know—for once in her life—my cat is actually terrified.

"Oh, my God, baby, come here!" I call to her, dropping to my knees and holding out my arms so that she can make a beeline toward me.

Out of the corner of my eye I see a shadow looming to my right, but I don't want to break my eye contact with Wonder. When Wonder tackles me, running straight into my arms, I turn, letting my breath out in a great whoosh.

A few feet from us is a wolf.

Zilla snorts, stomping her right front hoof, but because the woman is now unconscious on top of her, Zilla can't move too much without the woman falling off and possibly hurting herself worse. I stand quickly, holding Wonder tightly to me, holding the wolf's gaze as I hold my hand up to Zilla, trying to calm her and steady her.

The wolf has a massive, hairless scar across its snout, making it look even more vicious as it raises its lips in a snarl, hackles on its blackish back raised. I stand my ground, taking another step back. I somehow need to climb up onto Zilla's back and get out of here. I have to do this. I don't have a choice. I dig deep and find a scrap of courage and strength inside of me to try just that. I'm going to make a running leap for Zilla and climb up behind the unconscious woman, somehow holding her and Wonder on Zilla's back as Zilla runs out of the encampment. I think I can do it. I think I can do it— as I take a deep breath, ready to turn and bolt and leap up onto Zilla...

But that's when the wolf moves.

The wolf is impossibly fast, faster than I could have imagined. It launches itself into the air as I turn, and I feel its massive, muscular bulk hitting me squarely in the side. I don't have time to stop its lunge. I skid into the ground, hitting it squarely, the big wolf right on top of me.

Wonder gets knocked out of my arms, and she bolts for safety. Zilla rears up a little but remains with her four hooves on the ground, tossing her head nervously as she dances out of the way, picking her hooves up high as she tries to keep the woman on her back.

I stare up at the wolf who stares down at me, its wide eyes mad, its snout flecked with blood and spittle...

And somewhere, in the back of my mind, I realize...its eyes?

They look *human*.

The wolf rolls off of me when a force hits it very, very hard, force in the form of a woman rushing it. *Attis*. She's here. The wolf rolls end over end as Attis reaches down, grasps my hand and, in a single, fluid motion, pulls me to my feet. She holds her sword up, horizontal to the ground, as the wolf rolls, stops, shakes itself briskly and rounds on her, snarling, lips up and over very long teeth.

"I've got you," Attis whispers, glancing back at me with flashing golden eyes.

"Attis!" I yell, as the wolf attacks, launching itself and its wide, gaping jaws full of wickedly white teeth at her. It grabs her arm, and because she's not wearing her armor, when its teeth sink into the leather of her shirt, the teeth go through. All the way through.

Attis swings her sword down, but the wolf has the upper hand, dragging her backward as it twists to the side, the sword slicing past its body but doing no damage at all, because the wolf pulled her off balance. I step back, my heart in my throat, as Attis is pulled so far off balance, so quickly and viciously, that she doesn't have time to correct herself. She falls to her knees.

And the wolf lets go of her arm and darts

forward, bloody teeth aimed at her throat.

I react instantly. I run at the wolf, and then I hit it hard with my hands and arms. The wolf hardly budges, but its trajectory is slightly off because of my impact, and when the wolf snaps its jaws close to Attis' neck, it doesn't get her neck in its mouth, only a gulp of air beside her face.

Attis holds the sword up, blood dripping from her arm into the ground below us, but she still wraps her injured arm around me, holding me tightly to her.

"I love you," I tell her breathlessly, bracing myself as the wolf shakes itself, as it narrows its eyes, snarls, crouches in front of us.

Attis presses her mouth to the top of my head, grits her teeth, raises her sword, and the wolf charges.

And everything seems to...slow.

There's a flash of silver light, silver light that falls around us, like starlight. The light is so intense that it's all I can see for a long moment as my breath catches in my throat. I blink furiously, rubbing the back of my hand over my eyes.

But when I can finally see, I gasp.

The wolf is no longer in front of us.

It's...gone.

Starlight continues to fall like glitter from the sky, drifting gently toward the ground. This isn't the stars of earlier, falling to cobblestone streets and bouncing like light rubber balls. This is dusty light, pouring down, falling over everything. Powdered light that glows as it hits the grass and dirt.

Ahead of us, down the corridor of the encampment, I see something massive and silver, moving gently between the tents.

It's her. The bear. I take a deep breath as she gazes back at me with brilliant blue eyes. I don't know why, but when she gazes at me, I feel her in my heart, and I know that she saved us somehow.

"She saved us," Attis whispers. She gulps down air. "It was never the Ursa," she says then, voice soft. "It was the wolves who took Hera. I know that now. She's been helping us all along."

I turn to look at Attis, to kiss Attis, to hold her tight and tell her over and over again, as I sob out the adrenaline, that *we did it*. We survived. I want to tell her again that I love her, love her so much, and that I'm so happy that—across worlds—we managed to find each other.

But Attis isn't there. Nothing is there. Suddenly, everything is black, and the world around me fades away.

And I'm falling forward into complete darkness.

Chapter 14: The Beginning

I hit the ground so hard the breath is knocked out of me.

I lie there for a moment, shock soaring through me, my breath stuck in my throat. Then I gasp, breathe out, sit up, pressing my palms to the...

...to the *concrete.*

"Oh, my God," I whisper, taking in another deep, ragged breath as I push up, sitting up, staring around me.

Overhead, the single light bulb swings back and forth, back and forth. My suitcase lies open next to me, dirty clothing spilling out of it and onto the concrete floor. The washer sits in the corner, my laundry detergent perched on the lip of the washer.

Outside of the building, I can hear the familiar honking and screeching of brakes, the music of traffic in Boston.

I'm...home.

"No..." I whisper, standing up unsteadily, turning around. "No!" I yell, taking another deep breath and racing on unsteady legs toward the dark part of the basement.

But the dark part of the basement is smaller

than I remember it being. There are small holes in the wall, but they're only about a foot across.

There's no hole in the floor. There's nothing but standing water, and—out of the corner of my eye—a rat scurries past, diving into the nearest cavity in the wall.

I take a deep breath, staring down at myself. I'm wearing the Scooby Doo shirt, my leopard print bottoms. They look dirty. They look like they did when I left the tent. But I'm not wearing the werewolf coat.

I crouch down, bury my hands in my hair, try to breathe, try to understand what just happened to me.

I saw the bear. And then...I was back here.

I'm back home.

"Oh, God, Attis," I whisper, tears pouring down my cheeks as I stand up, as I pace in small circles, running my hands over the walls of the basement, trying to find an opening, a crack, a door...anything. But of course there's nothing there.

The portal opened and took me back through. And it's closed again.

I sink down to my knees, and then there's no more holding back the tears. They stream down my face as I put my head in my hands, as I sob out in the darkness of my basement.

Somehow, I manage to get to the elevator. I manage to punch the right floor button, and I manage to get up to my apartment. My keys are in the pocket of my bottoms, and I fumble with them at the door.

When I get into my apartment, I stare at what was once so familiar of a room. My living room.

There's my red couch with the teal blue pillows, the bright aqua walls and the terribly messy kitchen. There's Wonder, sitting on the counter, licking her lips as she digs into the bowl of wet food.

I stare at everything around me, breaking down inside. It was once so familiar, but now it's foreign to me. I hardly recognize anything, like I'm looking at it all with different eyes.

Which I am, I realize, as I sink down on one of my stools by the kitchen counter. Wonder saunters over to me, pressing her forehead against my forehead as I wrap my cat in my arms, drawing her close to me, and I begin to sob into her fur.

Getting home was all I wanted seven short days ago.

But I know this place isn't home any longer.

Attis is my home. Wherever she is is where I'm supposed to be.

But she's a world away.

αβ

Somehow, impossibly, it's the same night that I left, I realize. I stare at the date on my laptop screen in shock, but then, should anything shock me anymore? I shut the laptop, push it away from me across the bed and stare at the outfit I've laid out carefully on the chair in the corner of the room.

Tomorrow morning, the meeting with the trust committee is going to take place.

Like nothing ever happened.

Like my life didn't, in any way, change.

Part of me wonders if this was one long,

psychotic episode. That maybe I imagined all of it. But I know I didn't. I *know*. My clothes are dirty, Wonder has muddy mats on her paws and legs, and even without that physical evidence, the fact of the matter is that *I'm* changed. When I look in the mirror...there's a completely different person looking out at me now. I don't recognize her anymore, but—somehow—I think she's much better than the person who fell through that portal into another world. She's grown. She's changed. Irrevocably changed.

I place my hand over my heart, press down, trying to ease the ache that fills me. But nothing can ease that ache. The woman I love is a world away. And I can't reach her.

It's not fair. Life's unfair, I realize that, but this? This is *miserably* unfair. I spent a lot of time tonight yelling at nothing in particular, curling myself up into the tiniest ball possible on my bed, banging my fists against the coverlet. But my anger did nothing to change my situation, and now I'm so exhausted, I'm only left with my sorrow.

It wasn't supposed to be like this. I'd *made* my choice. I'd chosen *her*.

I need time to mourn this, to deal with this. But of course I don't have any time. This is my sister's death all over again. Somehow, I had to keep going with my life like the best person I'd ever known wasn't taken from me, when Ellie died.

And somehow, now, I have to keep going. I have to convince several people that a radio station they already don't believe in deserves another chance. Somehow, I have to keep living, keep trying, when everything seems like such a pale imitation of what life can really be like.

Because life? It can be *so perfect*. I close my eyes, I imagine Attis over me, her beautiful, soft smile turning up the corners of her lips as she trails a finger down my chin, to the skin of my neck. I breathe out, my heart racing, as I imagine Attis bending low to press that perfect warm mouth to mine.

"Josie," she'd whisper. She'd whisper my name like a prayer.

Wonder jumps up on the bed next to me, making a light meow, bumping her forehead against my elbow as I curl into a tighter ball, as I try to pick up all my broken pieces.

I pass a sleepless night, tossing and turning, feverish with heartache and sadness as I try to make sense of the past seven days, and somehow can't. Because, if everything that just happened is supposed to make sense, then I wouldn't have left Attis. I wouldn't have been taken from her.

I get up at six o'clock in the morning, and I call Carly, punching the numbers into my cell phone with blurry eyes.

"Yes?" is how she answers, her voice icy.

"Can we talk?" I ask her.

There's a long pause, and—for a long moment—I think she's going to tell me no.

"Meet me at the coffee shop in front of the trust building," she tells me, words clipped. And then she hangs up.

I get dressed, pulling on my nicest clothes with numb hands, lifting my chin to my reflection in the mirror.

The woman who gazes back at me looks empty.

☙

"Wow," says Carly, her brows raised when I walk into the coffee shop. She leans back in her seat, crossing her legs as she takes a sip of her coffee. "You look like hell," she tells me helpfully, her voice edged in sharpness.

"Something...happened to me," I tell her, licking my lips. "Look, I need to apologize. I was very wrong, and it was shit of me. I should never have made fun of you about the Boston Beast. You staked your professional reputation on it, you stuck your neck out—that took a lot of bravery. And I was wrong. The Boston Beast existed. I'm really sorry, Carly."

I think that if I'd told her Santa Claus was outside and wanted to meet her, Carly wouldn't have been more surprised. She stares at me with wide eyes, her mouth actually open for a long moment before she snaps it shut, leaning forward across the table. "What the hell is wrong with you?" she asks succinctly then. Her eyes narrow as she taps the tabletop. "Are you sick? Are you *dying*?"

"No," I tell her, though, inside, it very much feels like I am. "I was just wrong, and I owed you an apology. I wanted to make it right."

"How do you know that the Boston Beast was real?" she asks me, leaning back in her chair and holding me in place with her suspicious gaze.

"I...met someone," I tell her, pressing my

hands flat to the table.

Carly still gazes at me in suspicion, but her eyes are growing wider. "Who did you meet, Josie?" she asks me, her voice softening.

"Carly," I tell her, leaning across the table, "you wouldn't believe me if I told you. And, anyway, we need to prepare for the meeting." I'm so tired when I say those words. I can't imagine going in front of all those people, convincing them of...

"Wait," says Carly, leaning forward then, reaching across the table and pressing her fingers to my arm in the very first gesture of niceness she's ever shown me. "Just...Josie, please...trust me. And try me. I've seen some stuff you wouldn't believe," she says, her head to the side.

"Yeah," I tell her softly, biting my lip. "So have I." I take a deep breath. "What would you say if I told you that I met someone," I tell her, my radio brain taking over, "a veritable...knight in shining armor?"

Across the table, Carly actually pales, her eyes going wider.

"Josie," she says, leaning closer to me and dropping her voice, "I'd tell you...it's not the first time I've heard that story."

I don't know why, but I take a deep breath, and then I do something that is probably very stupid. I tell Carly everything. I tell her how I fell through a portal onto a lady knight. I tell her how I journeyed with this lady knight toward a city, how we went on adventures, and how—across the course of a single week—we fell in love.

And Carly listens attentively, making

sympathetic noises when the time is right, but—mostly—remaining silent. When I'm finally done, spent, leaning back in my chair, Carly leans forward, taking a deep breath.

"Holly... Well. It's a small, small world," says Carly, her eyes shining as she reaches across the table. She takes my hand and squeezes it, causing me to raise an eyebrow. "And I believe you, utterly," says Carly with a bright smile. "Because—"

I'm staring at her with wide eyes when the phone in my pocket begins to ring. I frown, reaching in... Who the hell would call me so early in the morning? I glance down at the phone, and then I take a deep breath.

It's Deb.

"The trust committee is a bunch of bastards, and they've moved the meeting up," she snaps the second I answer the phone. "They're trying to make certain you don't make the meeting. Where are you?"

I glance out of the coffee shop across the street to the building where the Moran Grant Trust resides.

"Believe it or not," I tell Deb, rising and gesturing to Carly to follow me, "we're right outside of the building."

"Oh, thank Freddie Mercury," Deb mutters. I can hear her take a deep inhale of a cigarette on the other end of the line. "Look, just get in there and do your best, okay? They're bastards. I don't think they're going to listen to you. But, hey, you're giving it a shot, so go you." Her voice is so dry and sarcastic, and I find myself actually chuckling.

After telling Carly everything, I feel strangely

light.

I'm going to go in there, and I'm going to give it my best. And that's really all I can do.

"Your stirring speech has moved me," I quip to Deb, surprised that I'm still capable of jokes. "Don't worry. We'll call you when we're out."

"Good luck," she mutters and hangs up.

Carly and I practically trot across the street and then the courtyard in front of the high-rise building.

"They moved up the meeting," I tell her, pushing through the rotating door. "It's now. They don't *really* want to meet with us, so they're being assholes."

"I figured that," she snorts. We race to the elevator.

"What floor is the Moran Trust?" I ask the guy behind the front desk.

"Eleven," he tells me with a frown. "Do you have an appointment?"

"We're with LEM Public Access," I tell him, as the elevator door slides open.

He's about to open his mouth, about to argue with us, but we're already in the elevator, and the door is already—blessedly—sliding closed.

The floors ding past, and then we're through reception and waiting in the plush waiting room, sitting on chairs, staring at one another.

"This is it," Carly whispers, licking her lips.

"They can see you now," the receptionist tells us, swinging open the board room doors.

There are eleven men and two women sitting at the broad table that takes up the entire room. At the far end is a podium and a sleek wall that a projector is projecting a white screen onto. Because the room is darkened a little, it's difficult to make out features of the committee members. They all look business-y...successful.

And they're all frowning.

They really, *really* don't want to hear this pitch.

But you know what? I just faced down a *wolf*. I faced down that wolf, and I—somehow—survived.

They don't scare me. Not even a little.

"Gentlemen—ladies," I say, clearing my throat and launching into my radio voice seamlessly. "I'm Josie Beckett, and this is Carly Aisley, and we represent LEM Public Access Television and Radio. I have it on the best authority that the grant that you so generously gave us each year has been revoked because someone on the board here was swayed by an argument by conservatives that our radio and television stations are liberal media."

A guy on the far right starts to bluster. "That's not true," he begins, coughing.

Bingo. Got him.

"But we'd like to demonstrate to you that public access programming is important for the city of Boston," says Carly smoothly, stepping up next to me.

Carly proceeds to show them the interviews she gathered with the people on the streets, projecting the raw footage onto the wall behind them. She speaks with passion for the radio station, and I watch her, feeling the energy in the room shift. Carly speaks for over half an hour, and when she's finally done, the guy on the far right—the guy who'd disagreed—starts up again.

"Be that as it may," he tells us, standing up, "there are better things we can allocate that grant to."

And that's when something inside of me snaps.

"Such as?" I ask him, venom in my tone.

He looks surprised. "Well. Ah...there's a golf company that—"

"At the end of the day," I tell the assembled board members, energy surging through me, "you have to ask yourself...did I do what was best for the city with the power given to me? There are voices on radio and television, voices that agree with us and disagree with us, but that bring to light stories and humanity in a way that's needed. Radio and television connect us; they show us that we're not alone." My voice catches as I stand up straight, as I imagine Attis staring at me with her warm, golden eyes, reaching across the space between us to curl her fingers through mine, like we fit together. "And it would be wrong to take that away—because it belongs to everyone. Not you or me," I tell them, breathing out. "But to everyone here in Boston."

The woman at the center of the table rises, nodding to us. "Thank you both. Please see yourselves out."

Carly glances at me, shaking her head just a little.

I blew it. We blew it.

It didn't work.

We're riding down in the elevator when the phone in my pocket rings. I take it out, stare down at it, feel my heart beat faster.

It's Deb.

"Hi," I tell her with a grimace as I answer the phone.

"It's done," says Deb, her voice light for the first time I've ever known her. "The grant's been reinstated. Apparently," she says, disbelief in her voice, "there was one guy who'd swayed them all, because—honestly, they didn't care much about it. And that's a direct quote from the woman who just called me. But she said that you obviously care, and they've rethought it. The grant's *reinstated*, Josie," Deb repeats. I have never, in all my years working for her, heard my station manager speechless. But she practically is right now.

I stare at Carly across the expanse of the elevator. I stare at her, and she has her head to the side. She mouths, "What is it?"

"They listened to us," I tell her, handing her the phone. "It's happening."

It shouldn't shock me, after the past few days I've had...but it does, anyway. And as emotion rushes through me, I know exactly where I need to go, the only place that—after everything—will still make sense to me.

So as Carly and I are about to part ways at the foot of the high rise, Carly turns to me.

"We have to talk," she tells me, her fingers finding my arm and gripping me tightly there. "It's really important, okay?"

"I'm exhausted," I tell her. "And I have something...important to do. Can I call you later?"

"Okay," she tells me, with a small grimace.

And then we embrace awkwardly—old enemies possibly becoming friends—and we each go our separate ways.

But my excitement from the grant being reinstated fades away almost completely as I put my hands in my pants pockets, as I begin the familiar path, walking the blocks, my head down, gazing at the sidewalk of my beloved city.

I walk all the way to West Side Methodist Church cemetery without even really seeing where I'm going, I'm so lost in thought. But I've walked this path so many times, I could do it in my sleep. As I slip through the small gate, as I walk up to my sister's grave, I feel so much in that moment that I'm breathless.

I sink down in front of her grave, pressing my fingers into the grooves of her name in the granite. I close my eyes; I take a deep breath.

"Ellie," I whisper. "Something...something *extraordinary* happened. And now I'm back home...and I don't know what to do. Would you believe me?" I tell the gravestone softly. "I went to another world. I met someone, Ellie."

Peace fills my head and my heart as I speak those words. I know that if my sister were alive, she'd be proud of me that I had made room in my life for happiness. I know that she'd want me to be happy, that she would feel bereft for me, that my chance with Attis was taken away from me.

She would want me to be happy.

As I crouch there, my palm flat against my sister's gravestone...something strange, but familiar, happens. I feel a little *zing* of electricity pulse through me, from the granite into my fingers.

I snatch my hand away from the headstone, shocked, gulping air as I blink away the tears, as I stare at the gravestone. I stand then, staring down at the grave, staring down at my fingers, utterly perplexed, my blood rushing through me.

And, for some reason at that moment...I look up.

Wind whistles through the trees, a light wind that brushes the leaves and branches together. A loud, rumbling SUV drives up the road beyond the graveyard, and somewhere close by someone talks loudly on their cellphone. The regular, normal sights and sounds of my city are all around me.

But there's nothing else.

I close my eyes. I press my hands over my heart. I listen to the wind in the trees, listen to the traffic, listen to the sounds of Boston living all around me, even here. Even in the cemetery.

And warm fingers curl around my elbow. Someone is behind me. Someone curls arms around me.

I'm imagining this. I must be. Because I feel a sweet, warm mouth on my neck, feel her holding me like she's never going to let go.

No. It can't be.

Attis is a world away.

I open my eyes. I turn.

Attis smiles down at me, her warm, golden eyes sparking with desire, with delight...with love.

"Hello," she whispers to me, her voice low as she gathers me tighter, closer, in her arms.

And then she kisses me.

It's searing, that kiss. Intoxicating as I drink in her warmth and softness and all that she is. But then I'm gasping, taking a step back, holding her out at arm's length, because she's *real*. I feel the intensity of her mouth, the strength of her arms.

Attis is *here*.

She's wearing a smartly tailored pair of black dress pants, a ruffled white shirt, a suit jacket and shiny black shoes. But I only notice that a little (though, admittedly, it's sexy as *hell*). What I really notice is that Attis is right here, right in front of me. That she's standing here, her warm fingers gripping my arms, her beautiful mouth curving up into a smile. I'm not imagining it.

She's real.

And she's in my world.

Attis steps forward again, and then she's wrapping her arms tightly around me as I hold her so close that a sob escapes me, gasping out into the air as she buries her mouth in my hair, on my cheeks, kissing away the tears.

"But *how*, Attis?" I whisper, staring up at her as she traces the pad of her thumb gently over my cheek, wiping away a warm tear.

"The Ursa," Attis whispers. "The Ursa helped me through. And because," she says, voice thick with emotion. "I chose you."

Behind her, I see something big and silver moving between the trees of the graveyard—but perhaps I imagined it.

All that matters is that, here and now, we hold each other, kissing and creating a brand-new, perfect memory.

And Boston rises around us, alive and thriving.

THE END

If you enjoyed *Forever and a Knight* and haven't yet read *A Knight to Remember*, it's available now! Read the knight story that started it all: Holly, a librarian, is starting to believe that love is impossible to find. But one night, during an unusually vicious storm, magic and romance appear in Holly's backyard in the form of a mysterious, gorgeous woman…wielding a sword.

Available wherever you purchase your eBooks and also available in print from most online retailers!

Author's Note:

I began writing *Forever and a Knight* when our beloved cat, Kit, was still alive. He would sing to me every morning, in his sweet kitty voice, and I told him that I was writing a character that was very much like him into the book as I held him, kissing his sweet head.

But halfway into writing this novel, Kit became sicker with his advanced kidney disease. And, one day, one of the most precious and beloved creatures I have ever cherished passed away in front of my eyes, while I held him, weeping.

For a long time I couldn't fathom finishing this book. I loved the story, the characters, dearly, but I had based Wonder on Kit, and I was so depressed after he died. But, one day, I opened the document and read the story I'd written thus far. I cried at the parts about Wonder, but that day, I wrote the next scene. And I felt a tiny bit better.

Writing this book, this story that I loved so much to create, has been a healing experience for me. Ever since I was a kid, experiencing horrific homophobia, I have turned to writing to help me through the darkest times and most painful moments of my life. And it always has.

This story has so much of my hope and healing in it, my pain and sorrow, too, and in the end, just like Josie, I got my second chance. Natalie and I have adopted a little kitten named Kai who will never, ever replace Kit--but he isn't meant to. He's a cherished creature that we love with all our hearts, just as we loved Kit.

And the story comes full circle.

Thank you so much for buying this book, for giving this story a chance. I poured my heart into it, and I hope, very much, that you enjoyed it.

Warmly,
Bridget Essex
January, 2015

More from Bridget Essex:

- *Don't Say Goodbye:* Maxine "Max" Hallwell has spent her entire life making the safe, responsible decisions. When her best friend, Jo, introduces her to her new girlfriend Fiona, a stunning, charismatic cake decorator, Max realizes that making safe decisions might have cost her the woman of her dreams...A heartwarming, poignant romance.

- *A Wolf for the Holidays:* Mandy's not having a great December. Her lackluster girlfriend has given her a massive dog--who looks a lot more like a wolf than a dog--as a gift. But all problems seem minor when she wakes up to a gorgeous, naked woman stealing jeans out of her dresser...a woman who swears she's a werewolf. A warm, holiday romance!

- *Wolf Town:* Amy moves to the strange little New England village, Wolf Town--but she finds more than a fresh start when she begins to fall in love with the daughter of the Wolf Town patriarch...who also just happens to be a werewolf.

- *The Sullivan Vampires:* A beautiful, romantic series that follows the clan of Sullivan vampires and the women who love them. Advance praise has hailed this hallmark series as "Twilight for women who love women" and "a lesbian romance that takes vampires seriously! Two thumbs up!"

- *Big, Bad Wolf:* During a terrible snowstorm, Megan thinks she sees a wolf. But when beautiful, hungry-eyed Kara comes into Megan's life, she brings more danger than a pack of wolves.

- *The Protector:* Elizabeth Grayson doesn't want a bodyguard, but when her life is put in danger, her father hires mysterious Layne O'Connell to keep her safe. And Elizabeth is beginning to fall for the woman who was charged with keeping her alive.

- *Dark Angel:* Cassandra Griman was in the wrong place at the wrong time when her life is saved by an angel. But first impressions aren't everything, and the captivating woman who saved her life is no angel. Can love save the soul of a vampire?

These and more are available now!
Search "bridget essex" where you purchase your eBooks or print books online!

22409902R00204

Printed in Great Britain
by Amazon